✓

Los Gatos H S Library

Fuentes,
    Distant relations

BC# 24988   DISCARDED

Los Gatos H.S. Library

DISTANT RELATIONS

Books by Carlos Fuentes

Where the Air Is Clear

The Good Conscience

Aura

The Death of Artemio Cruz

A Change of Skin

Terra Nostra

The Hydra Head

Burnt Water

Distant Relations

Carlos Fuentes

DISTANT
RELATIONS

Translated from the Spanish by

MARGARET SAYERS PEDEN

Los Gatos H.S. Library

Farrar Straus Giroux

NEW YORK

Translation copyright © 1982 by Farrar, Straus and Giroux, Inc.
Originally published in Spanish, Una familia lejana,
copyright © 1980 by Ediciones Era, S.A., Mexico
All rights reserved
First printing, 1982

Printed in the United States of America
Published simultaneously in Canada
by McGraw-Hill Ryerson Ltd., Toronto
Designed by Constance Fogler

Library of Congress Cataloging in Publication Data
Fuentes, Carlos. Distant relations.
Translation of: Una familia lejana.
I. Title. PQ7297.F793F313 1982
863 81-9904 AACR2

California Public School Library Protection Fund

BC#24988

For my friend Luis Buñuel,

in his eightieth year:

"Ce qui est affreux, c'est ce qu'on

ne peut pas imaginer."—M.P.

LA CHAMBRE VOISINE

Tournez le dos à cet homme
Mais restez auprès de lui
(Ecartez votre regard,
Sa confuse barbarie),
Restez debout sans mot dire,
Voyez-vous pas qu'il sépare
Mal le jour d'avec la nuit,
Et les cieux les plus profonds
Du coeur sans fond qui l'agite?
Eteignez tous ces flambeaux
Regardez: ses veines luisent.
Quand il avance la main,
Un souffle de pierreries,
De la circulaire nuit
Jusqu'à ses longs doigts parvient.
Laissez-le seul sur son lit,
Le temps le borde et le veille,
En vue de ces hauts rochers
Où gémit, toujours caché,
Le coeur des nuits sans sommeil.
Qu'on n'entre plus dans la chambre
D'où doit sortir un grand chien
Ayant perdu la mémoire
Et qui cherchera sur terre
Comme le long de la mer
L'homme qu'il laissa derrière
Immobile, entre ses mains
Raides et définitives.

JULES SUPERVIELLE

THE ADJACENT ROOM

Turn your back to that man
But do not leave him
(Avert your gaze,
Its dim barbarity),
Stand without saying a word,
Don't you see how nearly he fails
To distinguish day from night,
And the farthest skies
From the bottomless heart which troubles him?
Extinguish all these torches.
Look: his veins glisten.
When he extends his hand,
A breath of precious stones
From the circular night
To his long fingers flows.
Leave him alone on his bed,
Time tucks him in, watches over him,
Within sight of those high rocks
Where, forever hidden, moans
The heart of sleepless nights.
Let no one enter the room
From which a huge dog will emerge
Having lost its memory
And it will search the earth
And the ocean's breadth
For the man it left behind.
Motionless, between hands
Both hard and decisive.

DISTANT RELATIONS

1

My friend's pallor was not unusual. With the passing of the years his skin had become fused to his facial bones and his gesturing, slender hands had become translucent.

I had seen him shortly after his return from Mexico, which seemed to have somewhat dissipated his resemblance to a civilized phantom. Sun had given him density, fleshly presence. I almost didn't recognize him.

The return of his habitual pallor should have made him look entirely familiar, but there was something different about his manner. When I saw him alone at his table in the club dining room, I walked over to greet him and to suggest we have lunch together.

"Only if you join me here," he said, glancing toward the other tables, some distance from his.

His eyes were lost in depths far more profound than that of the vast shadowy dining room. The preferred tables, placed beside a large balcony overlooking the Place de la Concorde, escape the gloom. As these are the best in the club, it is only natural that they be allotted to the senior members. I accepted his invitation for what it was, a courtesy to a younger friend.

"I haven't seen you since you returned from your trip," I said.

He continued studying his menu as if he hadn't heard me. He was leaning forward slightly, his back to the windows. The bluish light of that early afternoon in November illuminated his bald head and fringe of gray hair. Abruptly, he looked up, but not toward me. He turned and stared into the distance beyond the square, toward the bank of the river.

"Order for me," he asked me as the waiter approached. He spoke with the sense of urgency that now seemed characteristic of all his actions. I wondered if he had always behaved this way, and I had simply not noticed it before. His small, darting eyes measured the square, focusing for a long moment on the tree-lined promenade of the Tuileries.

"Well," he said finally, after we had been served our wine and his restless eyes had found repose in its depths. "I had made a wager with myself, wondering if anyone would come over to speak to me, if I would find anyone to tell my story to."

I looked at him, bewildered. "I'm not just *anyone*, Branly. I'd always thought we were friends."

He touched my hand lightly, apologized, and said that when it was all over he would have to take stock of his life; it had all been very exhausting for a man of his age.

"No," he added, "I shall not resort to clichés, I will not say that at eighty-three I have become sated. Only those who have never lived say that."

He threw back his head, laughing, and in the same movement raised his hands, saying it was mere pretense to believe oneself immune to surprise. Perhaps, more than pretense, it was simple stupidity. Only a deep sense of insecurity would force a man to suffer such a foolish loss as that of his innate capacity to be amazed. He said death conquers only those who are not surprised by it; life as well. He blinked repeatedly, as if the light, less pale than the face of my friend, was painful to him.

"Until the time of my trip, I believed that I had achieved a certain equilibrium," he said, shielding his eyes with his fingers.

Then, with a graceful and lighthearted wave of his hand meant to dispel any hint of solemnity, he smiled. "My God!

I have experienced every kind of age, golden or wretched, every kind of decade, roaring or mute, two world wars, a leg wound at Dunkirk, four dogs, three wives, two castles, a dependable library, and a few friends like yourself, equally dependable."

He sighed; he pushed aside his wineglass and then did something extraordinary. He turned his back to me, swung his chair around and stared out toward the Place de la Concorde, as if he were speaking to it. I chose to think that in this rather bizarre fashion he was addressing me, wishing to emphasize the unusual nature of our meeting as well as of the story he had alluded to. Finally (for the sake of my own peace of mind), I decided that my friend actually meant to speak to us both, to the square and to me, to the world and to that plural *you* I represented at that moment, which, ironic and hostile, lurks in the *we* of the Romance languages, *nos/otros*, we and others, I and the rest.

Paris and I, Branly between the two of us. Only this interpretation could assuage my dignity, somewhat ruffled by my friend's strange behavior.

"The century is a brother to me," he said finally. "We have lived the same times. It is also my child; I preceded it by four years, and my first memory—imagine!—is of its birth, dominated by one special, I scarcely need add, unforgettable, image: the opening of the Pont Alexandre III. I remember it as an arch of acanthus stretching across the Seine for my benefit, so that I, a child, might learn to know and love this city."

I watched him finger the wide blue necktie and adjust the pearl stickpin that adorned it. Branly was staring into the distance, toward the Quai d'Orsay. I followed his gaze, as he explained how that image had been born within him—and now, hearing him, in me—the expectation that every evening, as on that distant evening when for the first time he admired the bridge over the river, for one miraculous moment the phenomena of the day—rain or fog, scorching heat or snow—would disperse and reveal, as in a Corot landscape, the luminous essence of the Île de France.

This is the equilibrium he refers to. He knows that each and every patient evening harbors that privileged instant. That hour has never disappointed him, and, thanks to him, I understand that neither has it disappointed me.

He smiles, thinking that the only exceptions occur, fortunately, when one is away on a trip, far from Paris.

 He met the Heredias in Mexico, only last summer. They were together on an excursion to Xochicalco organized by a mutual French friend, Jean, a longtime resident of Mexico City. My friend happily seized the opportunity to visit the Toltec ruins in the Valley of Morelos, especially in the company of Hugo Heredia, one of the outstanding archaeologists of Latin America. My friend's appetite for ruins has never been sated, and when he saw Xochimilco he commented to Jean that, in spite of what Valéry had said, civilizations do not die completely; they endure, but only when they do not progress.

As they contemplated the view of the valley from the high Indian citadel, he repeated his comment in halting Spanish to Hugo Heredia, and added that things that do not progress do not grow old: they alone survive.

"Nothing more logical," he concluded.

Heredia limited himself to a comment in French that Xochicalco was a ceremonial center, not a sacrificial site, as if he anticipated that question and wanted to make clear to the foreigners that violence is not an exclusively Mexican privilege for which he need apologize, but rather one of the few constants in the infinite variety of human nature.

My friend uttered a delighted aaah! in appreciation of Heredia's excellent French, but thought to himself, shrugging, that the archaeologist's remarks were intended to calm the sensibility of a rational Frenchman, sensual surely, but never mediocre.

He repeated this later, laughing, to Heredia, who replied that sensuality is but a chapter of violence.

"On the contrary," my friend responded.

The shapes in the valley that spreads out before the ruins of Xochicalco seem to approach or recede according to the caprice of the light and the speed of the drifting clouds. One has the illusion that he might touch the bottom of the ravine, as if it were rising from a prolonged geological dream; the dormant volcanoes seem forever beyond reach, longing for the return of their reign of fire.

My friend tells his hosts that only the swoon of the god whose breath is the wind, or the fury of the goddess that invades a cloud, was needed to invert that relationship of proximity or distance and make the volcano loom near and the precipice seem as abysmal as the lonely entrance to Mexico's paradise. "As far as I know, this is the only Eden imagined to be underground, there where Orpheus, Dante, and Sartre each reserved a site for hell."

"Look, Papa, look what I found."

Heredia's son had come running, out of breath, to the brink of the precipice; my friend reached out with the curved handle of his cane and hooked the boy's arm. He is convinced that he saved him from an accident; from the flat platform of the citadel to the surface of the pelota court below would be a fall of some fifty meters. The boy was highly excited, intent on capturing his father's complete attention, and the father granted that attention with an intensity my friend considered untoward. In brown hands cupped like an earthen vessel, as if fearful a drop might escape from between the chinks of his fingers, the boy held an object, a glimmer of fleeting brilliance.

"Forgive me," said Heredia. "I have not introduced my son, Victor, to you."

He hesitated, embarrassed, and added hurriedly: "Forgive me again, but I did not quite hear when Jean told me your name."

"Branly," my friend replied simply.

He forgave the clumsiness of the introduction: Victor, the boy, was absorbed in his discovery; his father, in assuring the boy of his undivided attention. Under such circumstances, introductions are best left for a more propitious moment. But Branly should not expect our standard of courtesy—what the English, in their incomparable way, call "good manners"—to be recognized, much less practiced, everywhere in the world, as he cannot expect the soft twilight of the Île de France—like a recumbent woman stretching out a hand to brush our cheek with her fingertips (that moment is approaching as I dine and listen to my friend speak these words)—to resemble what he calls, and he knows it well, the raised, gauntleted fist, the vertical, visceral, cutting light of eternal noonday, of the mountains of Mexico.

"Where did you find it, Victor?" the father asked.

The boy gestured toward the truncated pyramid, a temple that does not soar, my friend calls it, dominated by a girdle of sculptured fire serpents encircling its four sides, stone serpents devouring one another to make a single snake biting its own tail in the act of swallowing itself. The pyramid is surrounded by dry brush and restless dust.

"There," the boy pointed.

"May I see it?" asked Heredia.

Victor hugged the object to his chest. "No, later."

Until that moment the boy had been looking down, his eyes fixed on his treasure. Now, as he said no, he looked up at his father. My friend was surprised that with skin so dark and hair so black and lank he had such light-colored eyes. They seemed blue and dilated in the relentless light, green when his thick eyelashes shadowed them. He couldn't be more than thirteen; perhaps twelve.

Who knows? my friend is saying now, awaiting with me the arrival of twilight over the Place de la Concorde; maybe Mexican children remain small for so many years because the sexual precocity of the tropics requires a compensatory delay in other areas of growth. He had never seen such light eyes against such dark skin. Only then did he look with some attention at the father. Hugo Heredia was a Mexican Creole with ruddy skin, a black mustache, wavy hair, and studious, sad eyes behind tortoise-rimmed spectacles.

"No, later," said the child.

My friend refrained from asking whether an object found on an archaeological site should not immediately be delivered to competent authorities. After all, the visiting foreigner is warned that the Mexican laws are very strict in that regard; woe to him who attempts to smuggle an Aztec or Tarascan figure, bogus or not, in his flight bag. He wondered whether Heredia enjoyed special privileges.

He found the answer that same evening in Cuernavaca. My friend, and the father and son, were all Jean's guests. They dined on a loggia of pale wood and blue stucco, a portico open to the dual assault of the vegetal breath from the barrancas and the distant storm gathering on the crest of the mountains. My friend says he found the Heredias enchanting. The father had that quality so characteristic of cultured Latin Americans: the passion to know everything, to read everything, to give no quarter, no pretext, to the European, but also to know well what the European does not know and what he considers his own, the Popol Vuh *and*

[9]

Descartes. And, above all, to demonstrate to the European that there is no excuse not to know other cultures.

We tend to be somewhat uncomfortable with this attitude; we believe that knowing everything does not necessarily mean knowing something. But this was not the case with Hugo Heredia. For him, my friend says, a catholicity of culture was a necessity for him as a professional anthropologist. Simply put, he was a man who did not want to reduce knowledge to a single sphere, acute perhaps, but surely partial and therefore imperfect. Heredia, who often held his spectacles in his hands and mused with half-closed eyes, was unwilling to align himself with God, with man, with history, or with money, but neither did he deny any of them. As he listened, my friend dreamed of a different age and spoke of a library whose one or two shelves would contain all the knowledge worth knowing.

He tells me he recalled the two noblest faces in all painting, those of Erasmus and Thomas More, both by Holbein the Younger; he tried to find in Heredia a resemblance to them. This is a man who belongs to the century in which the New World was founded, he thought; since that time we have not known a universal man. And yet in the veiled eyes of that intelligence there was also a hint of patriarchal authority, a slight but firm warning of the boundaries that must be respected by others as they approach the gates of the domain where the discoverer of new lands is the master of all he surveys, empowered to dispose of lives and fortunes, with no distinction between his public and his private functions. A foreigner may not remove an archaeological artifact. A Mexican may. One cannot steal from one's own patrimony.

The hovering odor of the mangrove thicket was intensified by the approaching nightly storm that first would quench it before giving it even more powerful wings. Heredia was speaking of gods and of time, and his son was listening with something more than ordinary attention. The Mexican was saying that the expulsion of the gods by the modern city has condemned us to an illusory time, a time imposed by human limitations; we perceive, unclearly, only chronological sequence and we believe there is no other time.

"I don't know whether the gods exist; but I know the concept exists of a sacred world where entities are reluctant to be sacrificed. All ancient peoples refuse to abandon the old ways in favor of the new; rather than being cast aside one after the other, some realities accumulate in a permanent accretion. When this happens, all things are living and present, as is true among the peoples of Madagascar, who conceive of history as two flowing currents: the inheritance of the ears and the memory of the lips."

He commented that it is less interesting to take scrupulous care to relegate certain features of the present to the past than to celebrate the living presence of things we can recount and hear.

My friend, as he leaned forward to cut a piece of meat, could see Victor's eyes as he watched his father. The boy was absorbing a lesson. My friend tried in vain to intercept the half-lidded gaze of Hugo Heredia as he reached for the bottle of wine. Heredia was not speaking to my friend, he was not speaking to Jean, he was lecturing to his son, and they were both aware of it.

In a way, they lived in a universe of their own. Jean had informed my friend before dinner that Victor's older brother and his mother had died two years earlier in a plane crash. After Victor was born, Hugo and his wife had decided never to travel together. From that time, each of the parents traveled separately with one of the children, in turn. Jean wondered whether this was not a way to tempt the devil, to offer fate alternatives, forcing it to awaken from its dream and provide the final answer to the underlying question of the Heredias' game: which would receive the invitation to death?

"Then Victor could have been the one who died in the accident?" my friend asked his host.

Jean had nodded, and throughout the meal Branly understood and accepted the warm and private attention the father and son bestowed on one another. But he was also disturbed by the intensity of the relationship that, without being abusive (quite the contrary: father and son shared the ceremonious behavior that is the surest evidence of the Indian presence in Mexico; the Spanish, my friend said, are almost always noisy and rude), seemed to exclude the foreigners.

Then, as if the slight, but obvious, discomfort of my friend had been revealed in the sudden involuntary silence, the boy laughed and said an angel must have flown overhead. Hugo opened his eyes wide and smiled at my friend, who was dressed in white linen that night, and was illuminated, then as now, by an imaginary candle glowing just behind his left ear.

It was the last moment of the jungle and the barranca. Turning toward my friend, Hugo Heredia recalled Proust's words about a painting by Moreau: "venomous flowers interwoven with precious jewels." He asked my friend whether the night and the jungle, the flickering light and shadow of the barranca, did not remind him of Proust's words.

"No," my friend replied. "That is but one element of the scene, though admittedly the most sensual and immediate. I was thinking of something Madame de La Fayette wrote about the court of Henry II: '*Une sorte d'agitation sans désordre.*'"

As the tropical rain was unleashed on the roof of the loggia, Jean murmured in Spanish: "A sort of agitation without disorder." It was not my friend's intention to contradict Hugo Heredia, but rather to acknowledge the participation he was inviting. He put aside the incidents that had not entirely pleased him—the hasty introduction, the arrogant appropriation of the artifact, the prolonged asides during the meal—to accept the consuming reality of the relationship between father and son, which first confirmed its own intensity, its mutual supportiveness, then incorporated events that being tangential became involved in it, and, finally, once it had been satisfactorily defined on its own terms, opened unhesitatingly to include the host and the host's friend.

My friend did not hesitate to extend in return a cordial, slender hand as transparent as porcelain, the same hand now pointing toward the scudding clouds above the cupola of the Palais Bourbon opposite us. He comments that our symmetry of spirits tends to reinforce the recognition of a rational mind in a solid body; the symmetry of Mexican temples is the fearful symmetry of Blake's tiger in the night.

He mentioned this to Hugo Heredia that night in Cuernavaca, while Jean lighted the fire in the fireplace and Victor pulled on a blue wool sweater bearing the crest of the Lycée Français, then folded his hands across his chest as he had that morning to shield his newfound treasure from intrusive eyes. My friend conceded a point to Hugo; every time he remembered that brief glimmer he would associate it with the moment before the rain, and the strange flickering light in the fetid barranca.

The temple, Hugo was saying in reply to my friend, is a place apart, sacred, distinct from nature. But by the very fact that it was created to be separate from nature, it echoes it. However, my friend was no longer listening; the rain had ceased and the odors from the barranca were filtering in with a humid vengeance. The putrid river at the bottom of Jean's property continued along a mountain washed clean of the sun's wounds; from between river and mountain flowed a dark distant voice singing a song whose words were distorted by the metallic dissonance of the mountain and the vegetal void of the barranca.

Victor rose and walked onto the loggia; his hands grasped the wet railing as he began to whistle the melody of the song, which grew fainter as Victor joined in the tune. Hugo Heredia, his eyes again half-closed, was talking about men and space. My friend's eyes never left the boy, and his ears were tuned only to the play of the echoed melody, the solitary voice from the distance, the words indistinguishable, the voice recognizable as young, but not as male or female, and Victor's whistling, his response to the bird of night.

As my friend gazed at the boy, he remembered a few months earlier spending an afternoon in the Parc Monceau, watching children at play. As he watched, he wondered if they merely reminded him of the children he used to play with as a boy, or if he, now an old man and forever distanced from them, were actually seeing those children from his past. He says that at that moment he felt very old. Now Victor was offering him a mysterious opportunity to transcend those melancholy alternatives, to become involved in an unplayed childhood game. Who was singing in the barranca? It didn't matter whether this voice came from the past or the present.

The song ended, and for a moment, absently, Victor whistled alone. My friend once again became attentive to what Hugo was saying, to the scope of the ideas unfolding like a fan, but his eyes remained on Victor. A boy with light eyes and dark skin, a boy who still hopped and skipped like a child, as now, in response to a summons that only he heard; as only a moment before when he was accepting his father's teaching; as he would an instant later, returning to his place in the large chair before the fire. Without interrupting the conversation, Hugo will beckon Victor with a wave of his hand and the boy will go to his father and sit on his lap. Hugo will stroke the boy's hair and Victor will pat his father's hand.

During breakfast Jean told my friend that, as he'd seen, the father and son were unusually close; the death of the mother and the brother had undoubtedly cemented that closeness. My friend recalls then, as he does now, that his own father died at thirty, when he himself was a child of four. Beside his bed in the large bedchamber on the Avenue de Saxe is a photograph of his father taken shortly before his death. He, a man of eighty-three, gazes upon the youth of twenty-nine who had been his father.

Every night before going to sleep, he gazes at the photograph a long while, he tells me this afternoon in the dining room of the Automobile Club de France, as he told Jean that morning in Cuernavaca at breakfast, before their return to Mexico City and before the sun began its impatient race toward midday.

In vain my friend looked for the trace of a presence in the barranca. A young servant in sandals and white shirt and pants served the delights of the tropical breakfast, flamered fruits, tortillas, eggs smothered in cream and tomato and chili, and buns and breads as infinitely varied in savor as in name. The Heredias came down a little later, as the Frenchmen were drinking their second cup of coffee. Victor ate hungrily, rapidly, and asked to be excused to play in the garden that stretched to the edge of the barranca. He skipped away as Heredia said how pleased he and his son were to have met my friend; they had enjoyed the conversation and hoped they would soon meet again.

"I'm traveling to Paris in September for a Unesco conference," Hugo said. "Victor will come with me."

My friend still does not know why, but he almost asked them not to travel together. However, he realized just in time, he tells me, that since the preceding evening he had been experiencing a kind of vertigo, his mind racing simultaneously in several directions: he remembered the children in the Parc Monceau who no longer remembered him; he remembered a young man who was father to an old man; he tried to imagine Victor's dead mother and brother; and also the boy or girl who had been singing in the barranca. But most of all he tried to penetrate Victor's candid gaze, to become a child again and see through his eyes. In this way he might recapture the imperious innocence and the unanswered questions of his own childhood.

He was blinded by the sun now climbing the sky. Victor was a white, blurred figure in the glaring depths of the garden beside the barranca. As if with a gaudy flag, the Mexican sky proclaimed its intentions: high noon or nothing. My friend was on the verge of adding one more wrinkle to the travel plans designed to outmaneuver death. He was on the point of asking Heredia not to travel with his son; he almost offered to come himself to pick up the boy and take him back to France.

He says that everything was resolved, however, as is always the case with him, in a ritual of courtesy, because inevitably courtesy is the only reliable, true, honorable, and sincere means my friend the Comte de Branly can summon to impose order on human events, to offer them the refuge of civilization, to calm that orderly agitation, to exorcise the venomous flowers interwoven with precious jewels.

He invited the Heredias to stay at his home on the Avenue de Saxe while they were in Paris. It was only a few steps from UNESCO headquarters, he said, shielding his eyes against the savage glare of the sun. It would be a pleasure to welcome them, to renew their friendship, to offer his appreciation, he said, as he searched for his dark glasses to penetrate the thick lime-white light, the blurred landscape, of the garden where Victor was playing.

He returned to Mexico City that evening. The light faded suddenly, impatient now to cede its dominion to the abrupt nightfall of the high tropics. Resting his chin on his fist, my friend stared at the passing scenery sequestered by darkness. In the reflection of the car window he tried to re-create what he had seen that morning through the blinding sun after he had settled his sunglasses on his nose: the boy Victor on the lawn of the garden beside the barranca, beating Jean's Indian servant, throwing him to the ground and whipping off his belt to lash him; a tiny feudal lord, master of lives and fortunes.

3

The Countess, who never leaves their castle near Cahors, suddenly became ill, and Branly hastened to join her. He left instructions with his chauffeur to meet the Heredias at Roissy airport, and with his Spanish servants to look after his guests in his town house on the Avenue de Saxe. He returned as soon as possible; his train arrived in Paris at eleven in the morning. My friend found a taxi and forty minutes later arrived before the eighteenth-century façade of his residence.

No one answered his ring. Impatiently, he located the correct key on his key ring and opened the heavy door. Highly irritated, he stalked through the beautiful interior courtyard paved in smooth stone and past the service quarters flanking it, to a short flight of steps leading to the main door of the one-story residence constructed according to the dispassionate principles of the French baroque.

At the top of the steps he whirled with that imperious gesture of his slender, transparent hands that I have seen so often, transforming the overcoat, casually tossed over his ancient but martial shoulders, into something decidedly impressive, half hussar's jacket, half bullfighter's cape. He sought, in vain, a sign of life—the chauffeur, the cook, the valet. Though it was almost noon, his automobile was not in the carriage house.

He clasped the lapels of his greatcoat under his trembling chin on this deceptively sunny September morning in which a knife edge of air signaled the coming of autumn. He opened the glass door onto a foyer decorated, like the rest of the mansion, in the Empire style favored by the Countess, whose family owed its titles to Bonaparte. My friend, amused, shrugged his shoulders. Being newer, his wife's furniture was in better condition than his. From his ancestors Branly proudly claimed the house itself, the work of Gabriel and Aubert, a twin to the Hôtel Biron designed by those same architects. When my friend recalls, as he inevitably does, that the Biron mansion now houses the museum where the works of Rodin are collected, he quips that it is therefore unnecessary for him to open his doors to the public; he invites the public to visit the Rodin Museum instead. It is the same as coming to the Avenue de Saxe.

I told him it was not exactly the same. The public would be missing the gleaming ormolu of the superb collection of Empire candelabra and lyre-shaped clocks, the wooden cheval glass mirror crowned with winged figures and butterfly medallions, the Romagnese bas-reliefs and the spectacular malachite vases, the wedding of bronze, marble, plaster, and silver with amboyna, oak, beech, gilt, and mahogany. Their greatest loss would be the sight of the magnificent clock suspended from an arch of gilded bronze, with a seated woman playing an ornate piano with griffin legs, in a sumptuous mounting of motionless draperies and doors.

"Motionless, but poisonous," my friend added on the evening he had honored me by inviting me to his peerless table. "That clock is the work of Antoine-André Ravrio. He fashioned several similar pieces for the royal family. Perhaps that is the only way Hortense de Beauharnais had of airing her musical compositions, as the melody of a clock striking the hours."

"A clock may bore," I said to him, "but surely not kill. I don't believe in fatal tedium, in spite of the persistent efforts of several of our acquaintances to the contrary."

"No," my friend replied. "In his will, Ravrio bequeathed a sizable sum of money to anyone who could discover a means of protecting his workers against the deadly danger of poisoning resulting from gilding with mercury."

"You prove me right. Your home should be open to the public. Rodin can offer no such mysteries."

He laughed and said there was more mystery in the gesture of a statue than in the caprice of a queen. That morning my friend heard the metallic melody as he entered the large hall of his mansion. Stroking the gilded bronze, Victor Heredia stood before the figure of the woman seated at the piano.

"Careful," my friend said.

Startled, Victor dropped the key with which he had been winding the clock, and turned to look at my friend. He recovered his aplomb as they shook hands. My friend says he asked the boy about his father and the boy said he would arrive that afternoon.

"Then you didn't make the flight together?"

"No," Victor replied. "After what happened to my mother and Toño, my father thinks it's safer for us to travel separately."

"Your brother?"

With clear eyes and an imperceptible smile, Victor nodded and stared at my friend. "I've already told Etienne to pick him up at four tomorrow. How elegant! A Citroën with all the extras, and a uniformed chauffeur. That's class!"

He laughed, and my friend attempted to smile in response, but for some reason the smile seemed a bit forced.

"Where are Florencio and José? Didn't they prepare your breakfast?"

The boy looked at my friend inquisitively. "Oh yes, yesterday," he responded with a composure that was beginning to set Branly's nerves on edge.

"No, no, no. This morning. Where are they? Why didn't they come to the door? Where is everyone?"

Only then, as he turned to look for his servants, did he realize that his entire magnificent collection of candelabra was ablaze, candle after candle, all the bronze ram's-head bases, the garlands of blindfolded girls whose bodies served as candleholders, the bronze serpents whose fangs fastened on glass shades, the spirit lamp on a side table, the wall sconces in the form of bearded masks, the silver-winged Victories, the innocuous wax on the argentine backs of a pack of hunting hounds.

"They must be sleeping," said Victor, quite seriously.

"At twelve noon!" exclaimed my friend, incredulous in this familiar refuge now transformed by his young visitor into a forbidden, alien, distant space darkly funereal compared to the September sun outdoors, to the commotion of returning vacationers at the Gare d'Austerlitz, to the sharp contrast between the autumnal breath of an approaching St. Francis' Day and the St. Martin's Day hope of a late summer.

He pulled back the drapes, moved by an annoyance that contrasted sharply with the ostentatious calm of his young guest. As the sun poured in, its rays quelled the brief luminescence of the blazing candles, silver, and bronze.

Victor smothered a laugh as my friend caught a glimpse of his Spanish servants passing through the entry hall laden with shopping bags overflowing with the clamoring evidence of celery, carrots, tomatoes, and onions. My friend confesses that he, too, smiled. He had envisioned the ashen José and the florid Florencio bound to the foot of the bed, unable to free themselves to tend the wounds of bodies scourged by the feudal Mexican youth, master of lives and fortunes, young lord of gibbet and blade, eager to wreak vengeance on the brutal Spaniards who with blood and fire had conquered the lands of the Indian.

"Good morning, M. le Comte," murmured José, looking more and more like a figure from a Zurbarán painting.

"We're a little late," added Florencio, who looked like an exhausted jai-alai player. "There was a power failure this morning before you arrived."

Branly nodded with severity, and a little later, lunching with his young friend, said to himself, as now he says to me, that the soundest intelligence is that of one who has survived the tribulations of the prolonged adolescence we call maturity, with its seriousness and its obligations, to regain the authority of childhood.

"And the proof," he says, "is that as children we shape our worlds; as adults, the world shapes us. Adolescence is that wretched proving period when we must accept or reject the laws of adults."

That adults almost always triumph, he tells me, toying with the stem of his wine goblet as he had that afternoon during luncheon with Victor, makes all the greater the victory of those who have preserved the well-being the mature world calls sickness: childhood and its private domains.

"You see," he said during our long luncheon at the club, "there was a reason for the hospitality I extended to the Heredias, no less compelling for being cunningly conceived by my subconscious and hidden from my conscious mind. To put it simply, I wanted Victor to let me live his childhood with him before we both lost it; he because he was growing up, I because I was going to die."

I am accustomed to my friend's stoicism; although befitting his age, it is still admirable. But now there was something more than stoicism in his words. That morning, he said, Victor had invited him to join in his game and, stupidly, he had nearly missed the opportunity, nearly rejected it because of his passion for the order and reason that wear the solemn mask of maturity and veil one's fear that one may recover one's lost imagination. They ate in silence. Later, my friend passed the afternoon in his austere but comfortable bedchamber, a refuge from the Napoleonic delirium the Countess had imposed on the remainder of the mansion.

A rigorous delirium, rather than a delirious rigor, Branly thought as, following his custom, he gazed at the faded photograph of the thirty-year-old man who had been his father. A handsome man, the son thought now, his best feature the profile, at least in this sepia photograph in which the photographer, as if privy to the still undiscovered potential of his art, had transcended the sharp relief of the stiff family portraits of the epoch to create a diffused light of his own, a nimbus seemingly born of the intensely clear eyes of my friend's father. In fact, I say to myself when again I have the opportunity to examine that admirable photograph, he possessed the secret of being able to create an atmosphere around his subject, in the very way the suspended dusk of Paris, at this hour when my friend and I are being served our café filtre, is the distillation of all the dusks of all the epochs of our city. The atmosphere, I say to Branly, can evoke a time that is not our own, invisible, without end, and as secret as the ageless voices which, according to another of my friends, have remained suspended throughout time, awaiting the person who will rediscover and rearrange them.

My friend says that he inherited from his mother his least refined, but also his most resilient, qualities, the essence of stony, storm-hewn Breton stock. From his father he inherited only the hands—clasped under a cleft chin in the photograph—as if this Captain de Branly were praying with singular verve, given the fact that he's dressed as a soldier. He had not inherited his father's eyes, or the long wavy blond hair of this reserve officer, photographed before his death in 1900—not a death in battle but in a hospital room, and for causes that penicillin would have eradicated in twenty-four of our hours.

With measured affection my friend runs his hand across the face of his father, dead at thirty, as if wishing to close the eyelids and forget the eyes that in the photo look as if they were silver. Born in 1870. Now, that was a year for a soldier. The son, in 1914, would live and win battles, unlike the father, who could neither win nor lose during the three decades of peace he was fated to live following the triumphant return from Tonkin and the inglorious return from Mexico, the humiliation of Bazaine by Moltke and the bloody insurrection of the Paris Commune. He covered his father's eyes and closed his own.

He says that beside the father's photo he keeps a volume of the poems of Jules Supervielle, because in the presence of his father's likeness he always reads a few verses he is deeply convinced are appropriate. This isn't something he could explain, he adds, and asks whether I have ever had a similar experience with a book, say, or a painting.

"No. In my case it's a score, Branly, Haydn's Emperor Quartet. It isn't, as it is with you, that I associate it with a person, even less with someone dead. It's my way of relating to myself. When I listen to that quartet, I gain serenity or strength or forgetfulness, I experience the emotion I need at any given moment."

Branly smiled and said that perhaps it was the same with him, and that associating the poem with his father was more homage than mystery. Maybe I was right, maybe

Supervielle's poem made use of the photograph of the father to reach the son.

> *Voyez-vous pas qu'il sépare*
> *Mal le jour d'avec la nuit,*
> *Et les cieux les plus profonds*
> *Du coeur sans fond qui l'agite?*

Branly murmured, adding: "Supervielle, of course, was born in Uruguay; he comes from your world."

"Oh, Buenos Aires and Montevideo are my lost cities, they are dead to me. I shall never see them again. France is the final homeland of every Latin American. Paris will never be a lost city."

That afternoon Hugo Heredia arrived, without complications.

"Should I follow Master Victor's orders?" Etienne, the chauffeur, asked as my friend was overseeing the transfer of Hugo's luggage from the Citroën to the house.

"Of course. They are my guests. I am surprised by your question, Etienne."

"But, M. le Comte, you were inconvenienced by having to come from the station by taxi while I was taking the Spaniards shopping. That is not my custom."

"I repeat, they are my guests. Follow their instructions as if they were my own."

"The young gentleman's as well?"

Branly nodded, but something kept him from actually enunciating the word "yes." In spite of himself, his eyes questioned Etienne. The chauffeur realized it, and so that Etienne would not have to avert his eyes in embarrassment every time Branly gazed unblinkingly at him, my friend had no recourse but to ask if there was a reason for such a question.

"They won't tell you," the chauffeur said.

"Who are 'they,' Etienne?"

"The two Spaniards. José and Florencio. They're afraid to lose their jobs. They don't want to go back to Spain, you know."

"But what happened to José and Florencio?"

"Well, you know how Florencio looks out for José. Yesterday José was unpacking the boy's suitcases, as any good man would, hanging things up and putting his belongings in the drawers. Then young Victor came in and, according to José, flew into a rage for no reason at all. He whipped off his belt and began beating José; he drove him to his knees. Then he said never to touch his suitcases, not ever, unless he himself gave the order—and not before."

José, he added, had gone weeping to the kitchen and Florencio had said he'd go up and give that arrogant young man a good thrashing, who did he think he was? But José had smoothed things over. He reminded Florencio of how young Master Lope had treated them in Zaragoza, that's how young gentlemen were in Spain, and across the ocean, well! there they were young lords of gibbet and blade. Then they'd thought over their precarious status as immigrant workers and decided to leave things alone.

"You know how they are, M. le Comte. They know how to console one another."

A vulgar spark glinted from Etienne's rimless glasses, and this time Branly glared at him sternly, unblinkingly, until the robust Celt reddened, coughed, and asked to be excused.

My friend was not surprised by the fact that while tea was being served in the great hall of the candelabra the father and son pored over the telephone directory of the Parisian metropolitan area.

"It's a game we play," the father said pleasantly. "Everywhere we go, we look to see if we can find our names in the directory. The one who wins claims a prize from the one who loses."

"You were lucky in Puebla," said Victor, scanning the thick book.

"But you won in Monterrey and in Mérida," said Hugo, patting his son's dark lank hair.

"And in Paris, too, Papa." The boy laughed happily. "Look."

Father and son, arms about one another's shoulders, peered closely at the small print of the directory.

"Heredia, Victor," they read together, laughing, the son more quickly and gaily than his father. "Heredia, Victor, 54 Clos des Renards, Enghien-les-Bains."

"Where is that?" asked Victor.

My friend was still not quite at ease in the world the Heredias had opened to him, a world he consciously desired, though unconsciously—he knew now, free of the confusion of the morning—he was alarmed by the kinship that seemed to him in danger of closing a too-perfect circle, the union of alpha and omega. He replied with equanimity, not totally immersed in the game, nor totally outside it.

"North of Paris."

"Is it easy to get there?" Victor asked.

"Yes, you take exit 3 on the A-1 highway to Beauvais and Chantilly."

"Papa, I want Etienne to take me there!"

"That would be a waste of time. There's so much to see in Paris."

"But you lost, Papa. I want my prize."

"Isn't it enough to beat me?"

"No. I want my prize. I want to go there. You promised. We promised we'd give each other prizes, don't you remember?"

"But wouldn't it be a good idea to telephone your Victor Heredia first?" Hugo suggested with a certain resignation.

"Remember how surprised the old man in Monterrey was

when we showed up without warning?" Victor parried. "Remember?"

With his arm still around his son's shoulder, Hugo cupped his chin in his hand and forced the boy to look into his eyes. "No. I don't remember. You went alone."

The boy hung his head and his ears flamed crimson.

"He thought we were some long-lost relations coming to claim part of the inheritance," Victor added weakly, a tremor in his deliberately lighthearted voice. "The hereditary Heredias."

"Victor," Hugo said severely. "I'm delighted to play these games with you, but if they are to have any value we must never lie. Neither of us. Yes, we both looked up the name in the Monterrey directory."

The boy, with a hint of desperation that alarmed my friend, quickly explained that in Mexico the people of Monterrey have the reputation of being misers, like the Scots in Europe. That was the joke, did he see?

"But we did not go to his house together," his father said with a tone of finality. "You went alone. I allowed you to go alone. That was your prize."

Victor looked at my friend beseechingly and Branly said that of course one would have to telephone first; he would be happy to do it. He got up to avoid Victor's pained expression, and with the directory in one hand and his spectacles in the other walked to the library adjoining the great salon. He left the door half-open as he called the number in Enghien-les-Bains and heard first the firm but calm voice of Hugo, then the reproachful voice of Victor, followed by the angry voices of both and simultaneously the voice of the person who lifted the receiver to answer. As my friend spoke, the quarreling voices of the Heredias were stilled.

"Monsieur Heredia? Victor Heredia?" my friend asked, and the voice replied, "Who wants him?"

It is an old man's voice, my friend thought, and he says that in that instant he wondered if the Heredias were playing a game within a game, seeking, in addition to their names, and complementing that game, a correspondence between ages as well. He had just learned that the Victor Heredia in Monterrey was an old man; he guessed that the Victor Heredia of Enghien was also old. Had the names and ages of the Hugo in Puebla and the Victor in Mérida coincided, so that the father, who was the loser in names, was winner in the category of ages? Or it could be, ironically, that the ones with Victor's name were to be old, and those with the father's name young. The inherent nonsense of these combinations piqued Branly's curiosity and his sense of humor; it also occurred to him that this might be the reason for Hugo's unexpected irritation. Was my friend going to reward him with the news that this time the person who bore his son's name was a young man? He disliked having to disillusion him.

"I hope you will accept what I am going to say in good humor. Two foreign friends of mine looked up your name in the telephone directory . . . "

"My name?"

"Please bear with me. Actually, they were looking for their names and found yours."

"How is that?"

"It's a kind of game, please don't take offense . . ."

"Tell them to go play games with their bitch of a mother," spat the voice, and the line went dead.

My friend returned to the salon and reported the failure of a mission he should have realized was absurd but had carried out because of an overrationalization of his keenness to participate in Victor Heredia's games. This initial failure, he tells me, made him doubt his capacity to enter fully into the game, a game which even Hugo Heredia, at least a moment before, and to my friend's surprise, had seemed reluctant to join in. Branly was aware of the Heredias' restrained expectancy. My friend told them that he had failed, without going into detail. He waited, savoring the satisfaction of news withheld, certain that at any moment Hugo would ask the age of the man who had answered the phone. Was he old? Young? But the jesses of those questions were never loosed; they bound Hugo's lips and his son's as the falconer's jesses immobilize his falcon. My friend finally broke the uneasy silence to say that he was sure they would be interested to know that the man who answered, who had said he was Victor Heredia, had the voice of an old or at least a tired man.

Hugo displayed no glimmer of reaction. It was Victor who looked at his father expectantly and asked: "Then may I go tomorrow, Papa? Will you let me?"

The father removed his spectacles, as if to suggest that eyes can be as tired as a voice, old or not. But he nodded in acquiescence, as if finally conceding that fatigue and old age are synonymous. My friend sipped his tea and wondered where the line lay that divided the unity of the father and son from their efforts to dominate one another. Victor accepted Hugo's intellectual instruction; Hugo was not disturbed that his son whipped a servant. Both played the game of names together from the beginning, but Hugo refused to follow it to its conclusion and, if the occasion arose, to visit the man who bore his name. It was impossible to know which of the two was lying—the father, who perhaps wanted to protect his son from a risky encounter but not spoil an innocent game, or the son, who perhaps did not understand his father's unwillingness to participate in the conclusion of the game, and so, though only in his imagination, included him in it.

But that was not my friend's problem. He repeated this to himself the following morning as Hugo left for the opening meeting of the conference on the Place Fontenoy, and

Etienne drove them along the Seine toward Epinay and then plunged through a succession of the monotonous, haphazardly redeveloped towns of the Val d'Oise.

Branly attempted to entertain Victor with some comments about the countryside; Etienne barely masked his yawns. The thought crossed my friend's mind that he would have to find a more respectful and reserved chauffeur. He explained to Victor that they were approaching the region that from ancient times had been called the Pays de France, quite different from the neighboring provinces of Parisis, Sanlisis, Valois, Île de France, and Brie champenois; but all the time he was talking and entertaining Victor, believing he was concentrating on what he was saying, his mind actually was on what he is now telling me.

"It was only by a miracle that this lad and I happened to meet. I don't mean because we were separated by geography, but because in the normal course of events I would have died before I met him, or even before he was born. Or possibly the boy might have died before I could meet him."

He says he almost asked Victor to describe his brother, but just then Etienne, who in spite of everything, honest ham face and rimless spectacles, was very proficient at the wheel, turned from the highway and drove into the narrow business streets of Enghien, past the esplanade of the casino, the lake and the hot baths, beneath the railroad bridges, until he came to one of those magic, unexpected woods that redeem the ugliness of Parisian suburbs and obliterate not only the reality but even the memory of everything but these oaks lining the road, these arching chestnut trees filtering the fading September light.

As the Citroën turned into the private avenue of the Clos des Renards, my friend felt as if he were sinking into a world of undersea greenness. Once the automobile left behind the stone and iron arch displaying the name of the property, the avenue descended swiftly but smoothly and the trees, in conjugal embrace overhead, seemed to rise even taller. Below, lifting fingers of ivy covered the bed of this vegetal ocean. Cherry trees lent fiery grace to the deep, breathless coolness. Branly felt a sense of suffocation, as if in approaching this villa in Enghien he were descending in a submarine; the sea, too, cools as it drowns.

The car proceeded slowly over the thin layer of dead leaves. At the end of the avenue my friend could see a clearing, like the light at the end of a tunnel. He was eager, he confesses, to leave behind the suffocating darkness of the woods for what he could glimpse ahead, a French park, a garden of intelligence, a chessboard where the wild woods of a surely romantic imagination had been checkmated by a geometric precision of shrubs, greensward, pansies, and stone urns placed in perfect symmetry, like a brief prologue to the manor house, whose solitary façade rose as symmetrical as the garden, as if garden and house were reflecting one another, Branly says, in a nonexistent pool. In vain he looked for the element of order that as it duplicated would accentuate the symmetry: a mirror of water. The solid mansion rose from the level of the warning gravel—now crushed by an equally solid Etienne as he circled the garden and came to a stop before the entrance steps—to the crown of three slate-colored mansards and twin brick chimneys. And as if transported from the world of the forest, the villa became an undersea fortress, the useless barbican of a forgotten battle at the bottom of the sea.

A date was inscribed on the molding above the doorway: A.D. 1870. Etienne thought it was the number of the house and that he had made a wrong turn; he muttered curses against a municipal system that would assign two numbers to one house. My friend knew it was a date, not only by the reference to the Year of our Lord, which meant nothing to Etienne, but also because as he preceded Victor out of the car he glanced toward the second story of the house, where he saw hovering in the window a silhouette whose sail, like that of an ancient schooner, blended into indistinct waves of flowing hair—sail, fluttering curtains, white gown, all glimpsed fleetingly yet as one in the impression of antiquity they made on a man, my old, my dear friend, who had arrived with his young foreign pupil at what he thought was the end of a game but really was only the beginning.

4

They returned to the Avenue de Saxe. Branly tried to interest Victor in other outings, but the boy, although friendly, was wrapped in his own thoughts and said he would rather stay in the house. My friend watched him wandering through the mansion, familiarizing himself with it, perhaps memorizing it, while my friend read a book in the library, whose well-fitted bookshelves eliminated the need for further decoration. Wallpaper imprinted with Greek busts, acanthus, flutes, and staffs had not penetrated here, nor bas-reliefs in which Minerva holds a protective hand over the head of Eros. Instead, there was a whispered, measured, intermittent dialogue with Balzac and Lamartine.

The volume of *Méditations* fell to my friend's knees. They had tried to rouse someone. He had rapped on the beveled glass of the doors. No one came. He ordered Etienne to blow the horn. The glass panes of the door reverberated beneath my friend's fingertips. In spite of the isolation of the Clos des Renards, they could hear the murmur of distant buses and impatient traffic. But neither the remote noises nor the immediacy of the Citroën's horn proclaiming their presence before the pale yellow façade, my friend realized, seemed to distract Victor where he stood on a terrace guarded by two symmetrically placed, crouching stone lions.

His back to the house, the boy was staring toward what my friend then began to see—he tells me he knows now—thanks to Victor. Above the absolute contrast of woods and garden, the spirit of order that governed the garden marched toward an encounter with its denial in the woods. Order and disorder met without conflict among rosebushes, beeches, and a solitary willow, but especially in the birch grove bordering one wall of the manor house.

Branly again glanced toward the second story; what he thought he had seen was no longer there. In the sudden silence underscored by the absence of the sound of the horn, my friend heard Victor whistling a melody. As the boy walked down the front steps, his head bowed and his hands buried in the pockets of his corduroy trousers, gravel crunched beneath his feet. He walked to the end of the pebbled path and turned toward the long avenue through the woods. My friend says he could hear distinctly the transition from trodden stone to dead leaves, and only then what he is telling me now came to his mind: it was September, autumn was still some time away, yet the avenue of chestnuts and oaks was one long, uninterrupted path of dry leaves.

He still doesn't know why he called Victor to stop, not to walk any farther on the dead leaves, to return to the automobile. You see, there's no one here, perhaps if they came back another day they would have better luck. Docilely, Victor stopped, turned, and walked back to the automobile, where Branly awaited, holding the door open. After they returned to Paris, my friend did not insist again that they go out. Secretly, although without any reason, he hoped Victor would not be upset, that he would rather wander through the mansion on the Avenue de Saxe, the single story contained between the baroque cavern of the entrance, the courtyard of yellow stone, and the garden with its mani-cured lawn—unexceptional urns, and a thick sea pine placidly growing in sand that was in a certain way twin to the equally sterile asphalt of the street. My friend insists, however, that sand is a defense against the potential invasion of the street, and as proof he points out that the pine grows in sand but would be killed by asphalt.

In fact, in the moment he is now remembering, he corrects himself, he was thinking how unlikely it would be that his residence would be engulfed by the street, which would disdain the false oasis of the garden, recognizing it for what it was, a desert in disguise. But the woods of the Clos des Renards would not respect the fragility of plaster, stone, and slate of the manor house. Like the fleeting apparition at the window, there was something about the house that would not withstand aggression from its surroundings. He tried to draw comfort from the thought that, like the sand that nurtured the sea pine, his house provided protection.

Then he heard the faint murmur that penetrated as far as the library only because of the hospitable tranquillity of that September afternoon. It was as if the city, deserted during the summer, had not yet recovered its customary bustle in spite of the frenzy he had noted the previous morning at the Gare d'Austerlitz—workers coming in from the suburbs, tourists returning from vacations in Spain, and Spaniards coming to France to look for work.

He heard the striking of Antoine-André Ravrio's clock. On the hour, the bronze figure of a woman adorned in an Empire gown played a piano gilded, like herself and the doors and draperies of the motionless salon, in an opulent, and poisonous, bath. My friend tells me that as he listened, and only in that instant—as is wont to happen with our aural memory, and especially in the case of music, which reaches our ears naked and stripped of words, nameless, wishing to be heard for itself and not because of descriptive and identifying titles that make a symphonic poem little more than the background fanfare of trumpets for a scene we must imagine before ever we hear the music— only then did he realize that the clock was playing the tune Victor had hummed that evening at Jean's and a second voice had echoed from the venomous depths of the barranca in Cuernavaca.

He walked slowly, with no intent of stealth, he assures me, but, rather, a desire to preserve the instant, to where Victor, as when Branly surprised him on his arrival, was stroking the gilded bronze of the clock in the sumptuous music box, now striking the first hour after noon, its metallic tune ringingly marking the impalpable mathematical hours told by the hands.

Branly was again a boy in the Parc Monceau, playing with the other children, who recognized him, who loved him, who called to him because he was a child like them. And as they grew tired of playing amid the columns, pyramids, crypts, and rotundas commissioned scarcely a century earlier by the Duc d'Orléans, they all gathered together beside the pond— the imagined scene of impossible naumachiae—and sang that timeless tune they had learned in their homes, not in school, a madrigal filtered through thousands of children's and lovers' voices throughout history. My friend, in a voice broken by the emotion of his memory, placed a hand on Victor's shoulder and murmured the phrases that recall the beautiful fountain with waters so clear one cannot resist bathing there: *"À la claire fontaine, m'en allant promener, j'ai trouvé l'eau si belle, que je m'y suis baigné."*

He would place no obstacle before Victor's new invitation. They dined with Hugo, but no one spoke of the game. The father seemed to have forgotten it, his thoughts on the work of the conference. The following day, my friend Branly and his young friend again set off for Enghien-les-Bains.

5

The search for Victor Heredia, Branly is telling me, was not unlike an exhausting vigil before a mirror. He asked me to imagine such a vigil, yes, he says, as he seeks my reflection in the window closed to the bustle of the Place de la Concorde, simply imagine biding one's time before a vacant mirror, waiting for it to take on life, to regain its lost image.

"Do you mean," I ventured, "that, besides having the same name, the Victor Heredia of Enghien-les-Bains was a physical double of the boy?"

My friend shook his shiny bald head emphatically; his brow was unusually severe in refutation. That was not what he meant to imply, not at all. No, he meant precisely what he had said, keeping a vigil before a mirror, laying siege to it, a long and unremitting siege, until it was forced to reveal its image—not the reflection of the person looking in the mirror, did I understand? No, the mirror's own image, exactly so, its own hidden, illusive, reluctant, one might almost say coquettish, image.

For the second time, no one had responded when he knocked on the French doors at the end of the terrace of lions. It was Wednesday, racing day. Branly and Victor lunched at the casino, watching the passing throngs of elderly men and women who come every week to squander their pensions at the Enghien racetrack, and then, not content with losing on the horses, insist on losing at roulette. Their shuffling gait, their shiny dark-blue suits, their faded straw bonnets, belie—except in an occasional case of exemplary avarice—the success of such pursuits. My friend wondered whether our evasive Victor Heredia might not be found among the dispirited gamblers. Branly, you see, was still convinced that the person who shared the young Mexican's name was a man of advanced years. He says he had made that judgment when he heard the voice over the telephone. He admits that he rejected, a priori, the idea that the bearer of young Victor's name could be a physical double. At least, he said, he could find comfort in the fact that he had sensed what he was now trying to communicate to me, the feeling that he was keeping watch before a mirror, hoping it would dare incarnate the figure hiding within. At least, he says, he had that intuition.

"You see, I always believed that even if I found him I would need to continue searching, to wait patiently until he revealed his true face. I did it for the lad, I assure you."

As dusk approached, the old man and the boy, who had met purely by chance, who under normal circumstances would never have met, because the man should have died before he met the youth, and the boy might easily have been born after the man's death, strolled together to the lake at Enghien. They enjoyed the promenade and decided that this time they would walk to the Clos des Renards. Branly told Etienne to have a cup of coffee and in a half hour to pick them up at the entrance to the estate. As they walked, Victor kept lagging behind, inspecting and investigating and skipping in the childlike way that had caught Branly's attention in Cuernavaca. My friend, who walks straight as a ramrod in spite of his wounded leg, now hung his head in thought, wondering whether it was possible that the half-glimpsed figure in the second-story window was the Victor Heredia they were searching for. But as often as he considered this possibility, he rejected it. My friend had no way of knowing if the voice he had heard over the telephone was actually that of the French Victor Heredia. As he walked ahead of Victor, erect, occasionally resting his weight on his cane, he tried to reconstruct the telephone conversation. When he had asked for Heredia, the voice had countered with the question: Who wants him? And when he explained that he had looked up his name in the directory, the man was at first surprised, then insulting; he had never conceded that his name was Victor Heredia.

My friend tells me now, gazing at the goblet of sauterne scarcely less pale than the hand holding it, that as he walked along, followed by young Victor Heredia, and breathing the gasoline fumes, the train smoke, and the first mists from September woods decaying with their fruitless harvests, he wondered whether that voice could be related to the white sail-like silhouette that had passed so swiftly across the window of the Clos des Renards, whether the voice and the image, related or not, might belong to the person called Victor Heredia, or whether they merely served him, looked after him, taught him, tended him, recalled or awaited him. If the voice and the figure were not Victor Heredia's, my friend insists this afternoon, then Victor Heredia was cared for by a servant, looked after by a guardian, taught by a tutor, tended by a doctor, recalled by a kinsman, or awaited by a lover.

They were approaching the wall surrounding the estate of the Clos des Renards; my friend admits that he was weaving a mystery, and that doing so amused him. He stopped to wait for Victor, who was lagging behind, and saw him standing beside the high moss-covered wall, his head against the mustard-colored stone. Dusk was falling quickly now; Branly called Victor, beckoning to him; the boy left the wall and came running. He had a snail in his hands, which he showed to my friend. Heads together, absorbed in the mollusk, they walked toward the arch that marked the entrance to the woods with its avenue of chestnuts, oaks, and dry leaves that had not fallen from any of the surrounding trees. Branly started. Beneath leaden eyelids, his gaze shifted from the tiny snail to the lane that led into the estate, and he recognized what had been nagging at his mind, what until this instant had been suspended in mid-air, floating like the uncertain mist at the end of the lane over the house without a pool. This was the second revelation of this crepuscular hour: how strange that a house of this size and pretension had no mirror of water, no pond or fountain.

Etienne abruptly braked the car near the entrance to the private avenue and blew the horn; he explained that it was rapidly growing dark and he was worried about the count's health. Besides, for the first time, the chauffeur kept repeating, he had noticed a slight chill in the air. He was standing on the pavement beside the car, facing Branly and Victor and deferentially holding the door, waiting for his gentleman and the boy to climb into the automobile, where he had arranged lap robes for them. My friend says he is still trying to follow Victor's quick, nervous movements: the boy's hesitation, barely perceptible but real as a bolt of lightning, as he tried to decide whether to run down the avenue covered with dead leaves or climb into the car or do what he did—summing up his options in a kind of terrible desperation, slamming the door of the Citroën on the chauffeur's hand. Etienne himself, stifling a scream of pain, managed to open the door as Branly cast aside his cane to grasp the servant's arm. Branly hesitated, as Victor had just done. Should he help Etienne or stop Victor, now running toward the avenue of dry leaves beneath the leafy trees.

Actually, he says, he was saved the necessity of a choice when a figure hurrying toward them bumped into the boy and interrupted his flight. The man grasped Victor firmly by the shoulders and led him back to the scene of the accident, inquiring what had happened. At that moment, Branly had no way of knowing whether the man was a casual passerby or had come from the avenue leading to the Clos des Renards. The new arrival immediately dispelled any doubt. "Please. Come along to my house, I can help your man there."

Branly responded that Etienne couldn't manage the distance from the road to the house, and he invited the obliging stranger to get into the car with them. He cast a quizzical glance at Victor and climbed in behind the wheel. He started the Citroën and turned into the avenue of the woods. A hunched-over Etienne sat beside him, moaning between clenched teeth, wrapping a handkerchief around his bleeding hand. Victor and the stranger sat in the back seat, and from time to time my friend stole a glance in the rearview mirror through flashes of a sun setting at the very hour of the Île de France that he and I were now awaiting in the heart of Paris. On that day, it arrived just as he was driving the injured Etienne and glancing into the rearview mirror to observe a man wearing a wool-tweed hat whose brim did not obscure pale eyes above a singularly straight nose with no noticeable bridge and a thin-lipped mouth as straight as the nose—the mouth partly hidden behind the turned-up lapels of an overcoat, like the hat, of greenish Scottish wool.

As their glances met in the mirror, the stranger smiled and said, "Forgive me. My name is Victor Heredia. I deeply regret this accident at the very doors of my home. We will do whatever we can to help your chauffeur, Monsieur . . . ?"

"Branly," my friend said dryly.

Today he acknowledges an emotion that was either cowardice or prudence, or pure and simple fear, neither cowardly nor prudent: he did not introduce Victor Heredia to Victor Heredia.

Neither could he see in the mirror the boy's reaction when the man, whose age my friend still could not determine, as he could not absolutely identify his voice as the voice on the telephone, introduced himself. My friend stopped the car at the terrace. The French Heredia quickly got out, and between them they helped Etienne up the steps of the terrace and to the French doors. Heredia softly pushed them open and the three stepped into a cavern of dark wood marked by a strong smell of leather, apparently the foyer of the residence.

The owner, still in hat and overcoat, hurried up the stairs while Branly examined Etienne's injured hand. It was only after the master of the house had returned, removed his hat to reveal a white mane of hair, and begun amateurishly to swab the chauffeur's hand with iodine and to apply a simple bandage, that my friend realized that his host, although possessing a youngish face, was not young. And it was only after Heredia said they had better call an ambulance, and went to the telephone to make the call, that my friend looked about for the other Victor Heredia, and glancing through the French doors, spied the boy on the terrace, standing with legs wide apart, one arm akimbo, the other resting on the back of the crouching stone lion, the boy as motionless as a second statue, and, like a statue's, his gaze lost in the far distance.

My friend tried to follow the direction of that gaze. Heredia was telephoning for the ambulance; Etienne was gritting his teeth, cradling the injured, iodine-swabbed, bandaged hand. Branly moved toward the glass panes to observe the motionless boy, who was staring at the grove of birches suspended between the soothing mist of dream and the fading light of dusk that outlined the boy's slim whiteness seemingly born of the germinal mist. The sleek silvery trunks were the perfect recapitulation of the mist and the light of the setting sun—the sun, satisfied; the mist, indecisive. At that hour the woods were a misty curtain of light, wispy as the tree trunks, white as chiffon, against which one could barely see—interrupting the vertical symmetry of the trunks and as vague as the horizontal mist that veiled it and the oblique light that revealed it—the silhouette of a motionless figure observed by the motionless boy observed by my motionless friend from behind the half-opened French doors.

The spell was broken. The figure in the woods moved toward the house, whistling. The Mexican youth dropped his arm and then covered his face with both hands, as if trying to hide it. His back was turned to Branly, but my friend clearly recognized that gesture, as he heard on the lips of the figure moving toward them from the woods the tune of the timeless madrigal of the clear fountain and the beautiful waters.

6

The French Heredia said they must take Etienne to the hospital on the Boulevard d'Ormesson; he was afraid the fingers were broken. That wasn't the greatest thing that could happen to a chauffeur, he added. As Branly heard him say this, he avoided the eyes of the young Mexican, who at that moment was entering the house for the first time. My friend did not want to think the French Heredia was reprimanding the youth who bore his name; even less did he want the boy to think he was a partner in what was at the very least a premature accusation.

Similarly incapable of expressing overt disapproval, however, Branly glanced at his new host, and then said quietly: "Don't worry, Etienne. It isn't anything that won't respond to treatment."

"I suggest that you follow us in your car," said Heredia.

Branly again checked the irritation provoked by such freely offered advice. There was a peremptory tone in the Frenchman's voice, as if in counseling Branly to follow he were ironically acknowledging in the master a concern for his servant that he, Heredia, would never be so weak as to feel, certainly not to reveal. But the behavior my friend was beginning to perceive, as evidence of a common up-bringing, was not so much worthy of disapproval as some-

Los Gatos H.S. Library

thing to be overlooked; it seemed, even before such rationalization, undeserving of any comment. His attention was absorbed by a more serious reality. The young Heredia, like a character in a silent movie, had paused as he crossed the threshold, enveloped in silence, framed in a shimmering light that changed him into a trembling flame. If his eyes were not closed, they were nearly so. He was breathing deeply, and seemed tense, but content. It was the contentment that impressed Branly.

As the boy breathed in that aroma of leather pervading the entrance to the manor house, his breathing became more and more agitated. My friend felt that he could take the boy's agitation as the delayed reaction to the terrible act he had committed against the chauffeur, and he was about to point this out to the master of the Clos des Renards as courteous proof of the boy's repentance, but something stopped him, something intimately linked to his growing perceptions about the man with Victor's name. He shook his head, he tells me, with the certainty that the less one knew about what was happening, the better. Once more, the same feeling prevented him from introducing the two Heredias. With any luck, Branly told himself, the boy's natural curiosity, particularly in view of recent events, would be satisfied simply with seeing Heredia. After all, it was Victor's actions that had shifted attention from names, however closely related, to the injured chauffeur, whom the French Heredia, ignoring the Mexican youth's presence, was urging they take to a hospital. He would go with Etienne in the ambulance, the Frenchman repeated, adding on second thought that he could look after the chauffeur himself and the others could drive back to Paris. He would inform them in the morning of the poor fellow's condition.

"Not at all. Etienne is my employee, and any responsibility for looking after him is mine," said my friend, following a brief pause which at the time seemed natural to him but which in retrospect he considered deceitful. He still had not fathomed the French Heredia's intentions, and he had stumbled over an obstacle lying in the path of his inherent sense of propriety: the French Victor Heredia talked like a tradesman; his speech was in marked contrast to the nobility of his classic features, a contrast greater even than the physical contrast between the handsome leonine head and the squat body with its sturdy, squarish torso and the common, stubby-fingered hands.

As if to dispel any doubt about the extent of the responsibilities he was prepared to assume, my friend said *he* would accompany Etienne in the ambulance. But Heredia insisted. He knew the doctors on duty and that would facilitate the process. Branly did not want to tell anyone what he now admits to me, that he was trying to avoid having to drive at night on the always dangerous highways that by dawn are like battlefields, no less horrible for their repetitiousness; he is blinded by the aggressive headlights of drivers who view themselves as combatants in a modern joust. Visions of overturned trucks, little 2CV's flattened like the tin from which they are assembled, stretchers, ambulance sirens, and the flashing lights of patrol cars in the bloody gray dawn of the highways were suddenly fused into the single ululating tone of the ambulance coming to a stop behind the Citroën parked beside the terrace of the lions.

There was no time, Branly tells me, for discussion; it was as if everything had been planned, choreographed like a ballet. The boy would be all right, Heredia said. His own son would be arriving soon and the boys could keep each other company until the men returned from taking the unfortunate Etienne to the hospital.

"Yes, yes, yes," said Heredia. "I insist on it. You must spend the night here with my son and me. Tomorrow, M. Branly, you can drop by the hospital to see how this fellow is getting along; believe me, it's no bother; I'm a very late riser. You can just make yourself at home, my son André will look after you. Don't worry, the larder is well stocked, my friend; this isn't your common Spanish inn, eh?"

As they helped Etienne into the ambulance, he said: "I wouldn't want M. le Comte to put himself out on my account."

"Don't worry, Etienne," said Branly. "I repeat, everything will be all right."

Branly and Heredia followed the ambulance, my friend driving the Citroën very gingerly, and during the brief ride to the hospital he had an opportunity to clarify the reason for their visit and to explain the coincidence of the names. The Frenchman laughed, and begged my friend to forgive him for the language he had used over the phone. He hadn't known that such a distinguished person, a count no less, was calling; he'd thought it was some clown, it was almost an everyday thing these days to get that kind of call at any hour of the night or day, and when he'd answered that particular call—that is, the Count's—he was still half asleep. He'd already told him he slept late. Would M. le Comte de Branly forgive him? He wanted to apologize for that, too. He hadn't known he was a count or he would have used "de," *de* Branly.

Branly refrained from saying that he hadn't used it himself, but the irrepressible Heredia had already launched into a tale about a Cuban family that had emigrated to Haiti during the uprising against the Spanish at the end of the century, first assimilated into the French language in the heat- and salt-pocked marble salons of Port-au-Prince, and then, become rich in imports and exports, absorbed into the France of the First World War, riding the crest of a savory and aromatic mountain of bananas, tobacco, rum, and vanilla. Relatives of the poet? What poet? And of course, he concluded with an ostentatious air of ennui, they

[45]

had forbidden the use of Spanish, which for them carried only memories of restlessness, barbarism, and revolution.

"French is like my garden, elegant," said Heredia. "Spanish is like my woods, indomitable."

My friend can't remember his response to the French Heredia; it doesn't matter. Branly, who instinctively is courteous and hospitable to everyone, found something insufferable in the tone of this man with the pale eyes, straight nose, and white mane of hair. Heredia made a display of being courteous and hospitable, but this was precisely what bothered my friend. He suspected that Heredia's affability was a maneuver masking some overweening sense of physical or moral supremacy not immediately apparent to Branly but which Heredia hoped to minimize by lavishing attention on his guest. My friend was particularly repelled by the obsequious and at the same time ironic humility typical of the bourgeois parvenu who, terrified at the possibility of again becoming a servant, attempts to subjugate those persons he fears and admires.

My friend knows the world well enough to be able to identify those times when another person feels a superiority he does not want to show, but by that very fact, and by acting more than usually cordial, calls attention to what he wants to hide. He says he was on the verge of letting Heredia know by his actions that the opposite was more accurate, but the contrast between a French family of ancient lineage and a colonial transplant was so obvious that Branly felt embarrassed even for having considered snubbing Heredia. Undoubtedly, Heredia had too often suffered from French superiority and pedantry—which often go hand in hand—not to recognize the differences between them. He knew how to play on those differences and, in the case of those less cautious or less secure than Branly, how to ensnare the unwary.

In contrast to Heredia, my friend decided to practice

an impeccable courtesy based less on conscious will than on custom, running the risk that Heredia, in turn, would recognize my friend's stratagem.

That is why he is sure, he says, that he had done nothing to provoke the comment Heredia made as they parked in front of the hospital, facing the ambulance; and if the words were spoken, it was perhaps because they were, though for different reasons, in the minds of both men.

"You have no cause to look down your nose at a man who has worked for his wealth instead of inheriting it through no effort of his own."

Such an unexpected sally, especially one so close to the mark in regard to what really was passing through my friend's mind, evoked a swift response: "Everything one owns has either been bought, inherited, or stolen. Have no fear. We are not as different as you seem to believe."

But whatever Heredia's intentions—and Branly began to suspect that Heredia hoped to distract him, to involve him in a banal conversation, to challenge his honor, to provoke a long but courteous silence like the one that must have motivated the bizarre words Heredia had tried to thrust like banderillas into the neck of his guest—Branly freed his mind of the implications of this new and unexpected development, realizing with lucid clarity that a man like Heredia would not ordinarily worry about a chauffeur. Normally, he would not lift a finger for him, or go out of his way to offer him aid. Heredia had made up his mind, had acted, telephoned the hospital, before he knew who Branly was. His attentiveness toward Etienne did not spring out of compassion for the servant or adulation of the master, but from some other motive that Heredia had deceitfully hoped to obscure by proudly exhibiting the most repulsive emotion my friend and I know: resentment.

Branly did not hesitate for a moment. The instant Heredia got out of the Citroën, my friend slammed the door and threw the car into reverse. The lights of the ambulance blinded him, but they also blocked out the astounded Heredia standing on the sidewalk with one hand to his eyes, protecting himself from the luminous lances of the ambulance and the Citroën crossed in blinding white combat that terrified my friend, until, still in reverse, he found space in which to turn the car, and, shifting into high gear, followed the signs that would lead him away from the hospital, away from Heredia and Etienne—standing like statues, watching his desperate struggle to reverse the car and drive off in the direction of the Clos des Renards. He knew now that Heredia had wanted him away from there—why? He had wanted to lure him away and keep him away, but he would not succeed. The dazzle of the headlights did not prevent him from seeing a truth spawned in darkness, untouched by any light except a psychic certainty: if the French Victor Heredia was not interested in him or his chauffeur, then he could be interested only in the person who bore his name, the Mexican Victor Heredia.

My friend says he felt as if black shadows had congealed in his throat. The signs led him from the center of Enghien toward the highways that were the source of his night terrors, and in the prison of glass and lights surrounding him, the vision of his fatal accident and that of a park filled with children who no longer recognized him blended together like two crystalline rivers that for years had flowed side by side, finally to be silently joined that night. Victor needed him, he was in danger. That is why Heredia had lured him from the Clos des Renards, Branly tells me now, and adds that was all he knew—rather, all he needed to know—at this incredible moment in his life. He drove blindly, recklessly, certain that he was racing toward an encounter with his recurrent nightmare of death on a night highway. But, above all else, he felt that he was the object of an implacable hostility.

He could not identify its source. He did not want to consider Heredia capable of transmitting such sovereign hatred. Besides, he had left the Frenchman standing on the sidewalk of the hospital on the Boulevard d'Ormesson just now, blinded by actual lights. The blast of malice directed against Branly, Branly's vital juices informed him, his viscera, the shadowy taste in his mouth, sprang from a different place and a different time, a faraway time and place as distant in origin as the dead leaves swirling in the wake of the automobile racing along the avenue of the Clos des Renards— leaves my friend feverishly knew were alien to that place; they had not fallen from any tree in these woods, and who could say who or what had carried them here, or when or where they had actually fallen, in what dense forest.

7

Branly is an inveterate traveler. It is not unusual to see him one day, as today, in the dining room or swimming pool of the club housed in Gabriel's magnificent *pavillon* facing the Place de la Concorde, and then lose sight of him for months. He may wish to see his favorite Velázquezes in the Prado or the magnificent Brueghels in Naples, the diamantine lakes of southern Chile or the endlessly golden dawns over the Bosporus. The wish is father to the deed; wish, not caprice, he explains. Because he had known the innocent world before Sarajevo, he believes it would be absurd in this day of instant communications for men not to claim their right to use transportation to their own advantage, to fulfill their slightest whim, knowing that, like every new conquest, such privilege is also a notification of what we have lost: the visa-less intercommunicating universe he had enjoyed when one traveled to Kabul not in a Caravelle but in a caravan. The witticism attributed to Paul Morand could easily apply to my friend: he so loves to travel that his will stipulates that his skin be made into a suitcase.

So no one among Branly's friends is surprised by his sudden absence. He might be visiting the Countess at nearby Quercy, or be as far away as the Toltec ruins at Xochicalco. Neither will ever be dislodged from its site, and so, in keeping with a life based on civility and social niceties, my friend willingly goes to the mountains that will not come to him.

And such idiosyncratic habits serve a different end as well. They permit him, in keeping with his desire, to avoid any mention of occasional illness. Nothing irritates him more than the solicitous—sincere or feigned, though almost always hypocritical—attentions given the ailments that beset the elderly. He is no hypochondriac, and he detests the idea that anyone should see him reduced to querulousness or debility. When Branly finds himself in bed against his will, Florencio and José are well trained in informing callers that M. le Comte will be out of town for a few weeks, and if they want to communicate with him they may do so by writing in care of the prefecture of Dordogne, or perhaps by poste restante to the island of Mauritius. M. le Comte will undoubtedly be dropping by one of these days to pick up his mail.

Even those of us who suspect the subterfuge in all this are quite happy to attribute it to the combination of fantasy and reserve which in the Count are good and sufficient proof of his independence. In this way he cautions us to respect his privacy as he respects ours. It is only this afternoon, for instance, that I learn of the several days he spent in bed following the accident he suffered the evening he ran into one of the oak trees lining the avenue to the Clos des Renards. I acknowledge my appreciation of his confidence, though a barely perceptible gleam in his small eyes reveals

that if he has told me, it is only because the incident is indispensable to the story, the result of an automobile accident
—not uncommon in the life of one who travels so fre-
quently—and not a common cold.

"I am convinced that there are events that occur only
because we fear them. If they were not summoned by our
fear, you see, they would remain forever latent. Surely it is
our imagining them that activates the atoms of probability
and awakens them, as it were, from a dream. The dream of
our absolute indifference."

What awakened him was the whistled melody of the
madrigal of the clear fountain. He opened his eyes to the
shattered windshield of the Citroën and imagined himself a
prisoner in a crystal spiderweb before he verified the pain
in his leg and his head, before he put his hand to his brow
and felt his fingers sticky with blood, before he again felt
himself slipping into unconsciousness.

He remembers that when he again awakened he was
lying on a canopied bed. Automatically, his hand went to
his aching head.

"Don't worry, M. le Comte," said the French Heredia,
beside him. "You have been well looked after, I can swear
to that. I found you as I returned from the hospital. Why
did you do such a foolish thing? So many mishaps in a
single evening. My son André and your young friend helped
me bring you here. The doctor came, you were slightly delirious. He gave you a tetanus injection, just to be sure.
Your wounds are only superficial, nothing is broken. Your
bad leg is a bit worse for wear, and the doctor put a patch
on your head. He wants you to stay in bed for a few days.
It's the shock more than anything, you know. And at your
age you can't be too careful."

Branly waved away any concerns about his person and
inquired about Etienne.

Heredia laughed disagreeably. "Noble to the end, eh?

Your vassal is doing well, and is grateful for your concern. He spent the night in the hospital, and will be released today. He wanted to come by here, but I told him no, that you needed to rest. You're not really up to par, so here I am to carry out your orders. You just say the word."

As he tells me today, my friend was convinced that Heredia was again anticipating an unyielding silence, a reaction against the ever-increasing impertinence of the person in whose hands he was now virtually captive, and who intended to put to the test the limits of Branly's innate courtesy, challenging him to maintain his civility from a sickbed, especially now that he was dependent on the services of the man with the pale eyes, straight nose, and white mane of hair, who was caring for him in this bedchamber redolent —like the entire residence, and not just the foyer as he had first thought—of leather. The canopy of his bed was leather, as well as the chairs of this shadowy chamber closed in by heavy velvet curtains that made it impossible to tell whether it was night or day.

Yet, he told himself, it would be immature to refuse this disagreeable man the perverse pleasure of serving his guest, simply because, in serving him, the Frenchman would find further proof of Branly's feudalism, and a view of a world— which might actually be a relief for Heredia, as it was more Heredia's desire than Branly's—populated with serfs.

Unaided, my friend pulled himself to a sitting position against the leather-covered headboard of the castored bed, but he asked Heredia to arrange the pillows to make a more comfortable support for his arms. Then he asked if he might make a telephone call. He had begun to devise a policy of sorts for dealing with his unexpected and unsought host: he was beginning to realize that nothing would be more disconcerting than the continuing evidence of his courtesy, more than a counterpoint to the Frenchman's crudeness, a cool civility Heredia would find difficult to distinguish from aloof politeness, as in a rosary of identically colored baroque pearls gradations in size may not be readily apparent to the naked eye.

Heredia hesitated a moment, staring at my friend with curiosity. He folded his arms across his dirty white quilted silk dressing gown and finally informed Branly that there were no extensions upstairs, the only telephone being on the first floor. He would help Branly down the stairs, if that's what he wanted; however, he had noticed that the Count had been limping even before the accident. He didn't want to be held responsible, in case Branly should decide to file a claim for the second accident. Lucky for him, wasn't it, that the first had happened outside and that the boy was responsible.

Branly nodded, and asked Heredia to call Hugo, the boy's father. But, as his host was about to leave the room, my friend said: "No, on second thought, don't bother Señor Heredia; he might worry about his son, and there is no reason for that. Also, he is quite involved with his conference. If you don't mind, speak with my servants. They are Spanish, so they will have no difficulty understanding you. Yes, that's it, that way Señor Heredia will know where his son is, but will not worry about him. Could I trouble you, Heredia, to push my bed to the window? You can't tell the hour in this gloom. And ask the boy to come up later and visit. I am not at all tired."

Without a word, Heredia pushed the bed closer to the window. Branly smiled; he commented to his host that he was indeed a sturdy fellow. He took the cane Heredia had propped against the bed and pulled aside the curtain to allow the sun to shine in.

"Ah," he exclaimed with delight, and with a sincere impulse to share with Heredia his fundamental pleasure in life, the morning, and the sunshine. But the owner of the Clos des Renards had brusquely left the room. So, instead, instinctively seeking the signs of life his spirit had clamored for throughout the night, Branly looked out the window. His eyes took in the rational garden. He shook his head as he saw the spectacular evidence of his automobile's collision with the oak tree, and only when his quite contented invalid's eyes wandered toward the woods did he see the two figures standing hand in hand in the chiaroscuro of the birch trees. They stood so quietly they were barely visible; anything stationary in a natural setting succumbs to the universal law of mimesis.

He dozed, thinking that perhaps his host had been right, perhaps he was not yet ready for strong emotion; the world had deceived him through the years by leading him to expect the respect he felt he deserved. A resentment as flagrant and gross as Heredia's mounted in Branly's breast, an indication of the existence of a world that he had vaguely known existed but had never known. How long had it been since anyone had had the effrontery to thwart his wishes? How long since anyone in his presence had interrupted the priestly murmur of conversation typical of the French; in fact, of any civilized people?

Dusk was falling before his eyes, and as night approaches, the woods look like the sea. Vast, serene, inexhaustible, renewed in every breath. He felt suddenly suffocated, uncomfortably aware of the smell of tanned leather, and with a movement he then thought natural, but now, telling me, he recalls as violent, even desperate, he reached out with his cane and pushed open one of the casements of the window. As it swung open, he could hear the happy voices of the two boys, who obviously were playing beneath his window on the terrace guarded by lions.

Their voices, Branly says, dissipated the asphyxiating odor of hide and filled the room, as if it were a delicate, tall-stemmed goblet, with tremors of the beautiful, melancholy twilight, and also with the ineffable, the quintessential, joy of the boys, who were laughing and singing—now he could hear it—the madrigal of the enraptured nightingale: *Chante, rossignol, chante, toi qui as le coeur gai.*

Branly smiled and half-closed his eyes. There was an instant of silence and then the boys laughed again and began a question-and-answer game. He recognized the voice of the Mexican Victor Heredia. His was the voice responding to the questions posed by the second youth, the boy he still could not describe because he had not seen him clearly, only from afar, in the distance where the garden met the grove of birch trees. This André's voice was of an incomparable sweetness, midway between childhood and puberty, but free of the unmusical tones that often accompany this transition. His voice had retained the purity of childhood into adolescence, but at the same time it heralded a virile beauty in which the shyness, selfishness, and egotism of childhood were absent.

"Capital of Argentina."

"Buenos Aires."

"Capital of Holland."

"Amsterdam."

"Capital of Serbia."

"Belgrade."

"Capital of Norway."

"Oslo."

"No."

"Sorry. Christiania."

"Capital of Mexico."

"That's silly! Mexico City. That's like my asking you what the capital of France is, André."

"Enghien!"

Both boys laughed boisterously, as Branly sank back into sleep, lulled by the game that was like counting sheep, and remembering his own childhood, the games amid the columns, the triumphs in mock wars of the Parc Monceau in a time when the children knew him and he was not importuned by his past as he was now. In his childhood he had simply existed, unburdened by the mountain of IOU's that harass a being once content to exist without a conscious—even hostile—awareness of self. He fell asleep thinking that he was going to enjoy these days at the Clos des Renards more than he had imagined. He believed that he had found the real, if slightly painful, reason for his presence there.

When he awakened again, it was night and an early autumnal chill was seeping through the open window. The room was dark; Branly groped for his cane, and, without success, tried to close one of the windows. Another hand was helping him, taking his hand and guiding it toward the window pull. He felt the touch of rough skin guiding his hand toward the copper latch.

The window closed, and the intoxicating odor of leather returned, now mingled with an ancient perfume that Branly, even in his fascinated stupor, struggled to identify with a texture or with an odor half-wood, half-leather, a flexible, fragile wood, or if not quite skin, at least the leather of a glove: sandalwood, tanned hide, perfumed wood.

He awakened with a start. The light was on and Heredia —slightly ill-humored but with no sign of the vulgarity that secretly irritated his guest, now gripped by a strange vertigo —was offering him a tray holding wine, half a French loaf, and cold meats. Branly, still enervated, looked toward the window. It was tightly shut. The head of his cane rested beside the head of his bed.

"I hope you're hungry. You've been sleeping like a baby, M. le Comte."

"Thank you. Who closed the window?"

"I did. A moment ago. We don't want you to catch pneumonia on top of everything else. At your age . . ."

"Yes, yes, Heredia, I know. Do you have a servant?"

"Why do you ask?"

"I don't want to trouble you with bringing up my tray three times a day."

"It's no trouble. There's a dumbwaiter. Anyway, it's a privilege to serve a count. I wouldn't want to pass off that honor to a servant, now would I?"

These last words were spoken with the resentful self-assurance my friend found so annoying, but he made up his mind to contain his irritation. To a degree, Heredia was an open book, with the singular exception that what one read had to be taken in reverse and then subjected to a literal reading that canceled the original interpretation. This course, Branly told himself, was pointless, as pointless as the police inquiries in Poe's "The Purloined Letter." The searched-for object was always in full view. The "purloined letter" of Victor Heredia, Branly knew in that instant, was his son. He did not need to see the boy to know that the unique voice, the joy, that had moved him so deeply that afternoon belonged to a nature very different from that of the father.

The latter was looking at my friend with the eyes of a whipped pup. "Why are you so contemptuous of me, M. le Comte?"

Branly looked up. He nearly dropped his fork on the tin tray with a great clatter, but instead lifted his eyebrows.

"I said we don't speak Spanish in my house, but you didn't believe me, you told me to speak Spanish to your servants, that they would understand me, you . . ."

Branly says he was seized by a violent emotion. Contrary to custom, he was tempted to express it.

"But," as he explains to me this afternoon, "Heredia did not deserve my anger. A man who would bare himself in that way, whining and filled with self-pity, did not deserve my anger. Self-pity is merely a different manifestation of the resentment you and I find so intolerable."

"Had you set that trap for him deliberately?" I dare ask.

He insists that, in a manner of speaking, he had acted in self-defense. For one thing, Heredia had woven a web of deceptions, expecting that his discreet and courteous guest would not call attention to them. Second, his deception could be countered only with similar, tacit, deceptions —for instance, asking him to speak Spanish to Branly's servants. Branly had decided to dupe Heredia in whatever manner possible.

"I am amazed, M. Heredia, that in the house of a man of Caribbean extraction there is no image of the patron saints of that area, a Virgen de la Caridad del Cobre, a Mexican Guadalupe, a Virgen de Coromoto . . ."

He pronounced the names with a heavy French accent, the Vir-guen de la Ca-rhee-dad del Co-brhay, the *Ga*-da-loupe, the Vir-guen de Co-rho-mo-*to*. He was willing, he explains, to wager that the French Heredia was lying about his ancestors, and if so, he was lying about other matters. But he did not accuse him that night.

"What is important is that through my servants you relayed my message to Don Hugo Heredia."

He started to ask, "You did give them the message?" but refrained, not wanting to offer Heredia the opportunity, an opportunity silently solicited by the Spaniard of the Clos des Renards, to do as he did, to turn his back on Branly without answering, to pause on the threshold, and only then to speak, with a kind of hangdog rage. "Caridad, not Ca-rhee-dad, Gua-da-*lu*-pe, not *Ga*daloupe, Virhen, not Virguen, Co-ro-*mo*-to, not Corhomo*to*. This is not a whorehouse, M. le Comte."

He swept from the chamber wrapped in a dignity even more doleful than his initial self-pity. My friend smiled; Heredia had not dared refuse what Branly had asked as a favor, and because it was accompanied by a rebuff, Heredia had understood it to be an order.

As he was eating his solitary meal, my friend pondered the relationship between the other father and son, Hugo Heredia and his son, Víctor. As he tells me now in our conversation in the dining room abandoned by everyone except the two of us, he realized that between the two Mexicans there was a kind of understanding, an interpenetration, inconceivable between the French father and son. As far as he had been able to tell, the young Heredia of the Clos des Renards could not be less like his father. He did not have to see the boy; one had only to hear that voice to recognize the delicacy, the sweetness, the moderation of the youth, whose very being repudiated the crude insolence, the excesses, of the father. Yes, from that first evening beside the barranca he had accepted without question the unspoken understanding between Víctor and Hugo Heredia. He was sure that, because of their mutual confidence, the call from his unpleasant host had been sufficient to allay the anthropologist's uneasiness about his son's absence. Their understanding, Branly murmured in his temporary bed, and now to me at his customary table in the Automobile Club, was somehow connected with the boy's brutal treatment of the servant in Jean's house, and of his own Spanish servants on the Avenue de Saxe. Undoubtedly, he murmurs as he gazes penetratingly at me, and murmured then as he was again falling asleep, that feudal impunity of Latin Americans, as anachronistic, as picturesque, as delicious, as suicidal . . . Fermina Márquez in Paris, Doña Bárbara on the plains of Apure . . .

In a sterile landscape—but one that he dreamed was perfectly normal, even desired for its absolute absence of forms, colors, weather, or space, as if other landscapes, the accustomed ones, were the aberration and the names of its objects, forgotten and disgusting, were a perverse invention contrived to cloak the perfect whiteness of a self-sufficient cosmos, without need of trees, stones, flumes, blumes, and snew—captured in its own ineffectual, exhausted progression, advanced, without advancing, the sumptuous train of palanquins and trumpets, pages and palfreniers, prancing steeds and ragged beggars. And among the beggars he beheld the king adorned in all his robes and regalia, but icily ignored by all who surrounded him, soldiers and mendicants, as if he were but one of them, himself deceived, and on the litter of the king, borne on the backs of the palfreniers, traveled, in place of the king, a blond young beggar with black eyes, still a child, dressed in rags, with no crown but his golden curls, reclining languidly, unsure whether this was but another, innocent sport, neither cruel nor kind, but one the youth was inclined first to accept, and then renounce or accept according to his whim, as long as no one contested his place, and the king, whom everyone ignored except the dreamer who was listening from a different world, told how he had found the boy in an abandoned house, how to love him and care for him was to love or care for a little beggar.

8

He was awakened very early by a persistent humming. When he opened his eyes, he had the sensation that the room was swelling, but it was merely the early-morning breeze, the pungent, far-reaching, ebullient air of the Île de France that lends its flavor to this region—air, a still drowsy Branly told himself, he had been breathing for eighty-three years.

"One of the positive attributes of ancient peoples is that they have learned to respect their old, because in them they see themselves. In their rush, young nations deny their elderly their wisdom and respect—even, finally, life."

"You may be right," I interrupted. "Unfortunately, Europe wants today to see itself as young, and, as you say, denies the existence of her old."

"If for no other reason," Branly continued, as if he had not heard me, "I deserve to live because I carry a library in my head. Do you know that if tomorrow we awoke to find all the world's books disappeared, a few elderly men could, among us, re-create them."

I realized that he hadn't appreciated my interruption, even less its demurrer. In the moment he was narrating to me, the breeze was billowing the curtains like sails, like Branly's intelligent, curious eyes, half-open. He vaguely remembered a nocturnal visit from his host, but the empty tray from his haphazard meal was nowhere to be seen. And the window was now standing open. He could hear the morning sounds from the highways, increasingly feverish activity, laborers on their way to work. Branly could see them in his mind's eye, ruddy-cheeked, flushed by the early-morning chill and their breakfast of cognac, dressed in blue denim and turtleneck sweaters and, sometimes even now, the traditional beret. He heard their joking, their gravelly laughter, heard them humming the melody of the madrigal —*à la claire fontaine, m'en allant promener*—as they walked by. In the distance, crows flocked above the woods in Enghien; but in the garden that, by pushing aside the curtains, he could admire in the solitude of the white light of a complacent dawn hostile to any who would perturb it, a solitary bird seemed to echo the same tune in its melancholy salute to the end of summer—*chante, rossignol, chante, toi qui as le coeur gai.* And now symmetrical flocks of south-bound wild geese passed overhead, adding to the sense of farewell, blotting out all sound but their own, and in spite of their cacophony as intensely nostalgic as if fulfilling the

[61]

last lines of a bitter comedy. It was only as their honking faded into a distance gradually reclaimed from the dream of a landscape without space or sound that the mingled voices of the two boys rose from the terrace below, beyond Branly's view, singing of the laughing heart and the weeping heart—*toi tu as le coeur à rire, moi je l'ai à pleurer*—and then, still more distant, the voices of the workmen in a wordless melody, as the boys sang, laughing, that final, it is long I have loved you, I shall never forget you, *il y a longtemps que je t'aime, jamais je ne t'oublierai.*

"Capital of Bolivia?"

"Sucre."

"Capital of China?"

"Peiping."

"Capital of the Belgian Congo?"

"Léopoldville."

". . . French Equatorial Afr—?"

Branly tried to move closer to the window, glowing suddenly with light, not, as I have often said in jest, situated slightly behind his left ear, and lending a translucent luminosity to his entire head, especially the ears with the drooping lobes, a sign of age compensated by the pixieish helices proudly pointing toward the gleaming cranium, but this time within his skull, pulsing there like a throbbing drum. But before he could reach the window he heard the footsteps of the boys on the gravel, their laughter tracing the curve of their flight around the corner of the house. Branly settled himself comfortably in his bed to await the momentary arrival of Heredia with his breakfast tray.

My friend tells me now, with a smile, that it was waiting in bed, more than anything, that forced him to recognize how bizarre his situation was. In vain, he tried to remember a normal morning in his life, not wartime, not dawn in the trenches of the Marne in '17, not the bombardment and fall of Calais in '40, both the exception and the justification for a comfortable life, but one single morning in ordinary times when a solicitous servant had not appeared to place a breakfast tray across his lap, the bottom of the tray warm to the touch of fingers anticipating the temptations of steaming hot coffee and croissants warm from the oven.

After an hour of waiting, and fighting a mounting irritation he struggled to suppress for being as unworthy as capricious, he fell asleep, exhausted equally by hunger and by the battle against the stirrings of a tantrum that reminded him of long-ago mornings when a woman with exquisite blue eyes and colorless lips in a colorless face, named, yes, Félicité, had been late bringing his breakfast on the occasions he was taken to visit the castle of his grandfather and his father, the handsome officer whose photograph had always stood on his bedside table. He had been taken by the hand and led up a dangerous stone stairway with no handrail to an enormous cold bedchamber, where every night, as here, he had tried to push the heavy bed close to the window, imagining he was more secure there than in the unprotected center of the room. He had always been afraid on that stairway, and wondered if a rope, a mere semblance of a railing, would have afforded a sense of security.

The boys were far away. They were always so far that they were indistinguishable from the birch trees, and all morning, through the shutters formed by still-green branches, and amid the light and shadows of tree bark disguised as tattered Dominoes, he strove to identify their figures, and movements.

It was precisely that blending of the figures and the beautiful grove—a remarkable emblem of winter jealously guarded through every season, accepting the fleeting celebrations of summer without relinquishing its role as a symbol of winter—that allowed him, to a degree, to become one with Victor and André, to remember what they were perhaps experiencing there in the grove, invisible from the half-open window of the guest room when they stood still, barely distinguishable when they moved.

"Do you recall that moment when each of us discovers what other men have known throughout the centuries? The shadow of a tree, the fragrance of a flower, the veins in a transparent leaf. To know those things is to understand the absurd abyss that separates the eternal reality of things from the knowledge of them that only I—in spite of the realities and the knowledge of them thousands of millions of men have, or have had before me—that only I can acquire for myself, and which, lamentably, I can never transmit to any other being. Victor and André were discovering the world, and from my window I was watching and wondering whether an old man does not inevitably deceive himself when he imagines how it is to be young."

Today, more thoughtfully, he questions whether someday we will find a way to transmit the experience a man has accumulated by the time of his death, in the hope of sparing those still unborn the need to learn it all again, as if no one had ever been born before them. But the mocking response is always a vast Why?

"I mean, my friend, what right do we have to wrest their experiences from others, only to give a second life to our own? At that moment, I was trying to give credence to an old man's imaginings both of his childhood and of his old age. Were they false or true?"

He had awakened to the sharp, insistent pangs of hunger. It was eleven o'clock, and Heredia, his dishonest host, less honorable than the Spanish innkeepers to whom he did not want to be compared, still had not appeared with his breakfast.

With an effort, Branly struggled to the window. He cried: "Heredia! Victor Heredia!"

He looked across the clipped, symmetrical French garden to the birch grove where the two young friends were now playing. He extended his arm between the curtains of the open window and called out the name which, he realized, smiling in spite of himself, belonged to two persons in this house.

He says he is sure that young Victor was there, sometimes as motionless as the victim of a childish game of magic spells, as one of the tree trunks tattered like beggar's rags, other times, he is sure, as swift as quicksilver, weaving an ephemeral garland from tree to tree, fleeter than the eye could behold.

"Heredia! Victor Heredia!"

He waved his hand; the boy did not respond. Perhaps he wasn't there. But he couldn't be very far away. The silence exasperated Branly; he could see himself at the window, shouting a name, waving his hand, calling to someone who did not answer, veiled by curtains billowing like sails, and he told himself that if at that moment someone arrived at the Clos des Renards for the first time, as he had two days before, when from the woods of oaks and chestnuts he had seen a figure like his, that person, Branly admitted, would imagine he had seen exactly what Branly had imagined: the silhouette of a figure hovering in the window, fluttering curtains, white gown, all glimpsed fleetingly yet fused in an impression of antiquity.

They were playing amid the distant birch trees. They were not listening. They were not paying any attention. But something unfathomable was trying to make itself felt to Branly, to reach him. He fell back on the bed, exhausted, overcome by that dark and at the same time diaphanous sensation. He was trying to communicate with the boys, and they didn't listen. At the same time, something was trying to communicate with him, and he didn't listen because he felt something evil in that summons. Something evil was calling to him, trying to reach him. Did the boys feel the same when he called them?

He was wakened by the unexpected heat of midday, a prolongation of the year's tenacious summer, and by the voices of the boys from the terrace. Like the inverse of his dream, the voices were investing with normality the forms that had progressively dissolved in the repose of his consciousness.

"He's all alone."

"No. The lady lives upstairs."

"What lady?"

"I told you. The mother."

"Have you ever seen her?"

"Not very often. She never comes out of her room. She's always in bed. She prays a lot. She's very devout, you know."

"Is she very old?"

"I don't know. I think so."

"She'd be a good match for him; he's very old, too, isn't he?"

They laughed, and their laughter faded, slowly evaporating either because Branly dozed or because the boys were moving away like the workmen, the geese, and the melody from his own childhood in the Parc Monceau about the clear fountain with waters so beautiful one cannot resist bathing in them.

He dreamed about a woman he had loved in the past. He did not remember how old they had been, but he remembered the sentiment; it was a time when knowing one was hopelessly in love was enough for happiness. He clung to this sentiment because it was the only reality in a time when everything was moving so swiftly that events seemed to occur simultaneously. He had been born, as he had been told so often by Félicité, in his grandfather's castle on the eve of a new century. His death had taken place instantaneously, only now did he perceive it, at the very moment of the birth described by the servant with the blue eyes and colorless skin. His anguish arose from the fact that he must distinguish between the two and tell the world, and himself, that he had been born, but had not died. He heard laughter below his window, from the terrace, mocking his truth, reiterating with sarcastic incredulity that every time a birth or a death occurred, they occurred together.

In the midst of this temporal simultaneity, inseparable from the infinitely mutable landscape which was its twin in space, he had met the woman, and as they stood like statues in the middle of a park in flux, he had tried to tell her that what they were witnessing was not really seen by them but by someone who had the gift of seeing things through eyes that registered a rate of speed which, he thanked God, was not that of men: otherwise, if birth and death were simultaneous, they would be separated as soon as they had come together. Like statues, they gazed into the distance, but the woman's eyes were like two windows opening inward toward the interior of her body, her house; once inside, however, it was impossible to look outward through those windows. That was apparently the price of this gift.

He smelled leather and sandalwood; a woman was approaching with a tray in her hands. Branly did not look at her face. He was so hungry he had eyes only for what was on the tray. By the time he saw what it was, and had sought consolation in the woman's eyes, she had already placed his tray on his knees and covered her face, now veiled by sumptuously ringed fingers with gilded fingernails. The humors of leather and sandalwood were suffocating. He held out his own hands in supplication to the woman, leaving now, turning her back to him, trailing the white satin shreds of a high-waisted ball gown, the tatters of the stole tied beneath the décolleté neckline and bared shoulder blades. The tower of her hair seemed ready to crumble into ruins of powdered sugar and sticky cotton candy; her worn, flat-heeled slippers scurried like white mice; and my friend was left staring into the soup plate filled with dry leaves moistened by a foul-smelling liquid: his luncheon.

"Why doesn't she wear a veil?"

"I don't know."

"At least a mask, wouldn't you think?"

"Yes, it would be more comfortable than going around all day with her hands over her face. Say, have you read the story of the iron mask?"

"No, who wrote it?"

"Alexandre Dumas. Do you know him?"

"Oh, yes. I read *The Count of Monte Cristo* and *The Three Musketeers* in school."

"He came from Haiti, just like my papa. We would have invited him to visit this house, but he died the same year."

"The same year."

9

The year of his meeting with the Heredias in Mexico was swallowed up by the year of the Countess's illness and his decision not to travel any more, swallowed by the year of his last voyage to Naples to see the painting of the blind beggar leading the blind beggars, supplanted by the year he took a membership in the Automobile Club of France in order to exercise in the enormous swimming pool with the green and gold mosaics and iron catwalk, preceded by the year of the Second World War and the leg wound received during the debacle of Dunkirk, devoured by the year of his second wife's death, absorbed by the year of the First World War by the year of his last visit to his grandfather in the castle by the year when he had read *The Man in the Iron Mask* in his dying mother's garden with its clear fountains by the year of his father's death and the year of the inauguration of the Pont

Alexandre III and the year of his birth and finally the year that dissolved all the others, and he was again in a house not very different from this, gazing toward a grove of birch trees and an avenue of bare trees whose autumnal leaves rustled beneath the feet of the woman walking toward him. She was again dressed in a First Empire ball gown, although, of course, this could not be the time because he dreamed he was a young man, but flesh and blood, though the causal and persistent logic that in a dream seems so fantastic told him that the only time he could have met the woman now approaching through the trees and clad in a gown from the time of Napoleon was before he had been born. He stretched out a hand to touch her and tell her she would see, she need not worry, that the raging time in which birth and death occurred simultaneously was not their time, the sweet, slow time of all the lovers on this earth, their time did not demand that lovers be separated the moment they met. But the woman from the First Empire stared at him uncomprehendingly, seemingly unhearing. On one bare shoulder rested a white parasol twirled by sumptuously ringed white fingers with gilded fingernails. Abruptly the twirling stopped, and her expression changed to a dawning happiness based on the conviction that she did not remember this man, she owed him nothing, that their encounter was casual and his attitude impertinent.

Branly awakened with a cry of desperation lingering on his lips. He must beseech the vanished woman to recognize him soon, before he forgot her in that sweet and sad time when death and birth do not coincide. But more powerful than his cry was the insistent nearby dripping that interrupted the flow of the successive layers of reality being sucked into the infinite vacuum of dream. He was bathed in a sweat of nerves and hunger. With the aid of his cane he struggled to his feet and limped painfully to the small bathroom, very much aware of his inability to walk very far or to negotiate the stairs. The dripping that had been more compelling than his dream, than the name or the face of the woman in his dream, was coming from an ancient shower suspended like a stalactite from a rusty pipe: the perforations in the shower head were crusted with calcareous tumors from the water of the regions near the river Seine. My friend removed his clothing and, with some difficulty, showered. He again donned the nightshirt and bathrobe lent him by Heredia, and, supporting himself on his cane, left the room in search of the dumbwaiter.

The hall was long, and Branly was halt. He did not then know why, but the doors closed on the symmetrically placed bedrooms created a sensation of rising fear. Leather covered everything in this house, but the fact that it was used on hallways, bedrooms, and floors made it less precious, divested it of the uniqueness of skins destined for special purposes—footwear, book, coat, or sofa—a uniqueness only heightened when in our fantasy we imagine ourselves flayed and our own skin serving as coat or shoes for the person who has the indisputable right to strip it from our backs. In this house, however, the concept, the physical sensation, even more the evidence of less-than-perfect quality, turned these skins into little less than stained and sour wineskins torn ruthlessly from the backs of beasts.

The dumbwaiter was housed in a square pillar next to the stairway. Branly opened it and found a cold collation, seasoned this time with mustard that surely Heredia had daubed on the meats early that morning, for it had formed a crust not unreminiscent of the dry hides that covered every inch of the house. My friend managed to pick up the tray, balancing it on one arm against his ribs in order to free the other hand for his cane. He made his way back to his room, almost regretting that Heredia had denied him an opportunity for a mute reproach, would he condemn a guest to starvation? But, think what you will, to suppose that, first thing in the morning, Branly would suppose that cold meat was waiting in the dumbwaiter was to suppose a good deal!

"The image I had of myself at that moment was atrocious: an elderly pauper consigned to an asylum by irresponsible and cruel relatives."

He did not want to ponder further the subtleties of hospitality as they were understood by his most unusual host. Hunger claimed his attention, and constantly aware, for the first time in a long while, of a sense of humiliation and abandonment, he devoured the roast beef, sausage, and chicken leg as he watched dusk fall over the woods of the Clos des Renards, as once again the voices of the children, now nearing the terrace, rose to his bedchamber.

"I think I should go up and say hello."

"No."

"He must be wondering why I haven't come."

"Because you can't."

"Why not, André?"

"Just because."

"That's no reason."

"There doesn't have to be a reason, except that from now on we don't do anything we can't do together, do you understand?"

"Yes."

"You swear?"

"I'm not sure."

"I forbid you to do anything I can't do, and I won't do anything without you, and that's that!"

My friend says now that in that precise instant the feeling that something unfathomable but threatening was trying to reach him became a reality and the tray with the remains of his lunch fell from his shaking knees. But as soon as he stood and lurched toward the window, another, earlier thought materialized: the question of how accurately or inaccurately an old man can imagine his youth. And as he

parted the curtains with trembling hands, that doubt ex-
panded to include everything connected with the youth of
the two boys speaking the words that to Branly sounded so
cruel, words he had no reason or right to judge. He held
himself upright by clinging to the curtain, knowing at last
that to flee from danger was to rush to an encounter with
something worse, and aware that the strange, parallel compulsion of this moral certainty was causing him to hesitate—
as ruinous as the powdered-sugar hair of a woman he might
have loved in a different time, a man clinging precariously
to an ancient, threadbare damask curtain to keep from reeling and falling from the window to the stone terrace below,
where the children were resuming their game.

"Capital of Nigeria?"

"Lagos."

"Capital of Anglo-Egyptian Sudan?"

"Khartoum, Khartoum."

"Let's pretend that you're Gordon and I'm the Mahdi."

"Evil Mahdi!"

"Valiant Gordon!"

The boys laughed and then Branly heard the onomato-
poeic sounds with which children imitate an adult epic,
their voices simulating cannon fire and the charge of horse
brigades. Branly, still grasping the curtain, had a fleeting
memory of his own charades in a time when memories of
the colonial adventures of General Gordon were fresh in
newsprint and conversations. Finally, he peered from the
window and saw the dark head of Victor Heredia, but not
that of his young French friend, for André was wearing a
sailor cap and—all my friend could see from his perspec-
tive—a sailor suit as well, a sky-blue suit of heavy linen
trimmed in white, with ankle-length trousers.

With dusk came a fine, steady rain. For several hours
Branly sat at his window contemplating the woods. My
friend felt that in the same way the moon slowly ascended

from the familiar garden, from secret moisture between the oaks and birches rising after a long summer's absence to celebrate the return of the abundance of autumn when the woods are sovereigns of their moribund bounty, in the same way the real sounds of the landscape he was observing with such mournful and protracted delight were born in him.

The crows that are harbingers of night over the Île de France flew high overhead; below, a seething mass of invisible creatures released from the moist sand a sacred perfume that overcame the intolerable novelty of a house encased in hide. That powerful natural effluence, Branly mused, was an implicit rejection of the other anomaly of this lonely, leathery manor house: the dead leaves piled beneath the leafy late-summer bowers of the oak trees.

Branly thought of his town house on the Avenue de Saxe and of the sand in which his sea pine grew, lending in the very heart of Paris a touch of seascape to his garden. He smiles, remembering the scene from Buñuel's *Un Chien Andalou* in which the heroine opens her door on the sixth floor of a Parisian apartment house and steps directly onto the beach: Cabourg, sea, sand.

Now the scent of the moist earth of the Clos des Renards had the same effect, and my friend, a man who eagerly anticipates beauty, imagined the morning to come: the moist grass, the boughs wet with dew and rain, glistening with infinite pearls outside the window he would open when he awakened, and he would breathe deeply, grateful once again to be alive. How many nights had he delivered himself to sleep patiently resigned never to greet the dawn?

The serenity of the vista was ruined by an all too obvious proof of the indolent neglect of the master of the house. Branly's Citroën had been left abandoned against the oak that had interrupted his blind and careening flight two—or was it three?—nights ago. He tried to capture the idyll ruthlessly interrupted by an incongruous automobile, not unlike a Kurt Schwitters painting, another depiction of juxtaposed umbrellas and sewing machines set, not on an operating table, but in the middle of a garden designed by the heirs to Le Nôtre, which, as Branly is telling me now, smiling, almost playful in his allusion, is as if the flight to Varennes had been accomplished aboard a helicopter that lifted off from the Petit Trianon.

No less grating, no less disfiguring for having been hidden, was the last thing to catch his eye as he surveyed the area between the end of the avenue where the Citroën—in a manner of speaking—lay between leafy oak trees and the verge of the avenue of dry leaves, the graveled lane along which Etienne had first driven Branly and the young Heredia to this house, and the garden, properly speaking, with its precise disposition of shrubs, pansies, and greensward among arabesques of artichokes and rosebushes, whose geometry, gradually revealed in this first persistent rain of the coming autumn, was sundered by a long, deep scar, a knife slash through this rational and most perfect of gardens, an eruption of savage forest in a space designed to negate it: from the fallen leaves, across the gravel, through grass and shrubs, the rain revealed, as if in developer solution, an indecent trough, a cruel, oblique swath carved across the face of the garden, a garden disfigured by something resembling the track of a mysterious, lurking, nocturnal beast.

The color and texture of this scar were those of a match burn on human flesh—black, white, and gray. Branly's eyes sought the birch trees, the striated silver of their bark, and, among the tree trunks, the figures of the two boys. This time they were not there, unless they were hidden in the mist.

He shook his head. The crows soared. He massaged his temples. Night fell as he asked himself: How to describe the shadow of a dream? The insistence of the dripping shower drowned out the fine, expiring rain.

Heredia turned on the light, and Branly clapped his hands over bedazzled eyes. He wondered how long his host had been standing there in the darkness, observing him observe the garden, the rain, and the scar in the garden, revealed by the rain. Not long, he concluded immediately. Peculiar to Heredia—Branly is saying this November afternoon in the empty, darkened dining room of the Automobile Club, where only he and I remain, and we remain thanks to the respect in which my friend is held in this establishment— was his ability immediately to dispel serene contemplation, good humor, spontaneity of sentiments, and to make anyone who shared with him an hour, or a room, feel self-conscious, if not guilty.

After his host turned on the light, he picked up the tray he had set on a chair. He said, as he put it down, this time on my friend's lap, that his guest would not complain today, he'd see, a delicious *cassoulet*, no leftovers from some earlier meal, eh? don't you believe it. Branly did not reply at once. Though his eyes never wavered from Heredia's, pale as the bark of the white birch trees, he settled himself in the bed before affirming that of course the hot meal must be the work of Madame; he was happy to know that she had returned and would take charge of the kitchen. Heredia must permit him to state with some frankness—Branly figuratively wiped his lips before beginning to eat—that the food today had not been, how should one say, umh, up to the standards of a Spanish innkeeper, or even of a thatched hut in the Antilles, not even . . . But surely Heredia would understand what he was trying to say: how could he suppose that his guest, during a day in which, astonishingly, his host did not once appear—how could he suppose that his guest would guess there was a plate of cold cuts for him in a dumbwaiter.

"Didn't you get enough?" Heredia asked.

"I have eaten less under other circumstances," was

Branly's reply, as once again he ignored Heredia's impertinence. "That is not the point," he continued. "It was the lack of any warning. Had I known last evening . . . You might have informed me."

"Well, the fact is, you found the food. You'll know where to find it from now on."

Branly savored with pleasure a portion of sauce-soaked goose before adding: "Does that mean I may not expect to see you during the day, M. Heredia?"

"I told you. I get up late. I go to bed late."

"Are you a vampire?" asked Branly with his best worldly smile, not looking at Heredia, but concentrating on carefully spearing with his fork the green beans swimming in the deep dish of the *cassoulet*.

Heredia glanced at my friend from the corner of his eye and then did an extraordinary thing: he walked to the washbasin, took down the oval mirror, and carried it back to Branly's bed. There he bent over, holding the mirror in both hands so that its oval reflected both the host and the guest.

Branly tells me that at that moment, with all his attention riveted, as Heredia desired, on the undeniable reflection of their faces, and with the impatience of one who hopes for a solution to certain enigmas, so they will cease to be enigmas, and almost expecting to see only one face in the glass, his own, he overlooked the additional possibilities that only later would occur to him, and which, this afternoon, he outlines as follows:

"I could not, you see, distinguish between our two breaths, one perhaps cold, the other warm, or one actual and the other illusory. No, I did not know whose was the life that breathed moisture on the mirror, as I did not know whether, through me, Heredia's eyes were projecting a profile that was not in the mirror, perhaps not even in the bedchamber, or even whether the opposite was true and I myself was no more than an illusion traced on that oval by a nebulous finger drawing in the ephemeral mist on a mirror. You see, my dear friend, at this point I still did not know that a succession of dreams were merely disguising my ignorance of my own desires."

10

"*Il m'a eu,*" my friend thought later. "He put one over on me and I allowed myself to fall into the trap." Branly knew what his intention had been, to let Heredia know he was aware of the presence of the woman in the house. He wanted to confront him with the evidence, to see how he got around the proof gleaned from the inadvertently overheard conversation of the boys as they played on the terrace under his window, not suspecting Branly was listening.

And too, he confesses now, he had wanted to know whether or not his dream was real, whether that oneiric wakefulness of the past few days could survive something as destructive and commonplace as verification: your dream is true, your dream is true because it is your dream, your dream is not a dream if it truly happened, your dream is a lie.

But no; Heredia had caught him off-guard, had scandalized him with the exaggerated theatricality of the scene with the mirror; Branly himself had given him the opening with his unfortunate reference to vampires. Henceforward, he would be more cautious. He strongly suspected that Heredia was hiding something from him, that the vulgarity so repulsive to the involuntary guest was a sham, an attempt to divert his attention from the truth.

"I realized, you see, that the sentiments I have been describing, all inspired by Victor Heredia's uncouth behavior, were only *my* sentiments about the man. It was only fair to admit that I had never seen how he conducted himself in society, nor did I know what others thought of him. I even reproached myself: it was I who was crude, capable of viewing my host only in the light of my own standards, my own values, and—why not say it— my own prejudices."

But then he thought again of the vanished woman he had loved in a garden where birth and death were simultaneous. He rejected his impartial sympathy for Heredia to tell himself that the vulgar, uncivil, coarse host of the Clos des Renards had in his rasping voice sung him a pretty tune the night before only to distract him from one question: where is the woman the boys had been talking about?

And, as if on cue, their voices rose from the terrace. Branly listened attentively. The whole thrust of their conversation this morning was—in their games, laughter, sudden silences, snatches of the madrigal, intense secrecy—a reaffirmation of their decision that they would do nothing they could not do together, nothing from which one would be excluded. He imagined they were getting to know each other, as he believed he was getting to know them.

"Don't you like it?"

"No, André."

"It's hard for me to change."

"But I don't want you to."

"Then if you don't like it, Victor, I won't be like that. I'll be different."

Again, in the afternoons of his childhood in the Parc Monceau, a new child appears behind the windows of one of the handsome private houses that enjoy a privileged view of the garden which, though public, is the private domain of the nearby residents. It is difficult to see the boy's face, to which beveled windowpanes, the blinding light of the late-afternoon sun, and yes, distance, give the strange appearance of a blurred photograph, a lead-gray coin. The young Branly would let many minutes pass by once his companions tired of staring at the solitary child and returned to their games amid the columns, crypts, and pyramids of this garden, this folly the Duc d'Orléans constructed before his renunciation in favor of the Republican cause deprived him of his power of caprice (but, I dare interrupt, is there such a thing as power without caprice?), power which— surely he would know better than anyone, he who by now affected a revolutionary name, a name to enter the new century with—as Philippe Egalité he would soon forever divest himself of.

Branly recalls now, with a smile half-ironic, half-tender, his childhood in this magnificent place where an entire city's secret aberration flowers and dies, blooms again, and is nourished in unexpected fantasy before becoming frozen in the paralysis of counterfeit ruins. In Monceau, eleven years before the Revolution, there were, oh, any number of follies —a Roman temple, a Chinese pagoda, fake feudal ruins, a Swiss dairy farm, and a Dutch windmill. The bourgeois mansions that flank five of the six sides of the park are like Medusa eyes which petrified that final flash of desperate, dying aristocratic madness.

In one of the houses facing on the Avenue Vélasquez lives the child who never comes out to play with the others. Branly dreams him as he is, his face indistinguishable, but with pale, gleaming eyes fixed on the fake ruins of a century strangely obsessed with reproducing in miniature, to scale, with exquisite delicacy and love of *trompe l'oeil*, but not without a secret shudder, the whole of nature, as if nature were not sufficient in itself or unto us, but, rather, were guilty of the ineradicable sin of a past, an origin, attributable not to human reason but to divine insanity.

"Marie Antoinette's rustic hamlets at Versailles are no different from the battles between ranks of radishes and cauliflowers re-created on the lawn of Sterne's character's home when he was deprived of participation in the Duke of Marlborough's campaign, as the metallic gardens of Goethe, dissatisfied with real nature existing outside the realm of his imagination, are no different from the fantasies of Philippe Egalité in Monceau."

One day the solitary child crossed the frontier between his house and the park. He opened the gate of the small private garden and, dressed in his sailor suit, entered the play area, where the children were singing *À la claire fontaine, m'en allant promener*. But his physical presence does not make it any easier to see his face, the features condemned to perpetual oblivion, a disfiguring surface of silver-gray mirrors beneath a sailor cap. As Branly, himself a child, looks at the boy, he feels that their relationship lies in the future, like that with the woman he can only love, because he can recognize her, and she him, only in the fatal time of instantaneous denouements, time without enigmas because identification between life and death is total, not in normal time where they do not recognize each other when they meet.

The other children have gone back to their games; only Branly stands motionless, directing all his attention toward the newcomer. At first, the other children observe him with derisive curiosity, then with indifference, and finally they resume their games, neither curious nor derisive, more as if he were not there. And Branly recalls the instant in which he is ignored by all his playmates, as if he were already the man of eighty-three and not the child of eleven, but their indifference opens the way—he knows it, and a chill runs down his spine—to friendship and recognition with the solitary boy who today for the first time has appeared among them and who gives the impression of not understanding the ways of the world beyond his door. He stumbles clumsily, he shields his eyes with his hands, as if the light were too strong, and Branly does not know how to approach him and share with him a moment he knows is unique, because he does not know if the outsider who looks at him without seeing, through the pale eyes that are the only identifiable features in a blurred face, is by his actions —being there but not being there, open but impenetrable— trying to make his ignorance seem a mystery.

"Even today, dear friend, I do not know whether I was experiencing what I attributed to the stranger; whether it was I, standing there with one hand on my hip and the other clutching a large red ball to my waist, like this, who assumed the air of intrigue, you know, the insolence, of one who though he feels insecure and foolish has at least the doubtful elegance of transforming his defects into mystery."

There is more to tell today about that long-ago afternoon dreamed on a recent morning and recounted now as my friend and I persist in prolonging a November afternoon that doesn't yet warrant lighting the round streetlamps on the Place de la Concorde or extinguishing the subdued lights of the dining room in Gabriel's *pavillon*, which produce a transfusion of shadows, impalpable, though solid to the eyes of two men deep in conversation, Branly and myself (yes, from time to time I manage to say something, introduce a comment, provide a conversational opening for my friend), who call forth the very light that permits one to call the shadow shadow.

That something more, Branly continues, was the radical newness of the boy he had glimpsed so many times behind the beveled windowpanes that in some ineffable manner he had assimilated him into their group: clearly, the largely conscious transposition of ignorance into mystery practiced by the astute youth of eleven who was my friend Branly was, in the strange boy, something different, something which Branly, even on that long-ago day, recognizes without understanding, a missing segment of his soul that he will spend a lifetime searching for. In every hesitant gesture, in every

[81]

stumbling step, in every fiber of this newcomer bathed in the sunlight with which he seemed to maintain some strange relationship of fear and benefice—as if the light, Branly repeats, were injurious to him, as if it absorbed from him the very little it bestowed on him—in all the behavior that fortunately, almost charitably, the other children were not observing, Branly recognized, most of all, inexperience, pristine astonishment, withdrawal, and pathetic doubt.

The child Branly wants to laugh. He is in the presence of a fool, an idiotic, maybe blind, feebleminded weakling, and he is grateful that the other children are not observing him observe the imbecile or they would laugh at *him*, because he, incomprehensibly, is not laughing at this melancholy, helpless, faceless buffoon, this nervous, clumsy dullard shrinking from the sun as if from a beast crouched to spring, says my friend, as if protecting himself against the rain, the air, thunder, fog, everything, because everything, he has always known it but only today can he put it into words, everything, he says, was new to this child. Not ignorance, not mystery, his pathetic gyrations on the edge of the Parc Monceau were those of a star born but two seconds before, hurled from a galaxy expanding for eons toward the moment of explosion that freed this creature confined within its perfect death throes. For this new child the world is new, and because it's new—the outsider extends a pale, trembling hand toward my friend, and my friend does not know how to accept the offering—nothing is known.

The outsider holds out his hand. My friend drops the red ball and his insolent poise deserts him; he runs to join his playmates. The ball rolls to the feet of the cretinous child, who with clumsy, mechanical movements bends down to pick it up, mewing something incomprehensible, something not even a language, but my friend—today, an old man, he is still proud of it—resists the impulse to run back for the ball, to reclaim his property, to snatch it from the half-wit afflicted by the sun, who looks at the ball and looks at my friend and looks at the trees and looks at the park benches as if everything were not only new but incomprehensible. For him Monceau has no name, no history. It is what his eyes tell him.

"For those eyes were his entire identity, his entire intelligence, captive in a face I cannot remember; everything was incomprehensible, so everything was new and everything was strange."

From the corner of his eye he looks at the little boy who had slipped from the house on the Avenue Vélasquez. He prays that the other children will not realize he has not run to the newcomer to grab the ball that does not belong to him but to all the playmates who gather here every afternoon after school. The moment he turns his back to the child, he hears the sound of the ball and he stops, turns, and sees the extended hands, the ludicrous, almost-squatting stance, the ever-bewildered gaze, and the red ball bouncing toward him. My friend wonders, then as now, whether the outsider had returned the ball voluntarily or whether it had dropped from his inept hands.

He felt a fervor, a rush of tenderness, for that stranger; even today, he is grateful for that. It was a revelation about himself at eleven that would accompany him always, not a memory but a reality, and then as today, and also in the spiral times of dream, he feels that he was about to take the one step more that would have led him to the strange boy, to a sympathetic embrace, because two creatures who at last recognize each other are the very figure of compassion itself. Forget what separated them, remember what united them, recover something shared, the reason for his fervor.

He did not take that step. He did not embrace the boy. Still, the fervor of the experience, the outsider's gesture in returning the ball to him, his in not grabbing it from him, revealed to Branly that he had "what one calls a soul."

The wind swelled the room and again my friend had the sensation that an interior sail was moving this leather-lined house toward a destination far distant from its present location; the walls became gentle waterfalls, and my friend awakened.

The young Mexican Victor, the youth with the lank dark hair, was observing him intently, sitting at the foot of my old friend's bed. For a long time they looked at one another, unspeaking. As Branly emerged from the dream of his childhood fervor, he saw nothing in the eyes of the young Heredia to compensate for the categorical loss of the dream.

"You looked afraid," the young Heredia said at last.

Branly wanted to ask: then why did you not wake me? He knew he had not had a nightmare but that the dream from which he had emerged to meet the pale eyes of the boy he scarcely knew had been a pleasing one, the memory of an anointing, the recognition of his own, but shared, spirit.

"Then my face did not reflect my dream," he replied.

He held out a transparent, bony hand to touch Victor. He was aware that the youth represented something he missed terribly, something, in spite of his apparent proximity, as distant as the idiot of his dream. Here, now, sitting on Branly's bed, he merely accentuated the terrible distance Branly felt when Victor appeared in the birch grove or beneath his window, a disembodied voice accompanied always by another boy, whose face Branly had never seen.

"Have you spoken with your father?" my friend asked. The Mexican boy hesitated a moment, and then nodded.

Branly said he was feeling much better and that surely by tomorrow they could return to the house on the Avenue de Saxe. He lightly stroked Victor's hand, but he did not attempt to tell him how much he appreciated this proof of independence, the fact that he had come to see him in spite of young André's prohibitions and in spite of having sworn to do nothing that the two had not agreed upon beforehand, this Castor and Pollux from two such distant and distinct, perhaps not hostile but certainly not sister, cities. He hoped that his touch communicated his approval of what implicitly he judged to be Victor's rebellion against André; to have made his approval explicit would have been an almost irreparable faux pas. Victor surely would have retreated to the friendship with the boy his own age; what could he find interesting about an old man of eighty-three?

What, indeed, Branly's mind leaped to the thought, if not the fact that he had brought him here, that he had served as indispensable guide until the moment Victor had slammed the door on Etienne's fingers and the other Victor Heredia, the Frenchman, had come down the avenue of dead leaves to offer his spontaneous and generous assistance?

"Yes," said Victor, "it all depends on how you feel."

"Much better, as I told you. Thank you for inquiring. What news is there of our Etienne? Why has he not come for the automobile?"

"I don't know. As soon as you're better and can walk, you must meet the others."

"André? Your friend? Of course."

Victor again nodded, and lowered his head so that his long dark lashes shadowed the flicker of embarrassment in his eyes. "Yes, and her too."

"Who is she, Victor?"

"She says she wants to see you again."

"Ah, then she is someone I know?"

"I don't know. That's what she says. Ciao!"

He ran from the room, and my friend fell into a curious meditation, the gist of which he is now communicating to me in the deepening shadow of the dining room.

"But of course. He did not come to see me on his own, out of any affection for me; he came because the two boys

[85]

had plotted to deceive me, don't you see?—to upset me and mock me with this patent lie about the existence of another person, a woman, an acquaintance of mine, in the house."

He says that above all he was irritated by the contempt underlying the boys' ridiculous invention. He laughs as he recalls his thoughts that day: they think me so old and distraught that I can no longer clearly remember the women I have loved; as long as she is old, they think they can pass off any woman as mine; not only can I not remember her, I cannot even, it goes without saying, recognize her.

As he pushed himself upright in the bed, he almost overturned the breakfast tray with coffee pot, cup and saucer, silver, sugar bowl, and rolls. His first reaction, he says, was surprise that he had not smelled the unexpected breakfast he had been prepared to fetch later from the dumbwaiter where Heredia had left it in the dying hours of the night. He was adjusting to the schedule of only two meals a day, but the later the first, the less he suffered awaiting the second.

As he pulled the tray toward him, he realized why his sense of smell had not warned him. Everything was cold, the bread was cold, the coffee was cold, with no hint of the comforting warmth that for so many years had transmitted to palms of hands and fingertips a concern for his person that would never falter, and which, morning after morning, was manifested in this simple proof: a warm breakfast tray respectfully placed across his knees.

Had young Victor brought the tray this morning? He reproached himself, he had not thanked the boy. But his unfailing courtesy immediately gave way to an unpleasant suspicion, and to the question it inevitably posed. "Why was Victor, a young foreign guest in this house, serving the Frenchman who bore his name?"

Branly tells me that he felt distant eyes upon him. Again he heard the voices from the terrace.

"Where are you from?"

"From Mexico. And you?"

"From where I'm from."

Once more the voices faded into that strange litany, as soporific as a rosary of poppies, of cities no longer capitals of former nations or forgotten colonies.

"German East Africa?"

"Dar es Salaam?"

"Bosnia and Herzegovina?"

"Sarajevo!"

11

Sarajevo, my friend murmurs, trying to remember where he was on that bitter day, the 28th of June 1914. What was he doing while the Serbian terrorist Gavrilo Princip did what he did and what was he saying when the Archduke Francis Ferdinand ceased to speak forever? Had he just awakened late one morning following a pleasurable night, the perfume of the woman sleeping beside him filling his nostrils? He was barely eighteen, but he had already assumed his place in the world with all the pleasures and privileges ordained by name, rank, family, duty, and right. It was La Belle Epoque. The summer air, drifting through the windows of a balcony opened above the Boulevard de Courcelles and facing the Parc Monceau of his childhood, bore pollen from the chestnut trees. No one was preparing his coffee; the woman was almost invisible among the pillows; that novelty, the telephone, had not rung; the newspapers with their world-shaking headlines had not yet appeared; she would weep over the death of a morganatic wife that day in Sarajevo; she was sentimental voluptuousness and delicious indifference.

They did not care whether anyone saw them, whether anyone knew they had lain late in bed making love, and then he rose, naked, and, smiling, lightly caressed his lover's ankles. He walked to the balcony, looked out toward the park and the distant houses from which no one would be able to see his naked figure, young, erect, bathed in the sensual pleasure that was very new but fully accepted, no anxiety, no clumsiness. Yet, through the beveled panes of a distant window, he could see the eyes of the hidden, silent child isolated for all time, past and future, who only once had known the possibility of friendship, when it was offered him by an eleven-year-old Branly.

Shivering, he drew the drapes, and from the bed the woman said: Why are you doing that? It's such a beautiful morning. And he told her he had felt cold, and laughed: besides, why should anyone but himself see her like this, he wanted her all to himself, and paraphrasing Lamartine he whispered into her ear: I say to this day, stay your flight. She answered: But you drew the drapes; and he laughed: Then we needn't change the poet's words, *Je dis à cette nuit: "Sois plus lente."*

He read the headline as he left Myrtho's house at dusk. At first he did not understand its significance, because his imagination was still captive to Myrtho's bedroom on the corner of the Boulevard de Courcelles and the Rue de Logelbach, amid a mountain of sheets and pillowcases and eiderdowns and unlaced camisoles and black stockings and close-fitting boots, all the sensual paraphernalia of the clothing of that era, when everything, he tells me, was more delicious for being more challenging. And now he was sitting reading an incomprehensible newspaper in a café on the Boulevard Malesherbes, wondering whether at his age he should apply for an officer's commission or wait to be conscripted. In the window of the café he looked for the beardless reflection of his face, an adolescent disguised as a man.

Before the Great War, he explains, men became adult at

a younger age, because the average lifespan for European men was only thirty-eight to forty years (tuberculosis, diphtheria, scarlet fever, smallpox, syphilis, typhoid, malaria, tumors, silicosis, mercury poisoning from gilding). At eighteen, a man had lived half his life, and was not, as now, just beginning.

"Today everyone tries, at times obscenely, to prolong his youth. Haven't you seen the sexagenarians who insist on disguising themselves as Boy Scouts? Before 1914, one entered adulthood as soon as possible. We let our beards and mustaches grow, we wore pince-nez and bowlers, black suits, high boots, wing collars, and starched shirts. And who went out for a stroll without a cane and spats, except a workman or a beggar? Though there was very little difference between the two, I can assure you."

But the numerous, cumbersome, formal garments they wore augmented sexual pleasure, he attests: the prize was not easily won, the surprises were climactic, the anticipation formidable. Nights did pass more slowly; they obeyed, as a horse its rider.

He thought of the author of the *Meditations* several weeks later when he received the solicited commission; he was sent to the front as he had requested, and fully expected it was his destiny to die in one of the places where he had savored life. So many holiday retreats, his grandfather's castle near Vervins every Easter and Christmas, excursions to the banks of the Marne and into the heart of the Ardennes forest in summertime. At each instant in which death threatened, he repeated almost mechanically: *Et de mourir au lieux où j'ai goûté la vie!*

During his first leave, he decided to test the constancy of the places where he had enjoyed Parisian life; he hesitated whether to return first to the apartment on the corner of Courcelles and Logelbach or to the garden of his childhood years. Gradually, aimlessly, the lassitude of the uncommitted afternoon following a superb, gratefully savored solitary luncheon at the Laurent on the Champs-Elysées, the slight headiness of the golden cigarette between his lips, the sensation of being himself and at the same time someone different, yes, somehow different in the uniform of an officer decorated following the battle of Charleroi—defender of the cradle of the most vulnerable and violated poet who ever lived—and perhaps the thought of the young and handsome Rimbaud led him to the large house on the Avenue Vélasquez. He found the courage to ring the bell and ask for the child, the boy, that is, the young man, who lived there, who had lived there as a child.

The concierge told him that the family had moved some time ago, but if the officer wanted to see the apartment, it was empty now, it had a beautiful view of the park, ah, if someday when this was over, the officer should marry and be looking for a place to live, just look at this priceless view, said the talkative little old woman as Branly walked through the white-walled apartment, stroking the silky points of the brilliant mahogany mustache acquired in the campaign against the Huns, smiling, thinking less of this having been the dwelling of that strange child than of the amusing fact that from the windows of this room he could see the balcony of a Myrtho still unaware of the surprise her young lover had in store for that night that would be the slowest of their lives. The woman ten years his elder would open the door without recognizing him: how could they look the same, that young beardless aristocrat with languid, though not yet perverse, manners, so swiftly and satisfactorily ensconced in the center of his world, prepared to dispense and receive its rewards in the circle which, accepting him as its hub, deferred to him, and this young, mustached, tougher man, martial and stiff as a ramrod, who had seen others die and had fully expected to die himself at the Ardennes and at Charleroi.

"Oh, my God, M. le Capitaine. Are you all right?"

From the window overlooking a garden of open, blackened wounds, he sees a procession advancing through mountains of dead leaves down an avenue of oaks and chestnut trees green in summer. This time the palanquin is borne by a number of shrunken, white-haired old men in rags and tatters, who, in high shrieking voices almost indistinguishable from the dire cries of the birds in that blighted landscape, are singing the madrigal *Chante, rossignol, chante, toi qui as le coeur gai*—sing, nightingale, sing, you who have a happy heart—and behind them, flat-footed and ponderous, stumble ten or twelve naked pregnant women whose greedy eyes never leave the litter, shaking their heads like bitches emerging from water, dogging the palanquin that is advancing through mounds of dead leaves, borne on the shoulders of the miserable, filthy, shrunken old men.

In the litter lies a youth on the threshold of puberty, totally naked, bathed in gold, motionless as a statue, like one of Rodin's sculptures of young lovers, but without the girl to kiss. The statue is dead, Branly begins to scream, I warned you, gilding with mercury is poisonous, it should never have touched that body.

The motionless boy does not look toward him, but the shriveled old men do. They hail him, beckoning him to join the procession, inviting him with their shrill laughter, as the awesomely heavy, leaden women ask if he dares invite them to dine.

"Woman and death are the most sumptuous guests at the world's feast. Who will dare invite them?"

"Oh, my God, M. le Capitaine, are you all right?"

"What is the matter with you, Félicité? You look pale."

"A woman killed herself last night in the ravine in the woods, right here near Vervins, M. le Comte. They found the body the next morning, devoured by wolves."

"It was only by a miracle that we met. In the normal

course of events, I would have died before he was born. It is equally true that he could have died before we met, as his brother did."

"Marco Polo relates that twenty thousand persons were executed during the funeral procession of the Mogul Khan, to serve him in death."

"The mother of Victor and Antonio? Who knew the boys' mother? Did you know her, Jean?"

"There are things one loves only because they will never be seen again."

"Her name was Lucie."

"Where are you from?"

"From Mexico. And you?"

"From where I'm going."

"Do you remember me?"

"Not very well. Do you remember me?"

"No, I don't remember you. But I remember a terrible storm in August that stripped the leaves from the trees and left them naked; it seemed like November. Don't you remember it?"

"No, Victor."

"I also remember a country that was ours, our property. It was beautiful there, everything was always changing; nothing was twice the same, not grass or clouds or anything. Don't you remember it?"

"No. But I remember you."

"I don't remember you."

"You don't remember when Alexandre Dumas came to visit?"

"No, not at all. Only the places that changed, whether it was hot or cold, rainy or sunny. Things like that. What was Dumas doing here?"

"I think he wrote a book. But it was lost."

"We can find it, André."

"I remember you a little. I especially remember that you were supposed to come back. I remember that. You've come a little late."

"I don't know. I don't remember."

"You were late with your gift, Victor."

"No. I didn't forget that. I have it."

"You've brought it to me? You have it here?"

"No. It's in my suitcase."

"Get the suitcase. Please."

"I will if you want me to. We'll do everything together, won't we?"

"Yes. Now you see I won't do anything you don't like."

"Have you thought, maybe you were waiting for me?"

"Yes. I remember you, but not very well."

"I don't. I don't know."

"Speak more softly. Remember, he's listening."

"No. He's asleep."

"I don't know."

"Oh, my God, M. le Capitaine. Are you all right?"

"It is nothing, madame, it must be the heat, or perhaps something I ate," Branly managed to say. To avoid falling, he clung to the frame of one of the beveled glass windows from which eight years earlier a solitary boy had watched him, and from which Branly had not moved, that August afternoon in 1914, during the longest moments of his life.

"So long, my friend, that I decided to forget them. The forgetfulness was hastened by Myrtho when I stopped by to see her that evening. She was in the company of a general. I had to stand at attention. She looked at my medal and asked mockingly if it was chocolate; after all, hadn't we had to retreat from Charleroi? They decorated you for a defeat—and Myrtho laughed as the general turned his back to me, making embarrassed sounds. When I returned to the street, the Parc Monceau was locked. Disconsolately, I walked back to my house. She was right, I had not been able to defend the cradle of the boy poet."

12

He tells me that because he disguised his fear as timidity, he never returned to Monceau until after he was eighty, until recently, when he decided to relive the day of his leave in 1914, after the retreat from Charleroi and before following Joffre in the campaign that drove the Germans back to the river Aisne. We know what happened: the children did not even look at the old man, as the children of long ago had not looked at the lonely boy who watched them from behind the beveled windowpanes of the house on the Avenue Vélasquez.

He wished, as it sometimes happens in stories, that the children would gather round him while he told them tales of a time that everyone, with little justification, called the most beautiful and sweet, la Belle Epoque, *la douceur de vivre*. Instead, Branly leaves his park bench and walks slowly toward the Boulevard de Courcelles. As his eyes seek Myrtho's balcony, he concedes that the children are right to have forgotten him as well as the atrocious war of the dead and the cruel life of the living.

"Poor Myrtho; she so wanted to save herself from the poverty and sickness that devastated her mother. Before she died, I saw her once, ravaged and tubercular. Was that the sweetness of life?"

He says that, more than anything, it is the memory of those days that stirs him that evening—once the voices of Victor and André are stilled, and the woods of the Clos des Renards, as night falls, begin to look like the sea—to get up out of bed and test his strength. He sighed as he closed the window, and said to himself what he is now telling me:

"I hope they never grow up. Their mystery will be considered ingenuousness, or crime."

He flexed his leg with greater ease, and in the mirror above the washbasin noticed that the swelling on his forehead had gone down—the same mirror the French Heredia had used the previous evening to demonstrate, surely in jest, that he was not the Nosferatu of Enghien-les-Bains. The truth was, of course, my friend already knew, and now remembered as with simple physical movement he emerged from the vast dream of the day that had been a kind of dark epiphany, that Heredia had acted to distract his attention from the mystery the boys—and this, too, Branly had decided—meant to be a second deceit, the reverse of, but complement to, the first. He shook his bald, gray-fringed head. Heredia wanted to trick him into believing there was no woman; the boys, that there was. He remembered the first time they had seen this house. The white phantom in the garret window had caused him to realize that 1870 was not an address but a date: a time, not a place.

His cane helped him master the hallway of symmetrically placed doors. He had become accustomed to the persistent, penetrating smell of leather, but as he approached the narrow stairway that led to the garret, he had an amazing olfactory sensation. We all know that experience, he is saying as the afternoon loses its prestigious light to fade into mousy hues; it is that sudden sharpening of the sense of smell which at a fleeting and unexpected moment recalls through a scent a city, a season, a person. Even, at times, what we call a civilization.

"No, I am not referring to the expected. If I walk through the Carrefour de Buci, I expect to be greeted by that marvelous, both fresh and pungent odor of pepper and pike, goat cheese, and bunches of marjoram. No, I mean when one encounters that sensation elsewhere, when the familiar odor occurs in an unexpected place."

[95]

I said I understood what he meant. As an exile and a wanderer, I sometimes courted that sensation, but it came only when it was unsought. My lost cities of the River Plate, Montevideo and Buenos Aires, to me are the smell of hides, the dark river, cheap benzene, asphalt melted in the summer heat, wharves heaped high with wheat and wool, slaughter-houses and tea shops. I have found components of that odor here and there, in Nice and in Venice, along the Ramblas of Barcelona and on the docks of Genoa. It isn't the same, only an approximation, like the dry, oppressive air of the high plains of Castile and Mexico.

As he climbs toward the garret room of the Clos des Renards, Branly, the hall behind him, confirms that the olfactory summons was that of hides, of skins of specific origin, each proclaiming its antiquity with a mute call to the nostrils: we are ancient Spanish hides, ancient Arab and Roman hides, we are hides from the tanneries of the Guadal-quivir, the Tiber, the Tigris, we embellish desert cara-vans, the backs of long Christian breviaries, the sheaths of short Roman swords. And yet, to the sensitive nose of Branly—this friend so persevering and methodical in his passions and obsessions, whom I pictured sniffing like an old hound through the nooks and crannies of that villa hidden in the suburbs of Paris, a dusty oasis surrounded by commercial blight, discount stores, arcs of neon light—the farther he ascended the narrow staircase, the more that whirlwind of olfactory sensations was concentrated in a single superficially curious image, as if all the aromas of lost times and places ultimately had coalesced into an enor-mous painting of war trophies, a canvas with a David theme painted by a less harsh and less "disabused" Delacroix; a forgotten Imperial feast, decaying and decadent, Napoleonic splendor after the Maréchaux of the Grande Armée had looted the farthest corners of Europe and the Mediterranean to replenish the museums of France. He opened the door to

Los Gatos H.S. Library

the garret, the last gleam of daylight was a frozen star of dust, a milky winding-sheet, the perfect phantasmal crown for these trophies stripped from butchered beasts, cows, cats, camels, lions, sheep, monkeys, from the armies of the Carthaginians, the Ommiads, the Visigoths, all entwined in an absolute absence of historical connotation, vague rumors, crushed blossoms, a slough of names destined to be woven together in the scene that met his eyes as he opened the door, everything imagined or said or referred to resolved finally into a figure around which the hides, the skins stripped from the beasts of ancient armies, the trophies Masséna had plundered for France, were entwined like venomous flowers around precious jewels.

The woman beside the window was the very essence of an agitation not without order. Her Empire gown, white and diaphanous, high-waisted and with a long stole, was illuminated by the close, intense light of Ingres's female portraits, and like them, this was a Neoclassic figure on the edge of Romanticism, observed but at the point of observing herself, rational but on the brink of madness, alert but on the edge of oblivion.

Her hands covered her face, and her rings, as well as her poisonous fingernails, were gilded with mercury. She was Ingres become Moreau, and Branly reeled before the image, steadied himself with his cane and leaned against the terminal, supporting pillar of the narrow stairway to the garret. The curtains of the window beside the woman's figure were fine white muslin; they fluttered around her, animating her meaninglessly.

The French Victor Heredia closed the window and, with a circumspection Branly thought worthy of an old-fashioned chatelaine, rearranged the white curtains. The portrait of the woman in white illuminated by white lights and shadowed by the mask of her gold-tipped interlaced fingers rested against the vaulted wall of the attic.

[97]

"Ah, M. le Comte! I see we're on our feet and ready to crow! I won't ask you to help me with my 'Madame Mère' here, isn't that what you say, 'Madame Mère'? Bah, I don't know, it's so impersonal, the business of 'Madame Mère.' Every woman who doesn't have a title like Duchesse de Langeais or Princesse de Lamballe, say, should have a short, catchy nickname like La Périchole or M'selle Nitouche, don't you agree? But I won't ask you to help me find a place for my mamá; to each his own, eh? and as the saying goes, we have only one mother."

He laughed in his peculiarly irritating way, standing with arms akimbo, his hands hooked in the belt of a bizarre hunting outfit the likes of which Branly last remembered seeing in the second act of *La Traviata*.

"You know, M. le Comte? The ultimate freedom would be to have been born without a mother or a father. You wouldn't understand this, yourself, being a man who prides himself on his ancestors, but, if you will forgive my frankness, one who wouldn't have got very far without them. Ha! Don't deny it! Who would you be if you'd had the opportunities of a paid laborer or a washerwoman's daughter, eh? But when it comes to common, ordinary mortals like myself, who want to be responsible only to ourselves, we resent, believe me, that the debt we owe to those who give us life may be the very thing that allows them to take it back."

"Why, then, have you kept the painting?" Branly inquired calmly.

Heredia chortled, executing a strange little dance punctuated by the heels of his knee-high hunting boots; Branly could only ascribe this behavior to a celebration of the gathering darkness in the garret. My friend was so captivated by the figure of the woman in the painting that only now, in hindsight, as is so often the case, was he able to complete the entire scene. His host had been hugging the shadows, avoiding the Ingres light that, to borrow from

Quevedo's great sonnet, lent a tone of enamored dust to the painting of the woman from the First Empire. Heredia shrank from that light; he was dancing a jig because night was falling over the world.

He asked his guest whether he thought anyone, a public or a private buyer, might be interested in a unique painting not really appropriate for hanging in a dining room or a museum, a woman hiding her face with her hands. Why, you would as little consider hanging something like this as hanging a horrifying painting he had once seen in a magazine of a Jesus crowned with thorns, wrists bound, bellowing with laughter, revealing sound teeth that indicated the diet in Palestine left little to be desired.

Branly pointed out to his host that he had not answered his question: why had he kept the painting?

He tells me he was not truly interested, as he was no longer interested in the person of Victor Heredia, in the answer of this Frenchman dressed as if for a big-game hunt in the time of the President-Prince. He asks it, actually, so as not to leave the story unfinished, to assign it to its proper place in the text.

"Every unborn being is one half of a pair, M. le Comte, you wouldn't deny this, would you? it's even true of dogs. Can't you imagine, then, that the opposite is true, that young lovers are joined by the unborn child demanding creation through the souls of the young parents?"

Heredia looked at the painting and said, see, she seems to be pleading, the cold, the disdainful creature, interesting, yes, but disinterested; that was her manner, that was how she plotted to ensnare the ingenuous colonial, the Antillian planter, to capture his fortune by making him believe she didn't need it.

"By the time he realized, it was too late. She had everything. His revenge was to have her painted like this, shamed in a painting, as she was never shamed in the bedroom, the salon, or the tomb. You see, M. le Comte, I picture my mother as a jeering skull with teeth like castanets, laughing at us night and day."

"For her, there is nothing but night." said Branly, again recalling the line from Lamartine.

Heredia laughed and replied that he doubted it. His mother could organize a fandango in the catacombs of death, a dance of skeletons, with long candles and tall candelabra, to continue her mockery—the colonists again deceived, exploited, and mocked by the European vixen who had appeared in La Guaira on the very eve of Independence to dazzle the young men with manners brilliantly adapted to the needs of the colonials, who in Bonapartist opportunism saw the mirror of their own dilemma.

"To fight a revolution in the name of the people, but for their own benefit. A simple matter of take-from-you and give-to-me, throw out the Spaniards and up with the Creoles, and what better model than Bonaparte?" my friend asks me, summing up Heredia's lament. "The Creole revolutions weren't fought for *liberté, égalité, fraternité*, but to acquire a Napoleon. That was and still is the secret desire of the ruling classes of Latin America." I nod my agreement. "The Bonapartist consecration: my brother in Naples, my cousin the princess."

The story was too simple and too predictable to explain satisfactorily Heredia's rancor. But that evening the host of the Clos des Renards had nothing more to say, nor Branly more to imagine. The character, as my friend has already told me, fatigued him, but my friend also tells me that fatigue, paradoxically, was his greatest and most perverse strength. He was bored; the matter was easily forgotten. He forgot the context of the fatiguing apparition and lost interest in tying up loose ends.

That night, a kind of stupor, almost amnesia, prevented Branly from grasping the interrelationship of the diffuse images surrounding Heredia. He asks me now whether I— who have the advantage of hearing only the bare facts of the events, and was not, as he, immersed in the nonselective distractions of living twenty-four hours of every day—have been able to discern the connections he had not seen.

I hesitate before answering him. I know that if I say yes, I shall offend him; in spite of everything, he will take it as a presumption of superiority on my part, though I am his inferior in age and worth. But also, if I tell him no, he will take it as lack of attention or interest on my part.

"Perhaps this time you might have taken the extra step, Branly, the step that you did not take as a child that afternoon in the Parc Monceau."

As I spoke, my friend aged before my eyes. I am not being ironic; it is not age that makes us appear old, and Branly is a young man of eighty-three. His face openly displayed an emotion that in his words had until then been only the latent expression of the hostile and unknown. But if, while he was speaking, hostility had hovered about him, now, as I spoke, it became a reality.

"Why do you say that?"

I replied that perhaps the boys' deception had not, as he believed, consisted of trying to make him think that the woman in the painting existed, and remembered him; nor were they really suggesting, cruelly, that he could not remember the women he had loved; they were challenging him to remember the child in the window of the house on the Avenue Velásquez, whom, he himself admitted, he *had* forgotten.

"Do you remember his face, Branly?"

Sunk in thought, with an almost episcopal gesture of one hand, my friend sighed, "No." And he placed his fingertips to throbbing temples, and said that this was exactly what he had been thinking that evening with Heredia in the garret of the Clos des Renards, that his host was inviting him to imagine the true motive for an ancient rancor buried in remote places and times. But he, Branly, had seen this as yet another trick by Heredia to divert him from the truth of his involuntary confinement, as well as the true relationships between the boy Victor Heredia, the French Victor Heredia and his son André, and himself, the uninvited guest, the indiscreet and suspicious fourth, whose presence—he felt it now—the other three, once he had accomplished the mission of reuniting them, resented.

"The simplicity of the story Heredia told me in the attic made me believe that his motive was to satisfy my curiosity and send me on my way back to Paris. But that was not the heart of the problem. They all knew I would not return alone. The Mexican boy would go with me. That is what I saw behind those pale, narrowed eyes. I saw hostility, the unknown. Something that did not recognize me but hated me."

Branly fell silent for a moment, then drew in his breath, as if suppressing a cry, before speaking. "Now you tell me that in fact the equation was reversed. He hated me because I did not recognize him."

I did not dare ask Branly whether finally he admitted this was true. There was something too sad, too wounded, too anguished about my friend. I did not have to look in his eyes; his slumped figure conveyed his feeling that an opportunity had been lost forever.

CLEMENCITA

La bête épanouie et la vivante flore.
J. M. de H., "Les Trophées"

13

The French Heredia remembers with nostalgia that the wild January seas beyond the breakwater in the harbor of Havana—like holding to one's cheek an icy bottle swept from distant waters and bearing a message of crushed salt and splendid desperation —taste of snow. He remembers, too, the dark, quiet ocean along the sandy shores of Veracruz, where the exhausted Mediterranean flings itself on the beach with a flash of scales, like a suicidal fish. Especially, because it was where she disembarked, he remembers the sunny sea of La Guaira, an unruffled mirror stretching placidly at the feet of mountain and fortress, rocks and pelicans.

It is difficult for Branly to believe that Heredia can evoke even a modicum of tenderness. He prefers to suppose that he has slipped back into his interrupted dream, and that from the heights of San Carlos he is watching a small sailing vessel flying the pale colors of the realm of the bees sail into port. He strains to see the distant figures pacing slowly back and forth on the deck, men with hands clasped behind their backs, women with opened parasols. He wishes he were close enough to see them, and instantly his wish is fulfilled. Now he is on deck, but the ship is adrift, crew and passengers have abandoned her, and the woman, at the estate on the high cliffs, and cloaked in the mists of a La Guaira dawn, is instead wandering through corridors of ochre stucco, through dew-wet patios that open into passageways of salt-air-pocked stone that lead to other patios of lichen and dry grass, vainly seeking a mirror in which to see and remember herself; yet all she knows is what is whispered in her ear.

"Memory may be a lie."

She likes the feel of coolness against her face. From the heights of the mountain, rain, mud, and stones thunder down toward the port, but also clear streams still untouched by city filth. She dips her hands in the waters, peers into them, searching for her face; there is no reflection, the waters flow too swiftly. They have told her she should not seek her reflection, she might meet a wraith, but she guards her secret. The phantom appears only when at dawn she sits at her harpsichord, her father's childhood gift. It is her only memory of France, and when at dusk she sits for hours on a balcony overlooking wet red-tiled roofs and far below and in the distance she sees the ocean, she feels the tug of her French homeland, but she tells herself it is futile to think of it, more futile to return. If only she had never left. She cannot return to the country she left behind, after living here. France would not be the same. She should never have come, she sighs to herself, and tells her child-nana, much younger than she, when the little mulatto appears, dancing in a blond wig to amuse her.

"I had a Venezuelan nana," says Heredia. "She cooked delicious dishes, but one day she said she missed her homeland and wanted to go there to die. Since she was very old, and not a little befuddled, I went along with her, you understand? Oh, she was smug when she left here, that mulatto, wearing a kerchief she hadn't had on her head for thirty years, and carrying her wicker suitcases. She traveled in a circle from Paris to Cherbourg and from there by ship past Gibraltar to Marseilles, from which she returned to Paris by train, convinced she was back in Caracas. I prepared a room for her here with hammocks and parrots and a small greenhouse with arcades and red tiles to deceive her; but, the truth was, I deceived myself. Do you know what she told me before she died? 'The boat sailed between a cliff and a green shore, young Victor, where the sea was very narrow. I could see the houses plain as day, and the eyes of the people hiding behind their shutters in mortal fear, watching the passing boats as if they carried the damned. I looked high up in the masts, and they were swarming with howler monkeys smoking cigarettes. Oh, my God, I said to myself, I've come home.' "

"Did she never ask what you were doing at her destination when she should have left you far behind?"

"No. I tell you the truth, she was the one who deceived me. She knew the New World had left its impression on Europe for all time. Don't you agree?"

"The devil always knows what time it is," Clemencita murmured, "as long as it's somewhere else."

La Guaira is like a vine that keeps clawing its way up the face of the mountain to escape the unbearable heat of the coast, to reach the mist of the fort of San Carlos, from there look back toward Cádiz and Palos de Moguer to see whether the return caravels have sailed. At the balls of that long-ago summer she sparkled in her beautiful, diaphanous white gown with the high waist and long stole, the first appearance in these lands of Empire fashion. The salons of La Guaira—do you remember, Clemencita?—were cool, the bricks wetted down, the high ceilings, the high, cool wood, too, great beams, archiepiscopal shutters, unreachable armoires.

"You see, fortunes are like ships. They seek a safe port in a storm, and at times the instinct of money, that is, the urge to find that safe berth, blinds one, and confuses distance with safety. Laugh if you will, thinking how a French merchant in the Antilles—made rich by the wide-scale smuggling that accompanied the decline of Spanish rule and the instability of the Napoleonic wars, but based in the black colony of Haiti, where planters were hanged from their own palm trees and armies of mosquitoes routed the French armies as later the snow and mud of Russia were to do—knew better than any politician that what is up today

[105]

will be down tomorrow, and that the greater the pride, the greater the humiliation. It seemed grotesque to him to have to abase himself before the French Bourbons, masters of the meager lives and fortunes of his homeland, but not so before the Spanish Bourbons, with whom, in his unhinged mind, he had a clean ledger. Napoleon was unable to subjugate Spain, because the Spain of the Napoleonic era was not to be found on the mainland but in her colonies—which is where the French Revolution was to continue once it had been interred in Europe by dynasties alert to the fact that their true alliance lay with the third estate of dry-goods clerks and sawbones and pen pushers, and always against the common people, who will always be downtrodden even in the reign of freedom because they haven't the will to be anything but slaves, eh?"

Monsieur Lange rented a small boat in Santiago de Cuba, where he had taken refuge after the uprising in Haiti, and set sail for La Guaira with his dream of a liberal revolution without blacks, but—thanks to the good offices of a customs inspector whom he had taught to count—with stocks of their cotton and tobacco and rum, the harpsichord from which his precious sixteen-year-old daughter would not be parted, the daughter, and the three turkey buzzards that followed him through all the ports of the New World. He laughed: Caribbean buzzards, it seemed, were given to the sport of leaping from island to island, like Jesus in the famous account of crossing . . . was it the Jordan or the Dead Sea? Monsieur Lange knew very little about these things, but in La Guaira everyone became embroiled in a fierce rivalry over the beautiful French girl, even the Liberator, Simón Bolívar, who blew into town with gale force at the end of July, occupied the port, jailed the encyclopedist Miranda, who had been the lover of Catherine the Great, and then evacuated the port, and through it all, the royalists went on with their great balls, and Monsieur

Lange went on showing off his damsel—why else had he brought her?—she was bait, a hook to revitalize the wealth being drained away with the end of the Napoleonic epic and on the verge, inevitably, of vanishing altogether in the confusion of colonialist and wartime smuggling. A man of the storm-tossed sea, the Frenchman, with his daughter, disembarked in a colony in revolt, where the young men of La Guaira, the same as he, sought a port in the storm, an easy road to what was left of Spanish dominion in the Antilles— San Juan, Havana, or back to Caracas, whatever looked most promising, but always an elegant flight, picking one's way between insurrection here and repression there.

"But you see how things work out," said old Clemencita. "They pulled the wool over each other's eyes, and when the biggest know-it-all, the sweetest talker of all the fine gentlemen in La Guaira married the beautiful French Mamasel, she found out that the parents of her 'young gentleman' had cut him off because of his rebel doings; as for his rebel friends, he couldn't count on them for so much as a mass in Lent."

And where was our young rebel while an exiled Bolívar made his way through Curaçao and Cartagena and risked his hide in Puerto Cabello and Cúcuta? Well, he was discovering that after the news of the winter of 1812 no one would give the time of day for the vouchers and IOU's of an Empire that was going to end up with salt water on all four sides, young Victor, on St. Helena, an island without snow or birds or monkeys or anything, I swear it.

Among the vultures circling above La Guaira, she tried to make out the three that to the day of his death followed her poor father, so skillful in day-to-day accounts and shady dealings but so stupid when it came to what made the year's balance come out in the black. There is no one more dangerous than an idealistic merchant, and the logical man to succeed him was the one who hated him most: Francisco Luis de

Heredia, who had married Mademoiselle Lange believing she was an heiress, as Lange thought Heredia was an heir. How can Branly believe that this undying rancor that dares to become incarnate in dreams that aren't its own is anything but a sordid tale of money?

Heredia laughs disagreeably. Doesn't the Count agree that money can be the source of bitterness, tragedy, and evil; and loving money more than a human being—isn't that motive for enduring hatred? This courtly young man, handsome like a shiny green olive shedding brine as roses shed dew, said that what revolutions had enabled the father-in-law to do over there, revolutions would enable him to do over here, and he began to ply between Venezuela and Cuba, Haiti and Mexico, sailing contraband up and down the coasts, bringing in and taking out what Spain sent to and demanded from Havana, what arrived in Haiti from Europe for the squabbling, newly emancipated republics of New Spain and New Granada, and what the British purposely let seep through Jamaica.

"British colonies enrich British subjects," M. Lange would say during his lifetime, "but Spanish colonies enrich only the Spanish crown. Spain isn't growing rich, only the coffers of her rulers. You will see, it will be the same story with the rulers of these new republics."

She did not understand any of the things her father said. She played old madrigals on her harpsichord, and she went on playing them after her marriage to Francisco Luis. She never realized, and had she realized would not have understood, that her husband, heir to her dead father, was trafficking first in inanimate luxuries, silver and dyes for English cloth, then, though they say no, the animate luxury of a few souls, slaves in fact if not in deed, workers in short supply here but needed there, blacks from Gran Colombia, Indians from the Yucatan, octoroons from Cuba, aborigines from Tabasco, again for English cloth, always for English cloth, because in this part of the world where everyone dealt in gold and silver no one seemed capable of setting up decent looms or selling a good piece of cloth—what didn't Francisco Luis de Heredia traffic in, eh?, lord of gibbet and blade, cruel and growing older, the older the crueler, thanks to the cheap rum of the cantinas of Río Hacha and Santo Domingo, the crueler the sicker, thanks to the dark evils of the brothels of Maracaibo and Cap-Haïtien, what didn't he sell to cement his friendship with an indispensable signer of exequaturs here, a repulsive pockmarked notary there, the loutish Señor Coronel, chief officer of the garrison at Puerto Bello, a customs officer in Greytown who never seemed to dip a toe in dirty water but stood with one foot in Nicaragua and one in Costa Rica, and sometimes a Señor Ministro who might be fingering white flesh for the first time, what didn't he sell?

"When she was no longer of any use to him, he sent her off to the high cliffs overlooking La Guaira; that would be his final gift to her, she loved La Guaira so much: 'I'll let you stay right here so you can fill your eyes the livelong day,' cruel Señor, master of lives and fortunes," Clemencita recalled. But he was as pocked as the notaries who close their deals in whorehouses and then celebrate with women who wreak their own revenge on any man who celebrates with their wretchedness: you'll see. Now he was a livid olive, wrinkled and rotten. But what did he care if he had lost his looks; he would go on the way he always had. It had been a long time since anyone came to him because he was handsome, now they came because he was cruel, a swindler, and a good man for pulling chestnuts out of the fire, and here it all came down to getting chestnuts in and out of the fire, and the first thing he learned was that a pot of beans is a pot of beans no matter where you cook it, and in his sphere of influence, Mexico, the Antilles, and the new republics of Terra Firma, someone was always cooking up something, and that's the God's truth.

Not she; no, used up, solitary, she wasn't good for anything. Let her talk to herself, play her harpsichord, sing her madrigals, and stare the livelong day at the sea of La Guaira, where she had arrived as a young girl with her papá, the model of her husband, who never forgave the fraud of a dowry-less marriage, vile French deceit, décolletage and stole and diaphanous ball gowns.

"A white dress, that's best in this heat. I must wear it again. I must search through my trunks. It must be there somewhere. When I find my white gown, something extraordinary will happen, I know it here in my heart, Mamita Clemencita. Help me."

Her nana, but younger than she, only thirteen, the little mulatto come from Puerto Cabello to beg in the streets of La Guaira when the militia of the unstable republic of the cruel Creoles was killing people, including her father and mother; and she listened to her all those years, and hummed the madrigals she was forever playing on a harpsichord more tinny and out of tune with every passing day, and dressed up in a blond wig to distract her, and with her she pawed through the large trunks of fetid clothing wasted by heat and humidity, the tyrannical leprosy of the tropics that disheartens, lulls, and corrupts as it slowly kills.

"An eternal and languid contemplation of the moment of death. Do you know Moreau's painting, my friend? Do you know what the not disordered agitation of our spirit is? I will tell you: it is the opposite of the petrified disorder of the new Latin American republics."

THE MAMASEL

Fatigués de porter leurs misères hautaines.
J. M. de H., "Les Trophées"

14

But Branly had renounced, like the situation he evoked, any tone as moderate and conversational as mine. I am not sure whether relating events that are a part of time—a memory, a premonition, or the dream that thrusts itself between the two and is our present—means one must recount it, bring it to life, with the fervor that suddenly had taken possession of my friend. It was as if through this story of another time and a remote place he were fulfilling many of the latent acts that in his conscious life he had let pass unrealized.

The liveliness of Branly's account was in stark contrast to this shadowy hour in which—and only in deference to my friend—we were being permitted to prolong our after-luncheon conversation in such an unusual, not to say scandalous, fashion in the dining room of Gabriel's *pavillon* on the Place de la Concorde.

"Do you feel all right, my friend?"

Branly nodded energetically, as one of the highly attentive club waiters approached, carrying a silver candelabrum. In my friend's eyes I saw a series of questions illuminated and transmitted by intelligence. I prayed that my own eyes would not too flagrantly betray stupidity, and that the flickering candles which—in further deference—the waiter was bringing to us would illumine only Branly's intelligence and not my faltering comprehension of a story he insisted was but another bead on the oneiric rosary of the Clos des Renards.

I reflected on what he had told me. I reminded him (more myself than him, it is true) that this was the hour of the evening when the French Victor Heredia usually appeared to bring dinner to his guest and to talk awhile with him, until Branly fell asleep, and then, the next morning, was awakened by the pleasant chatter of André and Victor on the terrace beneath the sickroom windows. This is, I reminded him, also the hour you dreamed, surely the story you are telling me is part of that dream.

The intelligence in Branly's veiled eyes was not dimmed as amazement sparked there, and a hint of perplexity that reflected my own.

"I do not know yet," he replied, "because I have not finished telling you the story."

"But you know what happened," I insisted, rather inanely, as if still not conceding that this was not one of the ordinary conversations my friend and I habitually enjoyed after luncheon or before swimming in the club pool.

"No," Branly denied vehemently. "I shall not know until I tell it. That is the truth."

As he spoke, he held my forearm in a viselike grip, as if my arm were wood, something he could cling to in the vertigo that I could know only vicariously. I tried to imagine how it must have been for him to live—if one may use that word, knowing its insufficiency—what for me became a verbal account only after it had gestated, uncomprehended, in the receptive soul of my friend, who was now illumined in the trembling light of the candelabrum being borne toward us by a servant, and she said to Clemencita, Blow out the candles, don't you see that the light hurts my eyes, and I am dreaming of an earthquake that will toss us into the sea forever and uproot boulders with its force, Clemencita.

The mulatto patted the gray-streaked head of her child-grown-old, and said, Poor little honey bee, I don't know where you want to fly, but you can never go back home, never, you know that your husband with his new wife and his son won't want you near them there in Paree, but she said that none of it mattered, if she could only put on her ball gown and see herself in the mirror she was sure she would reign again as she had at the balls of La Guaira so many years before. And because the mulatto nana loved her very much she did not tell her there was no white dress in the trunks her cruel, sick husband had allowed her to bring with her. The absence of mirrors in the house had been Clemencita's decision, so her mistress would believe she was still young, so she would never feel that she was growing old. And her mistress played her harpsichord to drown out the plaintive call of the toucan in the tall grass.

"Then, do you understand, child, I had to cut corners, I had to pawn two or three things to scrape together the money to go to the port and buy the silks and fine lawns to make your poor mother a white ball gown she might never wear except to her own funeral, do you understand, child?"

When Heredia's second wife learned that the aged mulatto nurse was going around telling Victor such things, she asked Heredia to send her packing, back to the streets of Puerto Cabello to beg, but the cruel, sick Señor laughed at her and said that nobody, not even she, so distinguished, especially she, so respectable but so insipid, could compare to the beauty of the French Mamasel when she arrived in La Guaira at the time of the ball given by the Liberator, Simón Bolívar, who had just occupied the port and who had nothing but compliments and gallantries for her, thus setting Heredia's cockscomb aquiver with jealousy and ambition.

"And you have not stopped since then, Francisco Luis, but I do not know which has been greater, your ambition or your blindness. Out of ambition you married a French girl without a sou to her name, thinking she was a rich heiress; but of necessity you made a virtue, and following in the footsteps of your detested father-in-law, you replicated his life and fortunes in the shadow of the Independence. Now you again find yourself on the brink of ruin—naïve, fawning, bowing and scraping before the brother of the third

Bonaparte, involved in this Duc de Morny's financial adventures with the banker Jecker and his Mexican bonds. And do you see what Juárez has decided? I have just read in *La Gazette de France*: those obligations were contracted with the conservative government and are not worth the silk ribbon they're tied with. What are you going to do now, Francisco Luis? How can you support your son and me in the luxury of the court of Napoleon and Eugénie—legitimate or not? How are you going to pay Herr Winterhalter for the portrait I asked you to have him paint of me?"

It wasn't a bad thing for his son to believe he was the son of the Mamasel and not of this distinguished, proper, but insipid and affected girl from the provinces stuffing herself with the sticky-sweet pastries of her native Limousin. It might well cause Heredia's present wife to take stock of the highly precarious situation any woman finds herself in when she is, or ceases to be, the object of the caprice of a fine gentleman like Francisco Luis de Heredia, son of the Spanish enslavement of Indians, descendant of the patriarchs, judges, and jailers of the plains of Apure, with his face pocked and pale as the devil's shirtsleeve, deep in the ancient jungles of Hibueras, where more than one Andalusian conquistador left his soul and his bones.

"Don't you fret," Clemencita told her young lady. "No real gentleman goes around telling people what a fine man he is."

"That doesn't matter to me at all, Nana. I love him. I want him to come back to me. I am his precious Mamasel, that's what he called me."

"Branly, are you all right?"

"Look, child: the dress you wanted. Look, my boy: you don't know how your mother suffered. Look, my new Señora: I'll go when I choose, because your husband needs me as a living reminder of his remorse. Look, Master: you're a devil, and I wouldn't trust you or any of yours. You

Heredias would do anything to ruin and shame my little honey bee, who loved me from the moment I was rescued from begging in the steep streets of La Guaira, pure papaya peel and burning stone. But she knew more than any of you, for all your fine ways. She knew the secret of things. For example, how, not looking at herself in any mirror, she went beyond what I'd planned—which was to make her forget how fast she was growing old here alone in this big house on the cliff high above the sea—she went back to another time without mirrors when she was a little girl. She used to say, 'Clemencita, take me to the park because it's sunny today and I have a friend in the Park Monsewer or Monzoon,' I don't know how to talk that gibberish, young Victor, and she used to describe that beautiful park all filled with windmills and dairy farms and splashing fountains, it was 'precious' she said, like your papá called your mamá in the days when he loved her, before he dragged her down to the depths of shame, her first shame, and worse to come. I think her salvation was remembering her childhood games in that Monzoon or Monsewer Park in Paree, and her little playmate, because, she said, sitting there on her balcony overlooking the tile roofs and the still sea of La Guaira, 'he is my friend and he will never grow old as long as he remembers me and I remember him. He will never grow old if he dreams of me, nor will I, Clemencita.' "

"Is something wrong, M. le Comte? Remember, it's only a painting, eh?, not a real woman who remembers you and is waiting for you here, as the boys said. Have you seen a ghost? As old as you are, how do you know what true memory is? Live a hundred years and you will see you have forgotten ninety percent of your memories, those things that happened in the most profound well of the past. What do you think? I will tell you: memory is like an iceberg, it reveals only what it chooses. Do you remember the three buzzards that followed the French merchant everywhere?

Don't lose sight of them. Now they're circling above El Morro in Havana where Francisco Luis, ruined by the adventure of the Mexican bonds, has taken refuge among the Spanish colonists who when they become Cuban insurgents will also make my father pay for his crimes of smuggling, slavery, and prostitution. Now he must maintain us, his second wife and his son, in the comfort and the cult of appearances of the Second Empire. I say this in his favor. Everything conspired against him to sink him in a morass of poverty, but he would not allow it, his bitterness merely inflamed him. The blame for all this lay in the deceit of the Frenchman and his damned daughter, the Mamasel. But no one can sink Francisco Luis de Heredia, because he is a Señor, an absolute Spanish hidalgo in a land of brainless blacks and indolent Indians."

What could he scheme in the time of Napoleon's nephew that his father-in-law hadn't schemed in the time of the uncle? Obsolete arms for the Republic in Mexico, and contraband for and bonuses from that heaven-sent French intervention, with its hosts from every corner of Imperial Europe, Zouave battalions, Walloon regiments, bands of Czech musicians, Austrian hussars and Hungarian cooks, dancing masters from Trieste and lesser Polish nobility still reeking of cows, hams, and tile stoves, Prussian calligraphers and zealous young men escaped who knows how from the cold of Petrograd, all flowing together—thirsty, hungry, fevered, primitively libidinous and liberated in the land of El Dorado and of the noble savage with whose image the Old World had lulled itself for a century—on the distressed beach of Veracruz, where three buzzards wheeled above the fort prison of San Juan de Ulúa.

"Can you imagine that he would miss a chance for revenge, Frenchman? Hear me well, you through whose lips I speak, imagine how that devil will take his final revenge against my little girl-grown-old, very old, how he will snatch her from the dovecote where she lived without mirrors above the unreal mirror of the sea of La Guaira, he who already had betrayed and shamed her as a young girl, he who had dried up every drop of her youth and beauty, now in her old age how could he resist using her and shaming her, dragging my muddled baby to Veracruz, where he left her to the mercy of the drunken, jeering, cruel, bone-weary troops far from their homes. Ah, Clemencita, Francisco Luis told me, what a good idea to make your Mamasel's dancing gown again. For that's what she's going to do, she's going to dance in strange whorehouses filled with Indians and Flemings, peasants in rough white cotton and hussars in embroidered jackets, high-cheeked Hungarians and Jaliscans with lugubrious eyes. The great brothel belt of the Napoleonic invasion of Mexico, M. le Comte, from Guadalajara to Salina Cruz to Tuxpan and Alvarado, where soldiers sowed children with pale eyes and dark skin, who if their fathers had acknowledged them would have been called Dubois and Herzfeld and Nagy and Ballestrini, but instead were named after their mothers, Pérez and León and Gómez and Ramírez—and how will you remember all this, M. le Comte, no one has a memory that long."

"Ah, my poor little girl, all old and worn," the cruel proclamation, come one, come all, you see before you the Duchess of Lanché, the very one you read about as boys, here she is, which of you ever saw or touched a real authentic Duchess back in your homeland, a Duchess with a capital D? Don't pay any attention to her years, mon capitaine, distinction has no age, but if you want to know how to wring the best from our slightly aged Duchess, let me whisper something in your ear and then let you see with your own eyes and feel for yourself, open her mouth, that's it, run your fingers over her gums, what do you think of her, eh? not a single tooth, just a little marble nub here and there to spice up the broth, like the garlic in bean soup, eh, mon capitaine? No young girl can do that for you, eh, mon capitaine? What do you think of her?"

"Oh, my God, M. le Capitaine, are you all right?"

"Ah, my poor little girl, my little honey bee become a clown princess, far from her dovecote in La Guaira. One night I found her dead, dressed in her high-waisted white gown with the long stole, beneath a mirror in that whorehouse where the terrible tyrant Francisco Luis de Heredia had taken her to squeeze the last pittance from between her lips. He had never forgiven the deceit. Look what she had in her clenched fist: half a gold piece. Her last pay, and even then she was tricked by an officer who gave her only half a coin."

"My father had never forgiven the deceit, M. le Comte. My mother died in a brothel in Cuernavaca, where the Emperor Maximilian had a butterfly- and peacock-filled pleasure palace. But who knows where they buried her, because the Bishopric had forbidden loose women to be laid to rest in holy ground. Who knows what barranca they threw her into? But he had never forgiven the deceit, and he had published in all the local gazettes a funeral notice announcing the much-lamented demise of the Duchesse de Langeais. They say that the whole French court of Mexico had a good laugh over such a grotesque joke."

"But at the beginning you told me your mother would make fools of all of you, Heredia. I do not understand . . ."

"Don't you think it's her turn?"

"Perhaps."

"Do you know the names of every one of the Imperial officers who were stationed in Cuernavaca who visited Heredia's brothel in the barranca of Acapaltzingo on the night of August 12, 1864, to celebrate the seventieth birthday of the Duchesse de Langeais?"

"No, of course not. Don't you mock *me*, Heredia."

"Very well. Do you think it a coincidence, M. le Comte, when two people have the same name?"

"No. It is merely a matter of chance, of onomastic arithmetic, when names coincide."

"When they coincide, yes. And when they are sundered?"

Branly shook his head and consciously retrieved the rational tone he had decided to assume in his relations with the French Heredia. "Allow me, if you will, to express my doubts about everything I.have heard here tonight."

Heredia shrugged preposterously. "I am not to be trusted, is that it?"

"No. I must be frank. I am aware that everything you tell me has the effect of distracting me from something you undoubtedly want to hide."

"Suspect what you want, M. le Comte. But nothing will prevent what once was joined from being joined again."

Branly tried to see outside, but deep night lay over the woods and parks of the Clos des Renards; he realized that for hours he had been listening to voices as he stared into the nothingness of the night. The painted image of the pitiful woman known as the Duquesa de Lanché had disappeared into shadows far more obscuring than the hands that hid her face. Heredia exclaimed with feigned surprise and begged my friend's forgiveness for everything: the darkness, the late hour, for keeping Branly awake, for the long-winded obsession with family histories that had neither interest for nor any connection with M. le. Comte, whose most illustrious family had had no association with such ugly realities for centuries, of course not. Perhaps nine centuries, or a thousand years ago, yes, but certainly not a short century before, such a thing couldn't be. No ancestor of the esteemed Comte de Branly had been present at the whorehouse of Francisco Luis de Heredia one August night in 1864, nor had he been at the burial of the French

Mamasel in the barranca of Acapaltzingo, with Clemencita singing in broken French, as a kind of prayer for the dead, a madrigal the Mamasel had adored and always played on her harpsichord, *eló eté sibele*, laughed Heredia, that's how it sounded in Clemencita's broken French, a madrigal transmuted into an Afro-Hispanic chant.

Heredia had been laughing with every word he spoke. Now, with false obsequiousness, he lighted the candles of a silver candelabrum to lead his guest back to his bedroom.

"Follow me, M. le Comte."

"Please?"

"Is there something you want?"

"Nothing. Only that yesterday, when Victor brought my meal, I asked myself whether you were degrading him, Heredia, as your Francisco Luis degraded his wife."

"But, M. le Comte. The boy is serving you, not me."

Branly tried to smile. "Your father did not have such a good excuse. Perhaps he lacked an intermediary in his dispute."

"Doesn't it surprise you that he chose her as my mother?" Heredia asked unexpectedly.

"No," Branly said, adding with deliberation: "You yourself told me that, in your manner of thinking, one is free only if one is born without father or mother. Perhaps this is the intermediate solution, to choose one's parents."

"You are truly the good, rational, sensual Frenchman, M. le Comte." And Heredia laughed.

My friend nearly replied, "But never mediocre," and then remembered his conversation with Hugo Heredia on the day he met him: the high Indian citadel at Xochicalco, the edge of the precipice, Victor running toward them with his discovery, Branly hooking his arm with his cane, preventing him from falling fifty meters.

"A rational Frenchman, sensual surely, but never mediocre."

"Sensuality is but a chapter of violence."

"On the contrary."

He remembered, but he did not repeat, those words. Slowly, he followed his host, exhausted, leaning on his cane, and wondering whether the false Duchesse de Langeais of this hot-blooded and baroque story of the Heredias had fled his dream.

15

No. She returned punctually. But now she arrived laden with color, envisioned memories, signs and omissions more profound than her initial mystery. Then she had been separate from history, but now, Branly is telling me, it was in fact history that was responsible for making her more vivid but at the same time less real.

Nevertheless, though this invasion of his pristine dream of a woman eternally poised on the contiguous thresholds of birth and death by the concurrent, roiling tides of wars and passions, revenge and rebellion, the traffic of weapons and bodies, might have destroyed the pure essence of the woman now in addition mottled by a multiplicity of names, it made Branly realize that he was indebted to the Heredias for having interrupted his routine and its accompanying empty hours. This he acknowledged as he fell asleep that night, after he had been subjected to the schedule of his unsleeping host, and had judged a defeat the time spent with him, time that separated him from sunlit hours and the overheard conversations of the boys on the terrace.

At any rate, the elderly sleep very little; a drowsy old man is slightly ridiculous, my friend is saying now, as he consults the heirloom watch in his vest pocket, attached to an elegant gold chain.

"It is five o'clock."

Branly asks which I would prefer, that he continue the story or that we go for a swim in the club pool and then (and here he laughs apologetically, as if this were a benevolent imposition), if I wished, dine together at the Laurent he had known as a youth. No, that would not be possible, the restaurant has been closed for many years, perhaps the Vert Galant on the Quai des Orfèvres: he has friends there, too. Shall he reserve a table for nine o'clock? I was struck by the unconscious associations his words reveal. He knows that one restaurant is still open for business and the other not, but he is not ready to accept the loss of the owners of the place he frequented in 1914; to him they are as real as the restaurateurs he sometimes visits today. At the moment, his second suggestion seemed considerably more attractive, but some irresistible compulsion caused me to say: "No, Branly, I don't want you to interrupt your story."

I did not dare explain that a terrible sense of inconclusiveness was beginning to assail me; I feared that a prolonged interruption would seal, unfinished, the various stories beginning to fuse into a single narrative. He acquiesced, and then told me that the real mystery of that night he had spent in the company of the French Victor Heredia lay in the fact that when he returned to his bedroom he fell into a deep dream, so deep that all that had happened seemed to become a part of it: his ascent into the attic of the Clos, his encounter there with the man with the white eyes and hair, his discovery of the painting of the woman whose face was hidden in her hands, the stories about Francisco Luis and the nana Clemencita. But curiously, he says, within that dream, which was like being immersed in a body of water too deep for him to touch bottom, his head, above water and illumined by the moonlight, was experiencing a kind of extreme and undesired lucidity; drowned in dream, he plotted various detailed schemes for fleeing Heredia's estate the following day: he would call Etienne; why hadn't he come to pick up the Citroën? He would call Hugo Heredia; why his astonishing lack of concern for his son? He and young Victor would be back in the house on the Avenue de Saxe in time for luncheon; would his Spanish servants José and Florencio have everything in order?

"I do not know whether I make myself clear. In the dream, it was the everyday considerations that became fantastic; the rational part of my dream was the sudden and undeniable identification of fantasy with total reality. But you cannot imagine what I thought of to wait out the return of logic. While deeply asleep, within my dream though not reconciled to it, I entertained myself by counting, as if so many sheep, the Frenchmen born in the Hispanic New World."

He says that over the fences of his imagination, like figures in a transatlantic ballet, leaped Paul Lafargue, blown by a hurricane to London from his cradle in Santiago de Cuba to wrest a daughter from Marx, and, ever a cyclone, to whirl through the debris of the Commune and unleash socialist storms in Spain, Portugal, and France; Reynaldo Hahn, who came from Caracas with his gloomy songs and beautiful hands to rock the dreams of Bernhardt and Marcel Proust; Jules Laforgue, who had come to France because he had not wanted his flesh to grow old "more slowly than the roses" in Montevideo, and had exchanged the passage of a "sad and insatiable youth" beside the River Plate for the speedier universal illusion called death beside the Seine; and why did Isidore Ducasse emigrate, he too from Uruguay, only to die between an umbrella and a sewing machine on an operating table in one of the grim hospitals of Paris, when in Montevideo he had already found his Maldoror, his Mald'horror, his male horror, his mald'-aurora, the waters of the River Plate at first light, swollen with distended skins, the hides of slaughtered steers, of mutilated men, of children lost amid baled wool and sheep udders?

I listen to Branly speaking of my lost cities, and I exclude forever from his narrative that dual monster, the Comte de Lautréamont, that beast of prey whose poems were written with tentacles stained red with ink: "*C'est un cauchemar qui tient* ma *plume*"; yes, a nightmare stained his pen. My breath quickens as my friend makes room in his dream for another Frenchman from Montevideo, the lucid and magisterial Jules Supervielle, who was right to emigrate: there, facing the never-ending pampa, his brow would have remained forever naked, a "great empty plaza between two armies." And, following on his heels, José María de Heredia, the Frenchman from Havana, the disconsolate conquistador who returns to the Old World wearily laden with "the arrogant misery of his trophies, the blooming beast and the animate flower," the sun beneath the sea and the quivering of gold; drunk with "a heroic and brutal dream," the dream of the new continent, the nightmare of the old.

"Do you see, my friend? You, who come from there, should understand when I tell you that the New World was the last opportunity for European universalism; it was also its tomb. Never again, following that century of discoveries and conquests, was it possible to be universal. As it turned out, the New World was too vast, on too great a scale. No one there could paint, as Holbein the Younger here, the exact measure of the human universe as represented by the portraits of More and Erasmus. There we all became Heredias; enervated Creoles. I tell you, too many innocent backs bore the mark of the whiplash of Maldoror's cruel pen."

He stared at me with an inordinate, slightly sinister intensity, an expression that gave him the vaguely comic air of an ancient Roman senator plotting crimes in the baths of Diocletian. I feared this mood, because always when Branly verged on the sublime I was forced to swallow my amusement, along with a dose of ridicule. He lowered his voice suddenly.

And my inner laughter ceased abruptly as he placed his hand on my arm; I feared the twist my extraordinary friend would give to the things he was saying, feeling, remembering, foreseeing.

"Now listen carefully. This story was told me that night in the garret by several voices, those of Heredia and his father, the stupid and cruel Francisco Luis, and of his no less stupid, though benign, second wife, by the nana Clemencita, and by the Mamasel Lange. They were not telling me their own stories but the story of a different Heredia. The young one. The boy Victor Heredia. The story they told me was his."

My astonishment when I heard Branly's words was comparable only, I believe, to my feeling of inadequacy as I had listened to the narrative of the Caribbean Heredias, which, in turn, was punishment and compensation for my self-sufficiency when I pointed out to my friend that I understood, perhaps better than he, the real story of the two boys in the Parc Monceau.

He was prepared now, as we sat in the shadows of the club dining room, to grant the Duchesse de Langeais a place in the scene in the Parc Monceau; in that way he would not burden the shoulders of the young Mexican Victor Heredia with the misery and humiliation of the Heredias of La Guaira. He believed that the French Victor Heredia was the boy of the Avenue Vélasquez. But today he was a boy named André. And the Mexican Victor was André's prisoner.

"You exaggerate, Branly," I ventured, with a nervous start I tried to disguise by idiotically folding and refolding the limp table napkin.

He looked at me with gratitude and supplication. The first

emotion informed me that, as it had him, the exhilaration of the Antillean world was subconsciously beginning to dominate me. The second invited me to cooperate with him, to recover, to make possible, the original temper of our conversation, the priestly and rational tone of French dialogue, and, more importantly, its manners. As long ago as the sixteenth century, I exclaimed, Erasmus wrote that the French believe themselves the repositories of courtesy. And I shall not be the one to belie the wise man of Rotterdam. Branly reminded me that in the same paragraph Erasmus accuses the Germans of priding themselves on their knowledge of magic. He realized, at any rate, that explicitly I accepted, though implicitly held reservations about, his cult of *politesse*. One should not, he said, consider it a national characteristic, as Erasmus had done, or Lope de Vega, who had attributed equal virtue to the residents of Lombardy. It was, simply, his personal religion. In any event, he sighed, considering the historical destinies of France and Germany, was it not preferable to follow the modes of the French? I told myself that the undertaking would not be easy; the intelligent eyes of my friend told me, in exchange, that the story of the Heredias had infected us both. We were speaking like colonials; we were reacting like "enervated Creoles."

"But let us speak of Supervielle," said Branly, as if to break my vicious circle. "Do you remember his marvelous poem *'La Chambre Voisine'*?" he asked, his head curiously tilted to one side.

"Only because you mentioned it at the beginning of our conversation," I replied, attempting to avoid any implication of psychic communication, a possibility I found displeasing.

"It is one of my favorites," said Branly, closing his eyes and joining his hands under his chin in a posture halfway between memory and prayer. "I remember it because I had dreamed of them all, Lautréamont and Heredia and Supervielle, believing I did so consciously, when in truth, don't you see? I was projecting a partial solution to my enigmas, because the poem by Supervielle that I had begun to repeat in my dreams, *Tournez le dos à cet homme mais restez auprès de lui*, had anticipated me, it existed before the question, for the purpose of linking together the disparate parts of my dreams at the Clos des Renards and finally leading me to the truth."

Softly, my friend began to recite the poem. I smiled as I thought how, with Branly's recitation of the poem by a French Uruguayan, he was exercising the supreme gift of selection, synthesis, and consecration that France has reserved for herself through the centuries. Supervielle was a vehicle by which we could escape that tropical ennui in which the sublime constantly rubs shoulders with the ridiculous, and feelings of cruel guilt are all too grossly revealed, stripped of the pious veils we Europeans so quickly cast over our crimes against history, to enable us to accept the equally discriminatory and exigent French spirit of reason and good taste, but not to sacrifice the cutting edge of the fantasy, the displacement, the revelatory madness, of the vast, empty lands of the new continent.

> *Laissez-le seul sur son lit,*
> *Le temps le borde et le veille,*
> *En vue de ces hauts rochers*
> *Où gémit, toujours caché,*
> *Le coeur des nuits sans sommeil.*

I tried to remember, to anticipate, the lines Branly was reciting in the darkness, inseparable prayer and memory; but more powerful than the poem was a voice like the sound we hear in the heart of a seashell: there is nothing in its depths, but the ocean is captive in that intangible sound.

I had first the sensation, then immediately the certainty, that Branly was speaking words I was thinking an instant before he uttered them, the words of Supervielle's poem.

They could only be, I knew then, the words of his last dream at the Clos des Renards. How strange they had all been said before, by the poet, or by his reader, my friend Branly.

16

I feel as if black shadows had congealed in my throat. I feel, above all else, that I am the object of a relentless hostility. But, in spite of everything, I refuse to walk away from that boy who is observing me from behind the beveled windowpanes. I do not walk away, although I turn my back. I am not sure whether the barbarity I feel in my eyes is my own or a reflection of his gaze and of his baroque stories in which passion and vengeance are raised on a revolving altar of gold leaf and moon mist. I stand, unspeaking, my back to the boy who is watching me. A woman is approaching along a path in the infinitely mutable landscape of the Parc Monceau; the boy watches us from the window of the house on the Avenue Vélasquez. I do not know what time it is. I look at the boy and the woman, and I realize that for both it is difficult to distinguish night from day. I want to tell them not to worry, that what they are witnessing is not really being seen by them but by someone who has the gift of seeing things through eyes that register a rate of speed that is not, he thanks God, that of human beings, because otherwise we would all be destined, without exception, to be separated as soon as we have come together. But birth and death are not simultaneous for us. The woman does not understand, because she is not looking at me now, she is looking toward the boy in the window, and she tells him not to be troubled about distinguishing farthest skies from the depths of his troubled heart. The woman speaks to the boy as if I were not standing between them. But as she comes closer I smell leather and sandalwood. I hold out my hands in supplication, but she passes by, turning her back to me, trailing the white satin shreds of a high-waisted ball gown, the tatters of the stole tied beneath the décolleté neckline and bare shoulder blades, the tower of her hair about to crumble into ruins of sticky cotton candy. I stretch out a hand to touch her and tell her, you see, we had no need to worry, the raging time in which birth and death occur simultaneously is not our time. To us belongs the sweet, slow time of all the lovers on the earth and it does not demand that lovers be separated the moment they meet. But the woman stares at me, uncomprehending, seemingly unhearing. Her worn, low-heeled slippers scurry like white mice and she disappears behind the iron fence of the house on the Avenue Vélasquez. I am still in the Parc Monceau, awaiting her return, but now she is inside the house. There she croons to the boy as the mulatto had crooned to her, she protects him, and prevents anyone from coming near him, least of all a usurper like myself, for I am no longer a child and yet I presume to claim the attention and affection she reserves for the boy with whom she used to play, while still a girl, in the Monzoon or Monsewer Park, before leaving to fulfill her destiny among the steep hills of La Guaira and the reverberating barrancas of Cuernavaca. She places a finger to her lips, and tells us to leave the child alone in his bed; time hovers near, keeping watch over him. They had been reunited. They have emerged from graves in rotting barrancas of mangrove and plantain to be reunited on the high rock cliffs where moans forever concealed the heart of insomniac nights. Let no one enter that chamber again, exclaims the woman in the outmoded dress of the First Empire; nothing will leave this refuge, except an enormous dog that has lost all memory of the past and that will search the ends of the earth, land and sea, for the man it left behind, unmoving, in

the strong, decisive hands of the new mother and nurse, at
last reunited with the son she never had, but who chose her,
enclosed with him in the chamber where birth and death
are indistinguishable, and no evil, no ugliness, no humiliation, no intrusive vulgar demands can penetrate the seamless
surface of things that exist in instantaneous simultaneity:
this love, this proximity, this perfect awareness that time
will not exist between being born, loving, and the act of
loving, dying. I shall wait forever outside. Perhaps the dog
without memory will bring me the final notice of the moment when my birth coincided with my death. Both solitary.
She will never return. She has condemned me to death
because I was too impatient to remember the boy; to her,
this is a horrifying desertion. A crime. I am alone in the
Parc Monceau. They are reunited at last.

Reunited at last.

17

He opened his eyes. He parted the drapes. It
was day. He awakened convinced he had
dreamed everything that happened during the
night. His encounter with Heredia was a dream.
He looked out on the symmetrical garden cleft
by the secret wound he had perceived earlier,
blasted as if by gunpowder. The Citroën was
still there, abandoned on the carpet of dry leaves, beside the
oak against which it had collided. The tranquillity of the
sunny September morning was allied with the silence of the
garden and woods, with the play of the sun's rays among
leaves ravished by a dying summer, and with the only sound,
one Branly had not heard before, the long, plaintive, high,
far-off cry of a peacock.

He listened in vain for the accustomed voices of the boys.
Almost immediately the peacock was silenced by the sound

of hurrying footsteps on the gravel. Branly peered out and saw his Spanish servants, the sallow José, looking more than ever like a figure from a Zurbarán painting, and the florid Florencio, with his mien of an exhausted jai-alai player. Both walked rapidly, but in apparent confusion, suitcases in their hands.

Branly recognized the suitcases; they were the ones the young Victor Heredia had brought to the mansion on the Avenue de Saxe. José and Florencio seemed to be weighing the best path to follow. Branly threw back the bedclothes and seized his cane for support. He descended the stairs with a haste, he tells me, that disproved whatever fears his age or his health, or both, might reasonably have engendered. Barefoot and limping, he reached the foot of the stairway, crossed the dark foyer of the Clos des Renards, opened the French doors, and stepped onto the terrace of the stone lions at the very moment his servants were approaching the Citroën, dubious as to whether they should walk on the gravel or the dead leaves. Branly did not falter. He tells me that by that time the heavy veils that had obscured the recesses of his heart had been lifted. He was acutely aware of the denouement of the story, and he was prepared, as in the beginning, to extend the handle of his cane to prevent young Victor from falling into the bottomless crevasse of another's timeless memory, the memory of a being demanding a new soul as haven for its poisonous pilgrimage.

The servants opened the rear door of the automobile and again seemed to hesitate. Then Florencio, who was the more hardy, picked up one of the suitcases and heaved it into the Citroën, while José nodded and Branly hobbled toward them, spurred by fear, and confident of the wisdom of a different fear—that of crossing the greensward of the garden disfigured by the horrible scar that only he had seen from his window.

At his approach, José and Florencio looked at each other,

disconcerted. Branly watched as, like servants in some farce, they ran to hide beyond the boundary of the leaves that my friend, in his agitation and haste, could not believe to be the cause of José's greater-than-usual pallor, or the apoplectic semblance of his comrade. Branly stepped onto the leaves and opened the car door. He knew the interior of that Citroën; after all, it was his automobile. But this foul-smelling cave, transformed in the course of three days and three nights into a depository for rotting vegetation, swirling temperatures, and detritus, was, he thought at first, simply a monumental bad joke, the awful mischief of the boys who with the universal instinct of magpies look for places to hide their treasures, and themselves.

He saw them. The unbelievably smooth, prepubescent, olive-skinned, secret, and typically small body of the mestizo Victor Heredia lying on the seat, and a naked, white-skinned André crowned with blond curls that contrasted dramatically with the lank black hair of Victor, against whom he was pressing with soft moans, lips parted, from neck to waist as smooth as Donatello's David, but feet, legs, and groin a hirsute jungle tangled like writhing snakes and spiders.

Branly tried to shield his eyes. More than by the brutal copulation of the adolescents, he was blinded by the brilliance of two objects: André cupped his in the hand he held above Victor's head; Victor had removed his from the hastily emptied suitcase by his side; the hands holding the brilliant objects joined together, and a guttural groan was torn from my elderly friend. He threw himself into the car, on the naked bodies so vastly different in temperature, and tried to separate their hands even before their bodies: the two glittering halves, one in André's hand, the other in Victor's, were joined like a fused metallic mass; the united hands were like the blazing forge that melts and fuses metals. Branly touched that thing, first with the idea of preventing

[132]

the union of the parts, and then to sunder what had been joined.

He cried out, his fingers seared from the touch of that cold hard thing blazing like a coin, from the ice, flame, and liquid of a stream that but a few hours earlier had been pure cloud. He sucked his burnt fingers. With the other hand he raised the cane, prepared to thrash the buttocks of this monstrous André, whose back, in the male position, was to Branly, though the boy looked over one shoulder to laugh and wink a pale eye. Then, Branly says, he could see nothing but the doleful eyes of young Victor, their unfathomable pleading for compassion and understanding, the terrible and hopeless sadness, the gratitude for a farewell not unlike death, and Branly froze, bewildered by his own sense of compassion. Even much later, he did not know whether he felt pity for the poor youth lying there with opened legs, for the other boy, to whom he had not held out a hand so many years ago when a red rubber ball bounced between them, or for a girl who said she had played with him, though he did not remember.

"But, my friend, today I know that the pity I felt for Victor Heredia I felt on behalf of my two lost playmates."

In truth, he admits now, the eyes of the young Victor Heredia filled him with terror, because there is something stronger than love, hatred, or desire, and that is the simple will, when one has no will, or is nothing, to exist for another. Branly suspects that this is what the Mexican youth was communicating that morning to him, his cordial French host, pleading that he not interrupt something he could not understand because it came from so far away.

Softly, my elderly friend closed the door of the Citroën and merely repeated the words I had already heard: "My God, I hope they never grow up. Their mystery will be considered ingenuousness, or crime."

He spoke these words as he repeats them this afternoon, with a solemnity befitting the valley of death. Or, what is the same thing, an unattainable love. Standing there motionless on the dead leaves, Branly was aware of his sweaty palms, clammy cold, the trembling of exhausted muscles, and the bluish pain of fingernails which on other occasions had foretold the deaths of a lover, a friend, a second wife, of soldiers on the Western Front.

He vacillated; he says he was on the verge of collapse. A distant scream, which he attributed to the stiff-legged and plaintively vain bird, signaled the hasty return of José and Florencio. They grasped Branly by both arms, alternating excuses and chaste interjections: they had been here before him, here on the leaves, that's why they knew how he felt, he must leave, come, sweet gypsy Jesus, it was horrible, but everything would be all right if they left quickly.

"Take me to the house."

"Of course, M. le Comte, the taxi is waiting."

"No, this house, here, take me there."

"Please, M. le Comte, come home with us."

"But, do you see, I had already told myself that I had not come alone to the Clos des Renards, and I would not return alone to the Avenue de Saxe, where Hugo Heredia would be waiting for me in an Empire bedchamber overlooking a garden whose symmetry is scarcely disturbed by an evergreen sea pine growing in the sand."

"I know your house, Branly."

"I mean that thinking of Hugo Heredia's bedroom there forced me to think of Victor Heredia's bedchamber here. I had never seen it."

"Nor the boys' bedroom."

"That was the Citroën."

The servants had helped him beyond the perimeter of the leaves.

"I had never intruded on my uncouth host in the daytime. I had never asked him the reason for, or an accounting of, anything beyond an undeserved surprise, or gross indifference."

"This way, M. le Comte."

"No. This way."

"With my cane I indicated the most logical route between the two points, but also, according to the rules of propriety, the least acceptable. The French garden, perfect in its symmetry, lay between my servants and me and the house."

My friend says that not even in the most difficult moments of the Aisne campaign had he been challenged to make a more immediate or more difficult decision. The servants wanted to respect the symbolic space of that formal garden and to use the gravel path to walk around it.

"Unlike them, I knew that something—I did not and do not now know what—was dependent on my venturing to cross the garden by the route one could not see as one stood beside it, but, as you recall, only from the second story, a slash cutting through the garden like the phosphorescent track of a beast."

Trembling, José and Florencio had released their grip on his elbows, offering the excuses, the tentative explanations for their deplorable conduct, that Branly would never request, for, if anything characterizes my old friend—I know now better than ever, after listening to him and attempting to predict the outcome of his adventure with the Heredias—it is that he would never express his intense pride; pride is silent, it does not ask excuses nor offer justifications.

"M. le Comte, you told us that we should obey the young gentleman at all times."

Their voices were growing faint behind him. Barefoot, my friend followed the gash in the garden, seeing about him the infinitely mutable landscape of his dreams, as if the places he had dreamed of in his bedroom had always been here, within view of his windows, where a woman he had loved in the past had appeared.

"Yes, listen: in the center of the formal garden surrounding me, I saw re-created the most beloved—I realized it then—the most irreplaceable, landscape of my life, the Parc Monceau of my childhood, and in that moment I knew that whatever the end, whatever the meaning, of the life I have lived, I would owe to Victor Heredia, my young Mexican friend, this moment when I recaptured what I had most loved but had nevertheless forgotten. We imagine that the instant belongs to us. The past forces us to understand that there is no true time unless it is shared."

He pressed my arm affectionately, a rare gesture from a man of such correct and courteous, although never effusive or sentimental, behavior, and his silence allowed me to stammer that, in the end, whatever travels we have undertaken are nothing more than a search for the one place we already know, a place that embraces all our emotions, all our memory.

"Yes," Branly nodded. "Yes. Precisely so. And that is what I owed to the boy whom in the normal course of events I would never have known because he would have been born after my death. Why was that not so? When Victor Heredia was born, I was seventy-one. My father died at the age of thirty."

Branly was not looking outside. His back was turned to the windows overlooking the square, and before him there was but one face, my own, obscured by the shadows. This may be why he was speaking in this fashion, he may have felt he was talking to himself. Emboldened, I asked, as one asks oneself: "Do you wish you had never known the Heredias?"

"I did not *know* the Heredias," my friend replied after

[136]

a pause. "The person I came to know was myself, have you not realized?"

He spoke with a kind of affectionate intensity I found moving, because I know in all sincerity that in that affection were joined all the disparate emotions of his own life, as well as everything my friend felt for those of us, living or dead, who shared in it. This conviction was born of a vision: Branly, in the center of the formal garden of the Clos des Renards, had seen himself (perhaps he was also seen by the two boys, and by the French Heredia from his hiding place) again in the Parc Monceau; behind him walked a girl dressed in white and before him the stubbornly closed beveled windows through which peered a child whose face belonged to oblivion.

He walked toward the boy, leaving the woman behind. He chose the boy, he needed him, ultimately, more than anything in his life, because to no one had he given less. Now, this time, seventy-one years after he had forgotten him, he would not cheat him, whoever his lost friend might be . . .

He continued walking until he came to the crushed gravel bordering the terrace of the lions. Monceau, the house on the Avenue Vélasquez, its residents, all dissolved, and in their place appeared what had been there all the time, the massive, unexceptional, suburban manor house existing in the limbo of an outmoded elegance very much in the style of Louis Philippe, its yellow-painted exterior peeling slightly. He stepped across the threshold with the shield bearing the inscription A.D. 1870, and crossed the dark foyer. He walked through an even darker dining room lined with cordovan leather, a library which instead of books had piles of faded papers on its shelves, a kitchen with few signs of food but a quantity of tree leaves steeping in cold copper cauldrons smelling of rainwater. He passed the antiquated telephone, and the no less old and creaking dumbwaiter.

The upper story contained the attic. On the second floor

was the bedroom he had been occupying. Heredia's room should be on the same floor. And it could only be, he told himself, mentally reconstructing the floor plan of the house he had just explored for the first time, behind one of the symmetrical, leather-covered doors along the hallway between his bedroom and the dumbwaiter.

Again he was walking down the hallway, as he had that morning, though now it seemed immeasurably longer, the hall he had first investigated while looking for the breakfast he found in a dumbwaiter in a pillar beside the stairway. As he advanced, he rapped at each of the symmetrically placed doors.

"They were simply *trompe l'oeil,* my friend. Like the houses and streets on the backdrop of the Palladium's Olympic Theater in Vicenza, the doors had been painted on the leather. As I knocked, I heard no hollowness at all, only the dull thud of a sturdy brick wall." A flayed house, yes, but also, Branly tells me, a walled-in house.

One door sounded hollow, the one beside the column that housed the dumbwaiter. Branly opened it and, at the end of a vast gallery stripped of furniture or ornamentation, saw his host.

 The French Victor Heredia was clad all in black. Black shoes, trousers, coat, and shirt. The only white article of apparel was a clerical

18

collar as white as the hair, skin, and eyes of this disagreeable man standing in the corner of an enormous room whited like the sepulchers to which Christ compared the Pharisees. There was in the narrowed and satisfied eyes of Victor Heredia, in his ridiculous priestly attire, in the arrangement of the stubby-fingered, greedy hands clasping the lapels of his jacket, something utterly repulsive, which, added to the deathlike radiance of the room, provoked in my friend the biblical associations so uncommon in him and, generally, in the Latin cultures, which believe in Jesus only because he was legitimized by Rome.

The absence of windows added to the feeling of suffocation; but if my friend was aware of a sense of asphyxia, it was because of Heredia's words, welcoming Branly with his infuriating, accustomed vulgarity. "What's the matter, M. le Comte? Did you lose your slippers? At your age you shouldn't be wandering around without shoes. Why, you might catch pneumonia, and before you know it, pow! you'd find yourself pushing up daisies; then how could you ever make it barefoot over the coals of hell?"

He punctuated his words with strident laughter, and although Branly was not prepared to offer his host the least consideration and would have preferred to have announced succinctly his impending departure in the company of the young Victor Heredia, the spectacle of the older, guffawing Heredia garbed like a parish priest precipitated words that perhaps in other circumstances Branly would not have uttered:

"I have come to say goodbye. But not without informing you that I am aware that I have no reason to be grateful to you. Your duplicity has been unremitting. I shall simply recall to you the first of your tricks; that will be sufficient to disabuse you of any idea that you are still deceiving me. You offered to take care of Etienne if the boy and I returned to Paris. But you knew perfectly well that I would remain, because Etienne is in my employ. Wait, please. I want you to hear one thing. I fully realize that my chauffeur and I have been mere pretexts for getting the boy here. I wanted to tell you this before I left, and to admit that I may have fallen into your snare at the beginning, but today, as I return home, I am undeceived. You, sir, are a charlatan."

The French Heredia, Branly tells me, looked at him with theatrically exaggerated amazement. "Why the devil are you telling me all this?"

Branly drew himself up, supporting himself on his cane. "I am telling you that I am a man of honor and that you are an unconscionable swine. I regret that my age prevents me from giving you a thrashing, whether public or private. It is all you deserve."

Branly admits, the glimmer of amusement in his small black eyes piercing the shadow of the dining room, that if he had adopted such tactics it was to get Heredia to lower his guard, so he would go on regarding Branly as a kind of aristocratic mammoth chained in the dark cave of an outmoded ethical code.

"The ethics of a man like Heredia, if one can speak of ethics, originate in the supposition that we have exhausted ourselves under an outworn code; our true superiority consists in the fact that we maintain the code, although we live in the same world as the Heredias; ultimately, they will feel the lack of that ethical and aesthetic protection. Everything is politics in this world, and politics is above all a problem of legitimacy."

He placed his hand on mine. His obsession in that instant, he tells me, was to rescue the young Victor Heredia, and his words were a means of circumventing the coarse lord of the Clos des Renards, of finding the chink through which he and the youth might escape, and of returning him —yes, his honor demanded it—to Hugo Heredia. The obvious affection between the father and son that he had perceived that night in Jean's house in Cuernavaca flashed through his mind, Branly tells me now, with the blinding brilliance of a Mexican sky spilling down on a tropical barranca. Now, he thought, his only defense for the young Victor was to exacerbate Heredia's pride. He clasped his hands as only he knows how: long, pale, translucent fingers —prayer and memory.

"And allow me to add one thing, Heredia. The 'English vice' does not horrify me; it is even possibly a necessary part of a young man's education. But it does make a difference whether the, ah, partner is of one's own or an inferior class. One pays an inferior."

He stared at Heredia provocatively, arrogantly. The host, his smile never wavering, removed his hands from his lapels. "How many centuries of human corruption has it taken to produce those delicate, long-fingered hands, M. le Comte?"

"At least from the time St. Remigius converted Clovis to Christianity," my friend replied with indifference. I was about to laugh at his riposte, but he repeated to me his insult to Heredia: he did not want to leave without paying his debts; how much did he owe André for his sexual services to Victor?

Branly says he heard a sound like that of chains being torn from a cellar wall, and then it was as if the wall itself had fallen on him, scattering heavy, loose bricks over his body, as icy cold and as little to be warded off as the entire universe of this savage and yet strangely-to-be-pitied individual, who with insolent fury and tenderness raged: "He's an angel, an angel!"

"I realize something now, though because his physical aggression took precedence over any other consideration, I did not realize it when he threw himself on me. I should have suspected: he assaulted me in defense of his son. But there was something more, is that not always the case?"

True madness is neither passionate nor heated, my friend adds. His voice has the chill of winter, and glacially icy was the voice of Heredia when he attacked Branly, ramming him against the whitewashed wall, pinning him there with his stocky, graceless body redeemed only by the classic configuration of head, profile, lips . . .

What did he say, Branly asks. That Branly can know nothing about such things, that he cannot imagine what it is to know that your mother was thrown into a barranca, her grave so shallow that dogs and buzzards could feed on her body, devour it, scatter her bones to the winds, while a lonely boy waited for his father to return from making a new fortune in Cuba and Mexico, a lonely boy hoping that his mother would return too, but she never returned because she had been a banquet, first for the troops and then for beasts of prey, and he would make Branly pay for it, pay for the tenderness he had never known all those afternoons when ordinary little boys came home from school to play in the Parc Monceau but the boy with no recognized name or family stared from behind the beveled panes of a house on the Avenue Vélasquez, and only once another boy, he, Branly, was on the verge of accepting him, of playing with him, of admitting he existed, but he hadn't dared, he hadn't taken the extra step, and he would pay for that too, and how much had the French captain paid the Duchesse de Langeais? the so-appropriately named French Mamasel, for sold she was, in the brothel in Acapaltzingo that was one of the enterprises of Francisco Luis? Who was the inferior there, eh? the Mamasell, the Mamasail, the Mamasucker, or the sucked? Who should have paid whom, Branly, should your father have paid my mother or your mother paid my father? Who did the favor for whom, you bastard? And she? how could she know that things were not what she imagined if Clemencita had removed all the mirrors of the world and the Mamasel believed she was as beautiful and as young when she went to bed with the captain of the French forces in Mexico as when she went to bed with Francisco Luis following the cotillions held a half century before? What did I tell you, you bastard, what did I ask you? I told you that unborn beings are one half of a pair, M. le Comte, you can't deny that, it's even true of dogs, but can't you imagine then that the opposite is also true? that young lovers are joined by an unborn child who demands his own creation through the souls of the young parents? Generations are infinite; we are all fathers of our fathers and sons of our sons.

My friend was breathing painfully. He managed to avert his pallid face from Heredia's panting, the icy breath of true madness whistling from a winter that was all winters, remote from the sweating armpits, the dark-skinned belly, the pliant waist of that enormous woman's body sensually bedded on the waves between New Orleans and Cartagena de Indias, the Morro Castle and the Fort of San Juan de Ulúa, the blazing towers of Sans Souci and the banana- and melon-laden ships of French Martinique, British Jamaica, and Dutch Curaçao. That world, crouched in ambush, tamed only in appearances, again sprang to claw at us that last morning at the Clos des Renards, this slowly dying afternoon in the Automobile Club, as if in refutation of the prolonged calm of Cartesian reason my friend and I were struggling to save—did we truly believe that?—from the chaotic tropics of the Heredias, that torrid zone that somehow emitted from between Heredia's fleshless lips a breath of icy death, as if the baroque existence so removed from our world proclaimed itself in equal intensity in its antipodes, only there. Branly tells me now that as he felt Heredia's panting breath on his cheeks he imagined an ice-covered Antilles and found nothing abnormal in the vision of white cathedrals, white palm trees, white parrots and owls skimming through a colorless sky above a milky sea.

"You lie." Through clenched teeth, Branly's voice was strained, stern. "You lie, or you are confused, it makes no difference. My father was not an officer on the Mexican expedition; he was not born until 1870. You are totally confused. Mademoiselle Lange, Heredia's first wife, was then seventy years old. She could not have conceived. And she had no children by Francisco Luis. You are the child of your father's second wife, Heredia. But even this is a muddled lie, because you have decided that she is not your true mother. I attribute that whimsy to a legend concocted between you and the mulatto nurse. I do not see what any of this has to do with an unborn child."

"It is difficult work to make a child, I agree." Heredia's smile was particularly lugubrious and offensive. "But true generations have nothing to do with ordinary chronology."

"What do you mean?"

"Didn't you see him from the waist down? My poor child is not well made. The legs, the groin. Badly made, I tell you. It isn't easy."

"What?"

"What do you mean, Branly?"

"Wait." He pressed my hand. "I myself did not understand. As I told you, I shall not understand this story until I have finished telling it."

"In spite of having lived it?" I persisted.

"In spite of that. What possible relation can there be, tell me, between living something and telling it?"

"Perhaps none, you may be right."

"Forgive my violence," said Heredia, as he eased his lethal, crazed hold on Branly. "I am an insecure and fearful man, ha! ha! It takes blue blood like yours if a man is to feel he's sitting on top of the world!"

"You are unmitigatedly vulgar," said Branly with a twisted smile. "Unmitigatedly . . . Heredia? Is that your real name?"

The host of the Clos thrust his hands into his pockets and shrugged like a surly urchin.

"I would like, after all this time, to know the name of the

boy I did not hold out my hand to seventy years ago in the Parc Monceau. I know it is very late to make amends." Branly's voice was moved, grave, restrained. He sought, as he spoke, the pale eyes of the French Victor Heredia. His host was silent for a long while, grinding his heel into the whitewashed floor of this suffocating gallery.

"André," Heredia said finally. "My name is André."

"Like your son," said Branly, with one of those polite formulas with which one courteously fills the pauses in social conversation.

"No," Heredia shook his head. "Like myself."

"Like you, Heredia? Did I not say that I want to make amends for my indifference—my cruelty, if you prefer? Is that not enough? Must you persist in your low sarcasm?"

"Do you know why I never appear in the daytime? No, don't say anything. I will tell you. True phantoms appear only in daylight, M. le Comte."

Mincing like some elderly maiden, Heredia walked to the corner of the room. Branly, as he tells me now, was by this time sufficiently familiar with Heredia's tricks to anticipate, following this mimicry, some new and disconcerting revelation from his host. Accentuated by the newly assumed gestures of an ancient virgin, Heredia said that he feared the daylight phantoms, and his distinguished guest, the Comte de Branly, should fear them, too. Was it his hope to save the boys? Had he ever thought that maybe the boys did not want to be saved? How many things must there be that he never realized? Wrapped in his aristocratic arrogance, so remote from the black and rotting ravines where French mademoiselles in exile in the New World sing madrigals to frighten away the dogs and owls waiting to devour their dead bodies, so secure in his mansions and symmetrical gardens, so unyielding in a land that had never known an earthquake or the cholera morbus or trichinosis or the oil companies' murderous White Guards or the forced labor of

Indians or hurricanes bearing dead leaves in a gale that in mid-August can strip an entire jungle of leaves and fruit to scatter afar, beyond the sea, to impregnate with pure tropical pollen austere European wives who then give birth never knowing that seed travels, carried on the air, filters into nostrils, ears, mouths, asses, the uncountable orifices of a human body that is more water and pit and puddle than anything else, eh? Oh, there were so many things he didn't know.

"Do you know anything of my desire to give life to everything that could have been but was denied existence?" asked "Heredia," suddenly pulling himself to his full height and acquiring a dignity Branly would not have believed possible.

"André, then, should have been the . . . son of Francisco Luis and Mademoiselle Lange?" Branly stammered.

"He is, M. le Comte. You must believe me, he is. That is the only element of truth in this entire farce. Except that this time my little angel is going to be born whole, not as he was before, but whole again."

"Heredia" again seized my friend's arm, but now with a strength, Branly says, incredible not only in his host but in any man. He twisted Branly's arm behind his back, forcing his head and body in the direction desired by this monster of many guises, whose role at that moment my friend could not define: was he a dangerous clown, a harmless madman, an ineffective mythomaniac, or a wretched, defeated, lonely man deserving of pity?

"You see, you doddering old bastard, you senile old motherfucking asshole, you see, that's what you get for going around sticking your nose where it doesn't belong, trying to separate what was always joined and will be forever, you see, Victor Heredia doesn't belong to your time now but to mine, and at last my son has the companion I never had . . ."

With one arm locked around Branly's neck, "Heredia" with his free hand raised the door of the dumbwaiter and forced my friend's head toward the empty shaft, as if preparing him for the executioner's ax or the blade of the guillotine. Branly stared into the depths of the space in which the *monte-plats*, converted in English into the more obsequious dumbwaiter, ascended and descended. An icy blast rumpled his hair, tiny daggers of ice needled his skin, forcing him to close his eyes filled with involuntary tears. In that instant he had seen what he had to see.

Branly's hand still clasped mine.

"Have you ever paused, my friend, to think about the appalling concept of infinity, time and space without beginning or end? That is what I saw that morning in the shaft of the dumbwaiter. Infinity was like the flesh of a wet, bland squid, slimy and slobbery, a texture without color or orientation, the pure vertiginous *sensation* of a great white mollusk ignorant of time or space. Something interminable cloaked in perpetual fine snow."

"What do you plan to do, you pitiful old bastard? Do you think when you leave here you can set your police on me, accuse me, demand that I return Victor? Forget it. Victor and André are no longer here. Victor and André are no longer André and Victor. They are a new and different being. No one could recognize them. Not even I. They could walk past you in a café, or on a street, and you would never recognize them. You would never recognize them. True madness passes without notice."

"Heredia" again burst out laughing, and Branly, his senses reeling, deprived of any intellectual means by which to deal with this devil who was most satanic because he was incomprehensible, unknowable, and therefore to be feared, did what he had never done in his life, what no one had ever forced him to do.

"That morning—you must believe what I tell you—imprisoned by 'Heredia' 's arms, with that unutterable vision of infinite emptiness before my eyes, I did something I had not done in all my eighty-three years. I screamed, my friend, I screamed the way they used to scream in the Frédérick Lemaître melodramas our great-grandparents attended on the Boulevard du Crime. I screamed, convinced that my voice was my deliverance, my life, my only chance, my only salvation. Bah, of course, on more careful consideration, I believe I must have screamed that way in my cradle."

And with those words he withdrew his hand from mine, which he had held throughout this portion of his story. He clasped his own hands in that typical, gracious gesture that served in circumstances like these to dissipate any hint of solemnity and to return things to a properly rational level not without humor.

"Bah," he repeated. "The things one must do. I screamed, terrified by that vision and by the sensation of my impending death, I admit it. But as I screamed I turned melodrama into comedy. As I struggled against 'Heredia,' the hinges of the door of the suffocating, whitewashed gallery burst open under the weight of Florencio's shoulder. José rushed in on the heels of his husky companion with the visage of a Basque jai-alai player, and both rushed to free me from 'Heredia,' subduing him. I sank to the floor, out of breath, exhausted. In the struggle, 'Heredia' was roundly drubbed by Florencio: he staggered, and fell headlong down the shaft of the dumb-waiter. The two servants exchanged rapid comments in Spanish, peering down into empty space.

"Here now, we'd better go down to the cellar."

"But, Florencio, look at all the dead leaves rising up the shaft."

"I told them, my throat aflame, not to waste time. We had to leave immediately. Where was the taxi they had spoken of? Come, quickly. I would send Etienne to pick up the Citroën later, another day."

"The Citroën, M. le Comte? But Etién came to pick it up day before yesterday, as soon as he got out of the hospital and learned about your accident," Florencio exclaimed as they helped Branly to his feet.

"He said he was going to take it to be repaired. But he never came back."

"You remember, Florencio, Señor Heredia told us he thought the accident was his fault, because of the young gentleman, and he told Etién he should be careful driving with one hand, and if he wanted, he would go with him to pick up the Citroën and see you at the same time, M. le Comte, and young Victor as well."

"But you know how stubborn a hardheaded Frenchman can be, with all due respect to yourself, M. le Comte: no Spaniard could tell him anything, and do you think he would want to be indebted to some foreigner, heaven forbid! And that was that. It wasn't as if he were going by way of Tetuán to bring home monkeys, there being so many around here . . ."

"And that was that. He took his own car and drove off forever."

"What do you mean, Florencio?"

"Nothing, except I think Etién must have had an accident in his 2CV when he came here to pick up the Citroën for repair," said Florencio, as the servants gently led Branly toward the stairway.

"And I think Florencio is right. I think he was killed. Maybe. Anyway, he never came back."

"And Heredia? Hugo Heredia? What does he say?"

"Your guest left for Mexico this morning, M. le Comte."

"I must thank you, at least, for staying with me."

"M. le Comte is very generous to us, and treats us like human beings," said José, as the three reached the foot of the stairs.

"You should just see, M. le Comte, how the Spanish treat

their servants. It's 'do this' and 'do that.' 'You peasant bastard!'—begging your pardon, M. le Comte. 'You idiot, anyone can see your mother let you fall out of your cradle, you blithering simpleton, you thickheaded fool . . .' And on and on and on!"

"And the young gentlemen are the worst. They like to humiliate you, to run you in circles. 'Pick that up, Pepe. Now leave it where you found it, Pepe. Don't you hear me? Pick it up again, Pepe.' "

"Well, a pot of beans is a pot of beans no matter where you cook it, because that young Mexican was no better than the young Spanish gentlemen. Look, M. le Comte, what he did to Pepe the minute he arrived. So of course we came running with his suitcases when he called."

"And we asked his father, and he said why not, we should bring everything here . . ."

"And I laughed and told Pepe, Let's get out here quick or he'll be beating you again with his belt. What a one he is! A real little devil."

Branly, assisted by Florencio and José, stepped onto the terrace of the lions. He found it difficult to grasp what they were saying, or rather, to reconcile the inconsistencies in their words. He felt dizzy. His servants were playing up to him; they were contradicting one another; they had been there that very morning with suitcases in their hands; they had given them to young Victor in the Citroën. They, like he, had experienced physical fear when they stepped on the dead leaves. They had, finally, rescued him from the satanic fury of "Heredia," the confused scion of many places rather than any time, this man who, because he had no dates, no origins, carried the burden of unfinished stories: how could he be the son of Francisco Luis and the Mamasel, who had met in La Guaira in 1812 and been parted forever in 1864 in a brothel in Cuernavaca? how, even if he were the son of Francisco Luis and his second wife, the fat, dull, gluttonous girl from Limousin, could he have been Branly's contemporary in the opening years of this century, when my friend played in the Parc Monceau? How old was "Heredia"? How old was Francisco Luis when he died?

These reflections on the utter irrationality of their ages, so inconsistent with Branly's rational chronology, faded from his mind the moment he saw from the terrace of the manor the perfect symmetry of the French garden, the clear and intelligent space where nature was tamed by the geometric exactitude of shrubs, greensward, pansies, artichokes, and stone urns. In vain, he looked for a sign of the grayish scar in the grass.

The birch grove, the rosebushes, the beech and willow trees, seemed to exult in their own serenity, as if in homage to the vanished summer, and along the avenue of chestnuts and oaks, autumn had not yet passed, spreading its basket of spoils. The fresh, cool ground was swept clean; there were no dead leaves, only the enchanting play of light and shadow among green branches.

The Citroën was parked on the gravel drive where the avenue ended and the garden began. When Etienne saw them emerge from the house onto the terrace, he left off dusting the ornamental klaxon with his feather duster, touched one hand to the visor of his cap, and climbed into the car. The sturdy chauffeur circled the garden and came to a stop before the entrance stairway; he got out to open the rear door so that Branly, assisted by his servants, might enter. The surprise in the voices of José and Florencio rang hollow, less than convincing. Of this, at least, my friend has a clear recollection.

"Imagine. And to think we'd given him up for dead."

"Jesus! Sweet gypsy Jesus! The dead has risen!"

"You two get in with M. le Comte, go on, now, take good care of him. I'm going for his things."

Branly says he sank against the soft, beige, spotlessly

clean upholstery and refused to converse with the servants, even to look at them, to concede that he was aware of their disconcerted but conspiratorial glances, their shrugged shoulders, the upturned palms mutely inviting explanations.

It would have been very easy to say to them: Hugo Heredia bought him just as he bought you, except that his price was higher. One Breton peasant is tougher than two Andalusian peasants. It takes a little more effort to make Etienne stop remembering. For you, forgetfulness comes easy. A little more time, a little more money, that was the only difference. No one remembers anything. Nothing happened.

Etienne emerged from the house with a suitcase containing, Branly supposed, the clothing my friend had been wearing the night of the accident. He climbed into the car and started it.

"How is your hand, Etienne?" Branly inquired.

With a sheepish smile, the chauffeur looked at his employer in the rearview mirror and raised his bandaged hand. "I drive very well with only one hand, M. le Comte."

"Ah."

Branly turned to look back through the rear window of the Citroën. He read the date inscribed above the doorway: A.D. 1870. Etienne had thought it was the number of the house and that he had made a wrong turn; on that occasion he had muttered curses against a municipal system that would assign two numbers to one house. My friend had known it was a date, because as he glanced toward the upper story from the moving automobile, leaving behind forever the Clos des Renards, he saw hovering in the window a dancing, fading silhouette in diaphanous white, with a tall hairdo resembling towers of cotton candy. The peacock uttered its plaintive cry. But Branly listened in vain for strains of the madrigal, *Chante, rossignol, chante.*

19

The elderly sleep very little, Branly repeats now. They feel besieged by the need for vigilance, and in this, old age is wise. Adjustments are made so that it is not physiologically necessary to sleep as much as before, as in the days when one came home worn out after poking into every corner of one's grandfather's castle, or after playing in the Parc Monceau, after making love with Myrtho in a nest of rose-colored eiderdowns, or after nights beneath the sulphurous lightning flashes of the trenches.

At any rate, a drowsy old man is slightly ridiculous, Branly says, as finally we arise from the table in the club dining room and walk slowly through the spacious salon illuminated at this hour only by the streetlamps on the Place de la Concorde. It is just six o'clock, and the lights turned on at the moment we reach the reception hall seem blinding. An army of waiters and assistants, several of them mere boys, swarm in with rolled-up sleeves, tightly cinched aprons, and flushed faces, to prepare the tables, spread clean tablecloths, fold fresh napkins, and replenish the flower vases.

The servants apologize, bow, step aside impatiently, their servility bordering on hostility. They want us to know that we have delayed their chores, their getting off work, their meetings with children, wives, friends, their entertainment or sleep. My friend and I leave behind us a clattering of glass and silverware like the serenade of a silver fountain. The madrigal of the clear fountain is echoing in my head, as so often happens with those childhood melodies whose classic and insistent simplicity preempts from our memory, to our annoyance, compositions we would prefer to hear, in a kind of permanent and gratuitous high fidelity. For example, above all else, I love two compositions, Haydn's Emperor Quartet and Schubert's Trio No. 2 for piano, violin, and cello. I would have wished that those noble chords had accompanied our descent of the equally noble staircase of Gabriel's *pavillon*, not some childish tune about nightingales, sorrow, and joy beside a fountain.

The evening meal at the Automobile Club de France is being prepared as we, who seemed about to delay the whole process, oblivious of the obligations of others, walk through the ground floor of the green and mahogany library with its memorable engravings of the first French automobiles, and into the modern bar beside the large swimming pool. There are few members present at this hour, and Branly suggests that we might want to take a swim after we have finished our conversation in the solarium adjoining the pool.

I nodded, and he marched off toward the pool as I followed, marveling at how completely he had recovered his military bearing.

"No, it was not difficult to guess that Hugo Heredia had bribed all my servants. In a way, it was the inevitable corollary to this story, and the only act that could tie together all the loose threads. The father, I have stressed this from the beginning, was instructing the son. I hesitate to say this, my dear friend, since you are to a degree from that world, but his lesson was one of a false colonial aristocracy that equates nobility with a power of corruption and cruelty beyond punishment."

He paused for a moment on the fiber mat bordering the pool.

"Do you admit that?" he asked, tall, stern.

"It's probable," I replied.

"No. It is true," he said, and resumed his martial pace. "Think about it and you will realize that this is the point where all the stories come together—that of Hugo Heredia and his son, that of Francisco Luis and Mademoiselle Lange, that of the savage resentment of the master of the Clos des

Renards—in a common inclination of spirit, if we may call it that."

"It is probable," I repeated, slightly taken aback, adding that I felt more at home *here* than *there*.

In the dressing rooms, the attendants called up our numbers and we began to undress as our numbered swimming trunks and towels, along with the obligatory robes and scuffs, descended in the small lift from a collective loft concealed above. We members of the club have no right to take these articles with us but must entrust them to the club until the day, if not of our death, of our unlikely resignation of the privilege of belonging to it. Where else these days does one find such precise and uncommon rituals? We did not speak while the bald or graying muscular attendants in shorts and T-shirts attended us personally, soaping us with loofa sponges, scrupulously avoiding any contact with our private parts, before we proceeded to the showers.

After we had showered, we wrapped ourselves in the terry-cloth robes and went into the humid salon conceived of by the club not as a sauna or a Turkish bath but as a pleasant solarium. Sitting there was like spending a summer morning beneath a cloudy sky.

I maintained a discreet silence, which I believed invited my friend to continue a story that might otherwise have ended at the moment when Branly, barefoot and in pajamas, flanked by his Spanish servants and driven by his Breton chauffeur, left behind him forever the Clos des Renards. I dreaded the probability of Branly's accusation. His stoicism would have been extraordinary if at least once, and what better time than this, in the company of a friend, without witnesses, and with a solemn, if implicit, oath never to repeat a word of our conversation, he had not said what we were both thinking.

At least he could be sure of one thing, he said as he settled into the canvas chair beside mine: Hugo Heredia had returned to Mexico and would never again see or hear from his son Victor. Perhaps, as the terrifying Spaniard of the Clos des Renards had said, Branly, though he could never recognize him, had seen Victor in a café or walking down some street. He could even be one of the waiters who rushed in to prepare for the evening meal at the club; had I realized the number of adolescents who worked as helpers? I said I had, and added that this medieval system disguised as apprenticeship was preferable to turning the boys onto the streets, unemployed. Branly closed his eyes and said that we had not been talking about unemployment. His question was, had I noticed the faces of the young waiters, had I seen among them a face that might belong to the person "Heredia" had referred to: neither André nor Victor, but a new being, André *and* Victor.

I told him I had not. The idea seemed so extraordinary that it had never entered my head. Why here?

"To be near," Branly replied.

"Near you?" I asked quietly.

Branly fingered the heavily embroidered blue initials on his robe.

"Near the recognition I owe them," he said in a flat voice. "I find it difficult to recover my faith in my own reason, and yet the madness of the Heredias seems overly classic and therefore mysterious; it is a madness cloaked in civility."

He held out his hand.

I leaned forward to take it.

Almost imperceptibly, without seeming to do so, he withdrew his hand, and said: "First I must tell you, and then I shall not say it again, that I have asked myself over and over whether I could have avoided what happened. What should I have done? I blame myself for many things. I shall mention only one. I allowed, you see? my pride and my scorn for the French 'Heredia' to divert me from the responsibility of calling Victor's father, Hugo Heredia. You remember that instead I asked 'Heredia' to telephone my servants to inform them that we were well and would be spending a few days in Enghien. Actually, I should have telephoned Hugo Heredia myself. Why? you ask with a certain amazement. As things turned out, weren't all the Heredias as thick as thieves, as English detectives say? It is true. And yet how can I convince myself—though at the time I did not know— I was not remiss? I should personally have telephoned the boy's father, listened to his lie, to the tone of voice that as it lies reveals the truth of things."

I thought Branly was exaggerating his role in what transpired and I said that preventing what had happened would have entailed as much risk as any other combination of events. Victor could have died in the plane accident with his mother, instead of his brother Antonio. The possible combinations of chance, I added, were multiple. Hugo and Victor could have died in the accident; or Hugo and Antonio. Could Branly attribute any of the hermetic consequences to human will?

"There is one thing I could have done, something decisive," my old friend said, suddenly aged as he spoke.

"What, Branly?" I was alarmed by the ominous curtain of age that suddenly descended over habitually taut features.

"I could have let the boy fall from the precipice. All I had to do was hold out my cane, not hook his arm with its handle. He would have fallen at least fifty meters from the citadel to the pelota court in the ravine of Xochicalco."

I made no comment. This linkage of deaths in a barranca in the Valley of Morelos seemed excessive, if not offensive: first, Mademoiselle Lange, now Victor Heredia. The same barranca? Always the same dogs and owls? Branly looked at me with a trace of amusement.

"You must remember, if you truly wish to be generous in absolving my guilt, that I was on the point of asking the father and son not to travel together. I might have invoked —it is my right, shall we say, of seniority—an intuition, a sixth sense, a profound respect for the dead: Latins understand this. In addition, I was on the point of asking the father not to travel with his son; I wanted to offer to come for the boy and then accompany him on his return to Mexico, is that not so?"

"That's what you told me, Branly."

"Why, then, did I immediately invite them to my home, allow them to run the risk of traveling together, of being killed together, like the mother and brother before them?"

As he asked this question, my friend leaned toward me slightly. I repeated my thoughts as I sat beside Branly in my canvas chair. "I was thinking that courtesy is the only reliable means you can summon to impose order on human events, to offer them the refuge of civilization."

"And . . . ?" he asked avidly.

"There is more. I thought this was how you calmed that not unordered agitation, to use your own words."

He stared at me as if thirsting for my thought: "And to exorcise the venomous flowers interwoven with precious jewels, is that it?"

"You know better than I where the chance of human destinies ends and the art of literary selection begins."

Branly offered me a profile sketched with a silver nib. "Can they be separated?" he asked, finally.

He underscored his question with a nervous glance, and this time he pressed my hand.

Then he relaxed, sinking back into his beach chair.

We did not look at each other. Sitting side by side in the canvas chairs of the club solarium, we stared toward an undefined point before us, the tiled floor, the glass between us and the swimming pool and the bar.

Finally I interrupted this shared reverie by asking my friend whether he had subsequently had any news of the Heredias. My question, which Branly did not answer, included, I admit, another. What did you do when you returned to your house on the Avenue de Saxe? I framed it aloud, and Branly replied with precision.

"I discharged Etienne and my Spanish servants. The last time a servant in our house allowed himself to be bribed was during the time of the Huguenots. Imagine! Only Protestants and Latin Americans have dared."

"Or, if you will, a Hugo and a Huguenot," I said, with a weak attempt at humor, as if hoping to hasten a return to normality between us, knowing that the situation was not normal, and that my words were purely a reflex action.

"No wonder that in the court of Carlos III a bribe was referred to as 'Mexican pomade.'" My friend smiled.

His words were accompanied by the customary gracious movement of his hands, but now I saw in these gestures, in his banter, something more than an attempt to disavow the overly solemn mood of the occasion. Branly's hands moved as if performing the final rite of an exorcism: dissolving, blessing, dispatching forever.

"But, Branly, none of the small coincidences, the implicit analogies, escaped your attention."

I spoke in spite of myself; it was not my place to comment on what I had learned, since it was Branly who had told me, and his word was to be trusted. My friend started to get up, but then sank back into the canvas chair.

He closed his eyes. He clasped his long fingers under his chin and, instead of replying, recited a few lines from his favorite poem, which for me was becoming the mysterious leitmotif of this story that so often, I realized now, I had expected to be identical to the person who was telling it, yet, at the same time, independent of the teller.

My friend asked whether I remembered the title of the

poem. Certainly, I replied, "*La Chambre Voisine*," by Jules Supervielle, and again I said that I felt its lines had been with us throughout this long November afternoon.

"The eve of the Feast of St. Martin." Branly's eyes were still closed.

"What?" I struggled to follow the train of my friend's thoughts.

"We were speaking earlier this afternoon of that privileged moment in Paris when the phenomena of the day are dispersed and the day is crowned in glory. A luminous moment, as you know, in spite of rain, fog, or snow."

"Yes?"

"A true St. Martin's Day is the jewel in the crown, a summer day in mid-autumn, an unexpected gift for those of us resigned to numb survival in the glacial burrows of a primeval world, the hostile world of wolf against wolf, my friend."

A response seemed to be called for, so I commented that he was right, that in only a few days it would be the Feast of St. Martin, the eleventh of November, the Armistice Day of Branly's Great War. My friend opened one slightly self-deprecatory eye, as if that epic warranted nothing more than an ironic memory. He had mentioned burrows. Now he was telling me that summer could be even more savage than winter; the trenches along the Marne were a hive of insects, and all of them, officers and men alike, grew accustomed to awakening with faces covered with the flies that cling to a soldier's sweat, beard, and dreams. Flies make no distinctions.

"A St. Martin's summer's day is like a gift time grants to itself. It makes those of us who are older believe it is possible to prolong the sweetness of our days. Like the sauterne we drank at luncheon, you know. The golden sweetness of that wine is the result of November grapes, of fruit harvested after other wines are already in the casks.

[160]

Only the ripest fruit, grapes dried almost to raisins, shriveled from exposure to sun and the dying earth, give us the incomparable sweetness of a good sauterne."

"That may be so," I replied, "but it is impossible to distinguish the line between that golden maturity and the corruption that hastens, even precipitates it. A dark, repulsive fungus, Branly, call it noble decay if you will. And that's true of the sauterne."

"As I have told you, I could not anticipate the events of this narrative, even though I have lived it, because it was one thing to live it and another to tell it."

"But now the story is finished, and even though I didn't seek it, you have made me the new narrator of everything you have told me."

My friend seemed indifferent to my words, as if they were the accepted corollary to his story. I did not fully understand the nature of his disillusionment when, turning his heavy head to look at me, he replied that only part of what I said was true. I *had* become a probable narrator of his story, but the story was not concluded. No, it is the nature of narrative to be incomplete, to be contiguous with another story.

He answered my questioning look by wrapping himself more tightly in his white terry robe and asking with nervous severity, cold but inviting the heat the acceptance of his words would incur, what do you think a man like myself would do, a man in whom duty and pleasure have learned to live side by side, but only as long as they were justified and unified in the present, not in nostalgia, my friend, or hope, but in a sense of the present, the here and now, embodying the obligations as well as the potential of time; what is the meaning of being who I am and as I am, tell me, if I refuse to accept that sense of the present that others call responsibility, yes, but the ultimate responsibility that excludes, now listen carefully, any pretext of the *now*—"not this, it has already happened, or this, because it is still to come"—unless it encompasses a concept of *being*. Nothing dies completely unless we ourselves are guilty of condemning it to death by forgetting it. Oblivion is the only death; the presence of the past in the present is the only life; and this is what I came to understand after I returned to my house and reviewed my adventure with the Heredias. It is also what finally bound me to Hugo Heredia, in spite of everything that stood between us.

"What do you think a man like myself would do?" Branly repeated after an imperceptible pause.

"You went to Mexico to look for Hugo Heredia."

Again he closed his eyes, and said that he would tell me word for word what Heredia had told him late one October afternoon after Branly had located him in Xochicalco working in the excavations of the ancient Toltec ceremonial center beside the deep barranca that plummets from the altar to the floor of the Valley of Morelos and its profusion of extinct volcanoes.

"Every story is contiguous with another," my friend repeated. "I want to be as faithful as possible to the story of Hugo Heredia. Later you will understand why."

He asked that for the moment I limit myself to considering whether he and I were capable of re-creating with total fidelity the events of the afternoon from the moment I entered the club dining room and he saw me and suggested we lunch together. Could I see myself as I saw him? Could he see himself as I saw him? Could we both, through a supreme joint effort, re-create with verisimilitude the sonorous space about us, the tinkling glass, the heavy resonance of silver service plates, the murmur of voices nearby as well as distant? Could we remember, without error, the words of the waiter who served us? his face? his hands? "Listen then, through my voice, to Heredia's voice on that recent October afternoon in Xochicalco. We are talking about a figure created by narrative imagination, and as only imagination can reproduce a verbal account, it will be incomplete, it will be an approximation. In any case, that incomplete approximation will be the only possible truth."

He asked whether I accepted these conditions, and I said of course; I had never read or listened to a story without entering into the pact my friend, at this vibrant if perilous peak of our emotional and intellectual relationship, was proposing. But was the same accord possible between two friends in one another's presence as between an inevitably distanced reader and author?

"If you require the reader's proviso," Branly replied, "I shall introduce Hugo Heredia as a second author of this narrative, a second river in the hydrograph we have been tracing for the past few hours, you and I. Yes, you as well, you know it; you cannot turn back now. You, too, have become a river in this watershed whose true source we still do not know, as we do not know the multiplicity of its tributaries or the final destiny toward which it flows."

He courteously inquired whether I needed further information if I was to accept the reality of a narrative which, because it was narrative, must reside in the realm of the virtual. When did Branly travel to Mexico? On October 29, the eve of All Saints' Day and All Souls' Day, the day of the dead. He smiled. If he hadn't found Hugo Heredia, he would, in any case, have had a good pretext to witness those famous celebrations in a country that has never resigned itself to banishing death from the realm of life. Where did he stay? In the apartment of Jean, the mutual friend who had introduced him to the Heredias that same summer. He owned a penthouse with a broad vista of the exhausted smog, cement ruins, and shimmering dust of the Mexican capital. How had he located Heredia? Also through Jean, who had consulted the Ministry of Public Education to find out where the eminent archaeologist was. Had Heredia returned alone or with his son? Alone. How had he explained in Mexico City the disappearance of young Victor Heredia? As an accidental death. How? By drowning. Where, in Mexico or in France? In Normandy, on the beach of Dives-sur-Mer, at the foot of a high cliff where Romanesque stones tumble into an inlet of the cold turbulent sea. Were there witnesses? No; Hugo saw his son swim out to sea; he never returned. Did he report the death to the authorities? Yes; the boy's body had never been found. When did this happen? While Branly was recovering from his accident at the Clos des Renards and every day listening to the conversations of Victor and André, and being visited in his bedroom by the young Mexican. Had Heredia returned to Mexico at the time Branly's servants reported? Yes. No one in Mexico was surprised that he returned alone? Of course not. Heredia had already lost his other son and his wife; the death of Victor merely confirmed the family's fatalism, and fatalism surprises no one in Mexico. When did Branly reach Xochicalco? On the eve of the nocturnal vigil for the dead.

The narrator must imagine Heredia walking back and forth on the edge of the precipice of Xochicalco, sometimes interrupting his pacing to sit in a folding chair, and talking with Branly, who alternately accompanies him as he walks, or joins him as he sits down, while the sky darkens and one by one the candles of the funeral ceremony are lighted, as if each represented two souls, the soul of the one who lights the candle and that of the one being remembered. He must see the unmoving sculptured stone of the sacred serpents of the Indian world, and behind the hills of flickering candles, barely perceptible faces, as expressionless as the voices whispering night prayers, birdlike voices, birdcalls identical to the sorrowful remoteness of the rebozo-veiled dark faces, the hands with broken fingernails, the feet caked with dried mud, the bloody knees, the invisible eyes of the ancient peoples of Mexico, the contiguous memory, the image vanquished by the besieged mirror of our words, the conjugations of being born, loving, and of dying, loving, the names of the Heredias, all their presentiments, all their ancestors, reduced to one voice in this night of the dead: you are Heredia.

HUGO HEREDIA

Qu'on n'entre plus dans la chambre
D'où doit sortir un grand chien
Ayant perdu la mémoire
Et qui cherchera sur terre
Comme le long de la mer
L'homme qu'il laissa derrière
Immobile . . .

J.S., "La Chambre Voisine"

I shall not, M. le Comte, offer unwarranted apologies, nor shall I use your title again. I have not forgotten the lesson you taught me when we were introduced here in Xochicalco last summer. Forgive the social gaucherie of an archaeologist more accustomed to speaking to stones than with men. After all, one who chooses my profession does so because he seriously believes that the stones are alive and that they speak to us.

That night when we dined together in the house of our mutual friend Jean, I told you that ancient peoples refuse to banish the old ways in favor of the new. This is one example of how stones talk to us if we will listen. Yesterday's wisdom, and today's, instead of being cast aside in succession, accumulate in a permanent accretion. All things must be living and present, I told you, as among the Imerina peoples of Madagascar, who conceive of history as two flowing currents: the inheritance of the ears and the memory of the lips.

I stress this essential tenet of my vocation, because it is important if you are to understand behavior that otherwise you might consider far from rational. Yes, I appeal to you because I know no person more capable of understanding. I have lived among stones. The taluses of Mitla, the friezes of Chichén-Itzá, the terraces of Uxmal, have been more than the site of my professional activity; they are the throne—please forgive the word, but this is how I feel—of a kind of honor regained. Mexico is a land of upheaval, almost always violent, and, in such cases, endowed with a certain epic grandeur; but more constant and cruel and insidious, I can assure you, have been the periods of peaceful upheaval such as those we have known the last sixty years. As a result, the wounds in my country never heal; we never grow the new skin of an aristocracy; we do not have an elite that can close our wounds. The compulsion for upheaval, either periodic, as in the past, or constant, as today, prevents that healing.

You belong to a society that does not repudiate the virtues of its ancient executioners when they become victims. Your aristocracy has been shot, guillotined, and exiled. But the political, aesthetic, and social culture of France has been zealously guarded. Thus, someone like yourself can enjoy the benefits of a vanished order along with those of the newer republican regime. This is, allow me to say it, not the best of all possible worlds, though it is the better of two possible worlds. There is a difference, though I would be happy if that option existed in my own country. I was thinking about these things when you said the night we dined in Jean's house in Cuernavaca that Alexandre Dumas tells how Napoleon established an annuity of a hundred thousand écus in the name of the elderly widow of the Duc d'Orléans, whom you remembered, Branly, as the creator of the Parc Monceau. The motivation for his generosity was that in her salon on the Chaussée d'Antin the Duchesse was keeping alive the traditions of an aristocratic society that dated from the reigns of Louis XIV and Louis XV. Later, Dumas says that the first two hundred and fifty years of a life count only as memory. Would that were so of nations that vaunt their contemporaneity. I thought about your words all through the meal.

We Heredias of Mexico are what we are. Meat for the gallows, freed from the dungeons of Cádiz and Ceuta in exchange for participating in the conquest of the Indies. I shall not weary you with a detailed genealogy. Ten years after the fall of the Great Tenochtitlán, we had Indian wives and mestizo children in large numbers, along with vast expanses of land. Here, where there was so much land to be had and so many laborers to be enslaved, we could be what we had been unable to be in Spain. Hidalgos with a vengeance, immoderately indolent patricians, apathetic parasites. There was no reason to so much as lift a little finger in the New World, Branly. How then were we to demonstrate a power that like all functions atrophies if it is not exercised? Only with the enervation of appearances and the impunity of cruelty. History was to call this process the *encomienda*, royal grants of Indians, whole Indian villages, to Spanish colonists; the *mita minera*, forced Indian labor; peonage. Heredia is the name of many patriarchs, judges, and jailers in the new Hispanic world that survived for three centuries because we convinced that multitude of ragged creatures that they owed their very lives to our paternal protection, and to the consolation of our religion.

As a boy, I visited a hacienda that had belonged to one of my ancestors. It had been burned by Zapata's troops during the Revolution. It was a ruin, a ruin in the image and likeness of those who had inhabited it: ugly, black, and cruel. The huts, jails, and presses scattered about the burned-out shell of the old sugar mill spoke to me of a world without grandeur, a world consumed by injustice at the very moment of its apogee. But is this not the legacy of Hispanic peoples: the coexistence of grandeur and decadence?

I believe that visit shaped my vocation. I grew up and sought the means by which I might assure my place in society. We had fought tenaciously to maintain our position through the capricious regimes of the nineteenth century. The liberal reforms of Juárez dealt us the first blow, cutting us off from our traditional alliance with the Church. But very quickly our situation improved, when, after twenty years spent in inept bumbling in pharmacies, imagine! and legal offices and newspaper editorships, and of adapting badly to something then called "modern life," the dictatorship of Porfirio Díaz created conditions favorable to regaining a portion of our former universe: large landholdings. But a new aristocracy is not forged in thirty years, and when I was born in 1931, my destiny was sealed: find a profession or live by my wits. No other path was open; the Revolution had administered the *coup de grâce* to the vestiges of the old Mexican oligarchies. From that time forward, Branly, everyone in Mexico, like the impassioned followers of Bonaparte in France, would have a right to everything. Do you not agree that this is the form democratic oppression takes?

I am telling you this, and what will follow, because I want you to understand more than the complexity of my psychic and historical makeup; I also want you, my cordial and hospitable friend, to be interested in me as a person. Yes, I built my throne on the ruins of the Indian world; you must not be surprised by the paradox. It is time that we false hidalgos, we enervated Creoles, and, of course, we resentful mestizos, from what was once New Spain, at last recognize who we are, recognize that the foundations of this land, its most profound achievement, its ineradicable identity, insignia, and nobility, are to be found in our ancient Toltec, Aztec, and Maya stones. In them I, a grudging professional, a great lord without a fiefdom, a tyrant without slaves, I took refuge. I spoke to them, and they spoke to me. You must believe everything I have told you, Branly. You must devote even more thought to the enormity of the paradox I have outlined. I could not accept that my image was to be found in what Aldous Huxley called the "humpbacked" Spanish colonial architecture of Mexico; and in what had been the seat of our power, the hacienda, I found only the horror I have described. Such was the spiritual victory of the vanquished: I, a Creole in search of lost grandeur, could find it only among the monuments of my victims' past.

Professions deform one; archaeology is no exception. I spoke more with the stones than with my wife and my sons, Antonio and Victor. I had to travel constantly and our apartment on Río Garona Street became little more than a *pied-à-terre* for me. I met my wife Lucie in the French Institute of Latin America, that urban oasis on Río Nazas Street where my entire generation went to learn about film, literature, and, above all, about the civilization we thought it our personal responsibility to sustain during the years France was in eclipse. The first thing Lucie pointed out to me was that everything I told her about my ancestors was marked by that strange love for France which supposedly saves us Latin Americans from our ancient subordination to Spain and our more recent subordination to the Anglo-Saxon world. France seems like a safe and longed-for haven. Lucie was from one of the families of Barcelonnette in the Basses-Alpes who traditionally emigrated to Mexico. Her family made a fortune there in department stores, and now, as so often happens, she was atoning for the commercial sins of *her* ancestors by studying history and literature at the Institute. It was natural for us to meet, to fall in love, to marry.

I owe her a great deal. Unlike me, she found nothing

shameful in business enterprises; she had no such pride or pretensions. She complemented my formation, my culture; French reason is a good antidote to Latin American delirium. It is also its incubator, and Lucie delighted in reminding me that my country had fought a revolution for independence because a few men had read Rousseau and Voltaire, an enlightened counterrevolution because a few others had read Comte, and a new intellectual revolution inspired by Bergson. I leave to you your opinion of the success of these ideological transplants. But I confess to you, Branly, that Lucie's perception, her discipline, her capacity for work, were the goad to one of my own ambitions, my decision to read everything, to know everything, to find the interrelationships of all I had learned, and not to succumb to our century's gangrenous absurdity, which in the business world, in the very same trade that enriched my wife's parents—and, because they were grand hidalgos and never learned how to exercise it, impoverished my own—is today translated into mercilessly divorcing the past from the present, with the proposition that the past must always be something dead and we always something new, something different from that much-to-be-scorned past—new, and consequently thirsting for the latest innovation in art, clothing, entertainment, machines. Novelty has become the blazon of our happiness. So we drug ourselves against the realization that our destiny, too, will be death, the moment the future relegates us to the past.

No, I did not often speak with my family; I communicated to them only the lesson of the stones. I may never have known anything but the stones; this is my guilt, but I have purged it. Lucie applauded the "good lesson" of the stones, as she called it: the sense of the past, the obstinate refusal to sacrifice, to exile the past from a present that is incomprehensible except within the context of the past. This aspect of my work delighted her. But not what she came to call the "bad lesson" of the stones: the conviction that we belonged to a superior caste endowed with innate privileges that entitled us to reclaim the authority usurped from us by a world of parvenus.

Lucie was highly intelligent, and she feared my attitude, she said, because on our continent oppression went to even greater lengths than in Europe. The Europeans exploited peoples of distant lands and were able, without undue effort, to forget about them. We had our victims in our own homes, in ever-increasing numbers. They are the only palpable ghosts I know, my wife used to say: we see them begging in the streets, sleeping on garbage heaps, daggers of glass crystallizing in their resentful gaze.

"One day you will feel that guilt, Hugo," she used to tell me. "That good European conscience has a great deal to do with the remoteness of its victims. The day will come when the presence of the humbled among us will make it impossible to sleep."

Antonio was close to his mother and listened to her teachings; Victor was my favorite, and he learned mine. Believe me, Branly, when I say that those were the true and spontaneous motives for the fact that more and more often Victor accompanied me on my constant trips to the work sites. In doing so, he learned more about our country than Antonio, and I cannot deny that I did nothing to extinguish the spark of domination and hatred in his eyes when he saw what he had to see: entire villages of drunken men, women, and children: the men drunk because of the fiesta, the women because of pain, the infants because they suckled alcohol with their milk; the devout humiliation of Mexican churches, the incense haze of indistinguishable misery and faith; the pillage, the cruelty against man that is the watchword of the Mexican countryside. He scorned the people; he admired the stones, and in the latter, the "good lesson," he coincided with his mother and his brother.

[171]

One night I surprised my two sons as they were playing a strange game. Remember, they shared the "good lesson" of a finely developed respect for the past, and, in truth, there is no past without the sense of play that keeps it fresh. They were wagering on something. I felt a shiver when I understood on what. They were wagering on our deaths, theirs, and ours.

"Who do you think will die first?" asked Toño.

"Most likely it will be Father and me," said Victor. "You should see the little planes we take in the mountains."

"I promise that Mother and I will cry a lot," Toño answered.

"Father and me, too," said Victor.

I spoke with Lucie about their game. We decided, if decided is the word, to vary our responsibilities. We thought it morbid that the boys should identify their own deaths with that of one of their parents. They were right about one thing, however: the two of us should never travel together and thus expose Victor and Antonio to being orphaned. For my part, I would begin taking Antonio with me on some of the trips to explore the villages in the isolated mountains and barrancas of Mexico. I was an only child. My own parents were dead, and Lucie's parents, in spite of her efforts to maintain contact and visit them regularly, lived in remote French indifference. We told our friends this was a decision we had made when Victor was born. No one was surprised; some praised our foresight. No one *remembered*, you see, that occasionally *three* of us had traveled together—Lucie, one of the children, and I—exposing the other child to being the sole survivor of the family. But if we ourselves forget the logical order of our lives, how can we expect others to remember? In fact, Branly, this is the very essence of my profession: to reverse to some degree that amnesia about ourselves, that oblivion to what we were, to what our parents and our grandparents were, the nothingness that evokes the reluctant phantom that appears to tell us: this is what you were, this is what your people were; you have forgotten. The very mission of a ghost is to rectify the forgetfulness of the living, their injustice toward the dead.

Our decision to travel separately is common among families today, and Victor was right; the planes in which anthropologists hop from Palenque to San Cristobal, penetrate the sierras of Guerrero, or skim the ravines of Nayarit and Morelos, are as reliable as mosquitoes in a hurricane. Because in Mexico, Branly, even when nature is at rest, it seems to tremble threateningly. Bottomless chasms, slabs of solid basalt, treacherous peaks, the crosswinds of this delirious orography, the unexpected deserts, the thousands of pyramids disguised as innocuous hills. You are looking at them now where we find ourselves this evening.

Lucie began to travel more with Victor, I with Toño; but, though we never discussed it, the other child remained our true favorite. Toño admired and accepted only the mute beauty of the past, never the voice of its cruel power or its prolongation in the present. One evening in a hotel in Pátzcuaro a young Indian waiter carelessly spilled a glass of tomato juice over the new white guayabera shirt Antonio had put on to dine beside the lake. Imagine what Victor would have said, what he would have done. Toño, on the other hand, laughed, helped the waiter wipe the spilled juice from the floor, and then he himself rinsed the shirt and hung it to dry in the bathroom, giving thanks all the while for the invention of Dacron. In contrast, when Lucie returned from a trip to visit her family in France, she complained about how rude Victor had been to hotel and restaurant employees, especially when he discovered they were—as they so often are—Spanish.

"They were born to serve me," he would say, with a trace of arrogant humor.

I waited for another occasion to eavesdrop on the boys again. The opportunity came just a year ago, when the four of us went to Caracas for a conference on anthropology and had adjoining rooms in the Tamanaco Hotel. The writer and publisher Miguel Otero Silva had invited us to a masked ball in his home. As the hour approached for us to leave, Victor and Antonio thought we were busy with our costumes. This is what I heard them say.

"You were right," said Victor. "Father doesn't like to cry."

"Then do you want to trade?" his brother asked.

"If that's all right with you, Toño, why not?"

"It makes no difference to me," said Antonio, with the aplomb befitting his superior fourteen years.

"Then I choose to die with my father so Mother and you can cry over us, or I choose for you and Father to die together, so Mother and I can cry. The main thing is for Mommy not to die, because she's the best cryer."

They laughed, and I asked myself what Lucie had been crying about, what they had seen, what my sons knew that I didn't know. There was no chance to clear up this mystery. In the taxi on the way to the ball I touched my wife's hand and asked her if everything was all right. She said yes, today more than ever before; tonight we should not ask foolish questions, we must dance and be happy. Happy, but uncomfortable, I told her, imprisoned in the gold braid-trimmed uniform of General Bolívar from the time of Venezuela's war for independence. Lucie, on the other hand, floated into the salon a vision of beauty in her high-waisted, diaphanous Empire gown, long stole, and satin slippers, her hair combed into a tower of cotton-candy curls.

It was a warm night and the Oteros had decided to hold the party on their incomparable roof garden. As a confirmed traveler, Branly, you know how Caracas hides from its modern ugliness, withdrawing into walled secret gardens, though none, I venture, was as remarkable as theirs, where the play of lights—oblique and direct, soft and intense—seemed to sculpt anew the Henry Moore and Rodin sculptures displayed outdoors in the mild Caracas air.

From behind the statue of Balzac garbed in the monastic attire he wore when writing emerged a priestly figure. A man of average height, stunted by a sturdy, squarish torso, ennobled by a white mane of leonine hair, a man dressed as a parish priest, with the ubiquitous Venezuelan white-corn *arepa* in his hand. I heard the murmurs of amazement: had the man come masked as a priest, or was he a priest? Someone said in indignation that the cloth was not an appropriate costume, but either way, though this most unusual guest was wearing black, only his collar was clerical. He approached me at the precise moment the orchestra began to play; Miguel Otero asked my wife to dance and I found myself holding the stubby-fingered hand of the spurious priest.

"Forgive me." He spoke in a mellifluous voice. "You were pointed out to me yesterday at the opening meeting. As we have the same name, I wanted to meet you."

I must have stared at him with an extremely stupid expression, because he was forced to add: "Heredia. My name, too, is Heredia. The same name, you see?"

Though I said I did see, I had eyes only for Lucie. She looked magnificent, an ethereal, bewitched figure more beautiful than ever, her skin warmed by the tropics, her diaphanous gown swirling; and absentmindedly, out of simple courtesy, I asked this Heredia where his family was from; ours had come to New Spain in the sixteenth century. I anticipated his response.

"Ah, no. Our Heredias will be much more recent arrivals in the New World." Looking at him really for the first time, I saw that, despite my first impression, he could not be called old. "My mother," he said, "fleeing the Negro rebellion, came from Haiti to La Guaira. Very recent in comparison to your genealogy, of course."

I tried to recall a "Negro rebellion" in Haiti seventy to ninety years ago, but my memory told me nothing. The other Heredia clasped his hands pontifically, as if he had guessed what I was thinking. "Ah, so your memory does not respond?"

"No, frankly, it does not, Señor Heredia."

"But, nevertheless, isn't it true we have no memory but what we recall?"

"That seems rather obvious," I replied with some annoyance. My conversation with this Heredia was becoming grotesque. In fact, I thought I detected a trace of senility in the man's words and actions, and I tried to move away. He caught me by the arm. Extremely irritated now, I tried to free myself, but not before he forced me to listen: "If you ever need me, look me up in the directory."

"And why would I need you?" My rejoinder was brusque.

"We all need to remember at times," he replied affably. "I am a specialist in memories."

"Of course. Now, excuse me."

"But if you don't know my name, how can you call me?"

"Your name is Heredia, you have already told me."

"Victor," he said in the softest of voices. "Victor Heredia. Imagine: the Haitian uprising took place, I believe, in 1791, but that was the time of Toussaint L'Ouverture; the rebellion of Henri Christophe came later. I'm not entirely sure of that: in fact, I'm not completely sure of anything."

The door between our room and that of the boys was half-open when Lucie and I returned to the hotel. The boys were watching television, but only slightly lower than the sound of a song interspersed with jokes, we could hear clearly Antonio's voice, more serious every day, more indicative of his imminent adulthood.

"No, Victor. I'm backing down on our deal. I choose to die with Mother."

"*C'est pas chic de ta part*," said Victor, using one of the expressions he had picked up in his years of study at the French Lycée. As Lucie had taught the boys a very literary French, she was always surprised and pleased when she heard such phrases in her house.

"What difference does it make to you?" asked Toño. "You want Father and me to die together so you and Mother will be left to cry all you want."

"It isn't the same thing," said Victor. "I tell you it isn't the same. You traitor."

We could hear Victor punching Antonio, and I rushed in to separate them.

Lucie locked herself in the bathroom. I reprimanded the boys and told them that if they didn't behave themselves they would be on the first plane back to Mexico the next morning. My wife would not open the bathroom door, and when finally she came to our room, the boys had fallen asleep and she was no longer crying. I asked whether she had heard them speak like this before, and she said she had. And it was not just chance, she added. She was convinced that Victor made a point of bringing up the subject any time he knew she could hear. With a resigned sigh, my beautiful wife folded the Empire ball gown into a cardboard box and told me to do the same with my military regalia. The mulatto woman from the agency that rented the costumes had told her she would come by early the next morning to pick them up, the Señora understood, such outfits were rented almost every day; Lucie could leave the boxes outside the door and she would pick them up.

The four of us flew back together. That simple action, I believed, would put an end to the morbid, if playful, inclination of my sons. As the plane lifted off from Maiquetía,

La Guaira was a time more than a place, a cliff-rimmed port patiently awaiting the return of ancient ships to furrow the strangely calm and luminous sea. I tried to distinguish hands, faces, handkerchiefs waving goodbye from the large old houses and the Fort of San Carlos on the hill. I saw only the buzzards, which are the true lookouts of all the ports of the Caribbean. I closed my eyes and the hum of the motors blended with the memory of the plaintive whistle of the toucan in the Venezuelan dusk.

The accident occurred that Christmas, when Lucie and her favorite, Antonio, went to Paris to visit her family. The DC-10 plunged into the sea near the Azores. Their bodies were never recovered. No, there was no sign, no warning. Now that you and I know all the things we know, we might be tempted to believe that there was some connection between them and the death of my wife and son. That was not so, and this tragic event had its most grave consequences, as might be expected, in my home, and for reasons that would surprise no one: Victor's sadness, a sadness that moved me and moved all those who knew us, a sadness that caused our small apartment on Río Garona to become even more desolate, but a sadness my son refused to share with me. Because I had overheard the boys, only I knew the reasons. Victor found himself without a companion in his mourning.

You will understand, Branly, that as soon as I realized the truth, I determined to be a true companion in my son's mourning. But how could I take the place of his mother, whom he had expected to weep with him over my death and Antonio's? What did the boy expect of me? What could I offer him? I was not the first widowed father who had to answer such questions. I observed how Victor was changing, deeply affected not so much by his mother's death as by the absence of his mother as a partner in grief to weep over me and his brother. This sorrow had a different name: cruelty.

What was to be found in this soul that Victor and I shared, so to speak? I have already told you: scorn for men, respect for stones. I decided that because of the circumstances the boy could afford to miss a year of school. The important thing was for him never to be separated from me for a minute, for him to learn my lessons—the good and the bad, as his mother had called them—by accompanying me to the thrones of bygone honor and recovered identity represented in the great ruins of our Mexican past. With me, little by little, he would penetrate into the heart of Mexico: its villages, its churches, its world of dust and cheap alcohol, its cheating, its humiliated Indian, its cunning cacique who controls the stores, the brothels, the pawnshops.

"This is what we Heredias came from. Look closely. This is our clay."

I instructed him, Branly, to admire authority based on grandeur and dignity, and I pointed out the consistent absence of those qualities; I instructed him to dream of an ideal nation governed by a true aristocracy that would discipline both the masses degraded by vice and exploitation and the vulgar and rapacious exploiters of our nation.

I was not sure how Victor was changing, but I knew he was changing. That part of him about which I knew nothing was growing daily; I felt intuitively that there were things that only my son knew, only my son wanted. He wanted and knew things he was not telling anyone, and only I knew *that*. He had no true companion in his mourning, and my fear was that he would seek such a companion in danger; that is, in the unknown. That is the reason I kept him so close to me. I became aware of what you already know: the indefensible arrogance of Victor toward his inferiors, especially servants. I was not unduly concerned, in view of the fact that this is an attitude common among all well-to-do youths in the Iberian world; what did disturb me was that my younger son's behavior was causing me to long for the spontaneous camaraderie of my older son, Antonio.

And so, inadvertently, I began to undermine my own edifice, to compare the moments of coldness, the cruelty, of Victor to the natural joy, the spirit of celebration and playfulness, that had characterized Antonio. Another thing was happening that neither of us realized. Victor was forming me as much as I was forming him: like him, along with him, I sought and lamented my missing companion in death, my comrade in mourning: Antonio.

My perceptions of Victor's character became increasingly clear. One spring we happened to be in Aguascalientes at the time of the fair of San Marcos. That is a world of taunts, wagers, machismo, and intensified chance, a perpetual *all-or-nothing*, Branly, a cyclone whose eye is centered in the cockfight. There, everything I have just mentioned reaches a peak of frenzy not unlike that of the most ancient forms of communal games, mysteries, and hazards. I arrived at the ring at the last moment; I heard the shout "Close the doors," and bets flew thick and fast. The cocks were sprayed with mouthfuls of water and alcohol, released, and set in confrontation for the battle that everyone, even the roosters, knows is to the death. I scanned the eyes, hands, heads, of the crowd transformed by the hysteria of betting into a great undulating serpent. Only Victor, in the middle of an excited crowd, sat totally motionless. He didn't lift an arm, a finger; his icy gaze never shifted from the center of the ring—which for this single reason, because one person was watching in this manner, ceased to be a ludic circle and was converted into an arena of execution. Do you remember the Hitchcock film in which all the spectators at a tennis match follow the play of the ball except one: the murderer? My son's unflinching stare told me that for him the death of one or both of the cocks was a matter of total indifference, since from his viewpoint this was the fate to which they were destined. The two cocks had been trained to fight, and armed with razors on their spurs; they were the playthings of their masters, but also masters in their own combat, and, ultimately, it was better to die in the ring than in the poultry market.

That all this should be translated into such absolute moral indifference made me believe that for Victor the cult of aristocratic authority was being converted into a cult of fatalism and blind power, and I asked myself what had been lacking in an education intended to illustrate the unity of time, a time that does not sacrifice the past, which, after all, had been my goal in my relationship with my sons. I soon found out, the first time we went together to Xochicalco—before I met you, Branly. I was working with the team of the Swedish anthropologist Laura Bergquist one afternoon in the area of the pelota court you see below us, when we all heard, from the heights of the citadel above, a terrifying cry that some thought thunder, the thunder that long in advance announces the July late-afternoon rains in the Valley of Morelos. I looked up and saw Victor standing at the edge of the precipice, right here, Branly, where you caught him with the handle of your cane, right here where I am standing now, imitating Victor's actions for you. His bleeding hands were extended from his body, like this. I ran toward him. Fortunately, Bergquist and two workers followed; Victor fell, but he fell into our arms.

We had cushioned his fall, but that night the boy was delirious. His hands were badly cut, and he kept repeating the words, "I forgot," "I forgot." When we returned to Mexico City, he told me what had happened. He had been half-playing, half-exploring around the site of the Toltec temple, when he discovered a chink in the talus at the pediment of the plumed serpents. One of those frogs that seem to hop through the dust, guiding us to hidden mountain rivers, slipped into the opening and Victor tried to catch it.

[181]

But instead of the rough, palpitating body of the batrachian, he tells me, he touched a surface of incomparable smoothness, something, he said, that felt like hot glass. I can never forget the vivid and perfect image. He removed the object, and when he saw it (as he was telling me, he again became feverish), he gazed upon something indescribable, a unity so perfect, so seamless, like a potent, concave drop of gold, that it needed no added embellishment, carving, or detail. If I understand what Victor was telling me, human hands could add nothing to its perfection, though it was not the work of nature. It had been crafted, he knew, because on the crown shone a relief, surely a sign, that seemed born of the very essence of its substance.

Now this is important, Branly. My son confessed that he felt an irresistible hatred for that perfect object that could owe nothing to him, or to any man. He picked up a sharp stone and struck at the object until he split it in two, divesting it forever of the beauty inherent in its wholeness. In the frenzy of his task, Victor cut his hands. He hurled half the object from him. Holding the other half in his hand, impelled by the force of his shame, he ran to the precipice; he threw even farther the second half, which, he said, was burning into the cuts on his hands. Only then did he cry out, and fall.

I let Victor sleep in my bed that night, but I turned my back to him. I had failed. Victor had learned the uses of arbitrary power, but in the process he had forgotten the memory of the unity of time. This was never my intention, I know you believe me. On the contrary, I had wanted human authority to serve the memory of past civilizations, and the awareness of the present to serve everything that had preceded us.

The reason I am telling you all this, Branly, is that I feel we Heredias owe you a debt. I could read the thoughts that passed through your eyes the night we met. I am sorry to have deceived you. I am not a universal man from the century of discoveries. I am only a slightly resentful Mexican Creole, like all the rest of my compatriots marked by mute rage against their inadequacies. Mine is a selective culture. What can save me from the *capitis diminutio* that is the curse of being a "Latin American"—which is to say a man who turns everything he touches into melodrama? Tragedy has been denied us; even our deepest sorrows come under the label of the circus of disaster. Listen to our songs, read our love letters, hear our orators.

Several months went by in which communication with Victor was difficult, if not impossible. He resumed his studies at the French Lycée. I observed him closely, and kept repeating that ridiculously obvious phrase I had once heard. "We have no memory but what we recall." It began to haunt me, I couldn't get it out of my mind. Does what we forget cease to exist, or is it we who are diminished when we forget something? Does what we have forgotten exist whether or not we remember it? These thoughts quite naturally were in my mind during my work at archaeological sites. The vast treasures of Mexican antiquity are no less real because for centuries we had ignored their existence. Perhaps the work of the archaeologist can be reduced to this: to restore, however imperfectly, a past.

I thought about this when I visited the city of the gods, Teotihuacán, the first true city of the Western Hemisphere. Its great avenues and pyramids are like a diagram of the ancient relationship of all things with all things. I remember our meeting here on a different afternoon, in a different space destroyed because Victor was with me, and today I believe that the limitations of my lesson were related to the changes that were taking place in our lives because of Victor. For, Branly, if you want me to summarize the most profound lesson of Mexican antiquity, it is this: all things are related, nothing is isolated; all things are accompanied by the totality of their spatial, temporal, physical, oneiric, visible, and invisible attributes.

"When a child is born," I told Victor that intensely pale afternoon, "it is accompanied by all its signs; it belongs to a day, a physical object, a direction in space, a color, an instant in time, a sentiment, a temperature. But what is amazing is that these personal signs are related to all other signs, to their opposites, their complements, their prefigurations. Nothing exists in isolation."

"Give me an example," Victor said, and I sought his eyes. I felt that our ability to play together was being reestablished, and I explained, as an example, that if your day was that of the eagle Cuautli, it would correspond to the signs of the lofty flight that watches over the earth like a sun, but that this grandeur would find its complement in the sacrifice that must accompany it, in the figure of the god Xipe Tótec, who gives his life for the coming harvest, and who in order to escape from himself sheds his skin like a snake: the grandeur of the eagle's flight and the painful misery of our flayed lord.

First—yes, how banal—we played dominoes; then cards; increasingly complicated games, as if challenging one another. I resurrected the disturbing game of faro from Pushkin's *Queen of Spades*, with its secrets of enormous power, immense riches, but, also, infinite death. Victor responded with tarot cards. I compared the somnambulistic indifference I had witnessed at the cockfight of San Marcos with an enthusiasm of sorts displayed one afternoon when we went to see the bulls. I had explained that the *olé!* of the bullring comes from the ancient Arabic *wallah*, an invocation, an address to God. Victor did not shout it out that afternoon, watching the veronicas of El Niño de la Capea; he murmured it like a danger-fraught prayer that would save the matador's life because only he was repeating it.

We played games with photographs, Branly: Victor remembering his seatmates in grade school; I, mine. We cut up photographs to create unlikely pairings, entire families with faces transported through time and space. We bought old newsreels, projected them, each trying to incorporate himself (one always had to be the spectator) into the ambience of the film: automobile races, wars in Manchuria and Ethiopia, a dirigible disaster, the rallies of Perón's followers in the Plaza de Mayo.

It was Victor's idea to look up our names in the telephone directories of the towns we visited. The two Hugo Heredias, the half-dozen Victor Heredias, in the Mexico City phone book created a certain amused excitement, the first I had detected in my son for a long time. The novelty of the game needed no justification but this: pretended surprise, a shared laugh. In Mérida, however, the fact that there was but one Victor Heredia in the directory was a temptation: we called him, he laughed with us, we hung up. In Puebla the game grew more complex; Victor proposed that the loser should give the winner a prize.

"And who will determine the prize?" I asked with a smile.

Victor, unsmiling, replied: "The one who wins, of course."

In Puebla there was only one Heredia in the directory, a Hugo.

"My prize will be for us to speak normally about your mother and your brother. It's been more than a year now, and we've never mentioned them. Don't you think it's important for us to begin remembering them?"

Victor did not reply. We called the Puebla Hugo Heredia. He growled at us in a hoarse voice, and hung up.

"Have you noticed, Father? It's always old men who answer."

"Well, we could bet on whether the next Victor will be young and the next Hugo old."

Victor laughed and said that I wasn't old; I replied that

when one is twelve, anyone over thirty seems as old as the tomb.

"But some people never grow old."

"Who are these fortunate ones?" I spoke lightly.

"The dead." My son's voice was grave. "Antonio will never grow old."

Jean had spoken of you often, Branly. In UNESCO, many people I respect know you. I have enjoyed your spontaneous, perhaps excessive, hospitality. I have seen the world that surrounds you. I know your interests. I have leafed through the books in your library, read what you have underlined in a few books more affectionately abused than others: Lamartine, Supervielle, Balzac. That is why I know I would offend you if I asked you to be discreet (worse, silent) in this matter. I should say nothing more. A true secret is one that is not told as a secret, but is kept so as not to lose the friendship of the person who told it, whether or not he knows.

You could say, with justification, that you didn't solicit my story. That is true. It is no less true that among gentlemen the things that must be said will not be repeated. You will tell me that I am mistaken to speak, that pride is silent. I will have to ask your forbearance, Branly, and say that I am swallowing my pride to apologize. We have used your name, your house, your automobile, your chauffeur, in carrying out a pact whose consequences, even today, I cannot accurately foresee. This is why I must speak, and also why I must ask you to tell no one what I say. I will explain. In everything I have said until now, it is implicit that it is not necessary to ask you not to repeat it. But what I am going to tell you now demands a silence which if violated would violate an agreement my life depends on. So, you see, I am telling you these things because you deserve an explanation; there is no other reason. If what I have told you previously is accurate, and verifiable, what I am about to add is open to any interpretation. Even I, who lived it, do not understand it. Am I telling you these things to have you share in my amazement, my doubt, my perplexity? Possibly. It is also possible that I would never have spoken a word of this if you had not sought me, exposing yourself to my violence or my betrayal in the same way that in receiving you I exposed myself to yours. I am trying to understand, as I see you here tonight, while evening begins to fade and the candles of the night vigil for the dead begin to flicker; you deserve my words, as I deserve your silence.

In Monterrey we found one Victor Heredia in the directory. My son called him from our room in the Hotel Ancira. Victor put his hand over the mouthpiece so the man couldn't hear him, and said: "He says he remembers everything."

I felt the hair rise on the back of my neck. I took the phone. I told the man who I was. A voice replied that he was glad to have our call, he had been expecting it for some time, and he invited us to come to tea in his apartment across from the Bishopric in the old part of that city shadowed, in the past as today, by a barbaric sun filtering through the dust. Monterrey does not inspire confidence; it is too indifferent to its own ugliness, as if the city existed only temporarily, in order for its grotesque oligarchy to make money and carry it off to heaven. That may be why I didn't tell my son about Victor Heredia's invitation. It was Victor, because he was the winner, who asked me to take him to meet his namesake. He asked in a tone that implied that if I denied him this request I would jeopardize the fragile edifice of our games and, consequently, our mutual trust. Our reviving affection, Branly.

I didn't tell him about the invitation. We arrived without warning, as Victor told you the evening the three of us were having tea in your home on the Avenue de Saxe, do you remember? But there was no surprise on the face of the man who received us that afternoon in a run-down apartment tastelessly adorned with silver paint and shabby furniture from the thirties, the kind one still sees in France in the Galeries Barbès.

I was the one who was surprised. I recognized the man who had appeared from behind Balzac's statue in a garden in Caracas while my beautiful Lucie danced in her swirling white gown. The surprise Victor detected on Heredia's face must have been surprise at my surprise. Victor's agitation that afternoon in your house, Branly, when I denied having gone with him to Heredia's apartment in Monterrey, was the predictable alarm of one who does not wish to be left alone in a decision which, nevertheless, ultimately excludes the possibility of being shared.

Yes, I recognized the man from the garden that night in Caracas, even though this "Heredia" was not exactly like the other man; he merely reminded me of him. I had sufficient presence of mind to tell myself that this must have been what the man meant when he characterized himself as a specialist in memories. I have described the moment of our arrival at Heredia's apartment. An instant later, the old man, who received us wearing bedroom slippers and a shabby white quilted bathrobe, and was holding a cup of Mexican corn-gruel *atole* in his hand, himself pretended great surprise, and asked whether we were the long-lost relatives that always come swarming out of the woodwork like termites when they scent the death of an elderly rich relative.

You will say when you read this that my son Victor was telling the truth, that it was I who lied. No. Please try to understand something very difficult to explain. We were both telling the truth, both Victor and I. Neither of us lied. He went alone, and we went together. "Heredia" was aware of my surprise when he recognized me, but he pretended surprise with that nonsense about poor relatives. And this happened, or, rather, the two things happened, Branly, in the wink of an eye, instantaneously, in that apartment with its splintered floors and silver paint, where, through dirty lace curtains, one could see the squat, gray, crumbling, graceless buildings of Monterrey. A presence was succeeded by a nonpresence, an attitude by its opposite, an affirmation by its negation, I by him. "Heredia"—he looking at me, I looking at him— standing there with his cup of *atole* in his hand, controlled the conversation, Branly; as he spoke to one of us, he excluded the other, not only from his words but from his very presence. I realized this only later when in the most tentative and uncertain way I asked Victor whether he remembered something "Heredia" had told me that afternoon. Victor said no, staring at me with curiosity.

I didn't ask any more. I knew, too, that I hadn't heard what "Heredia" told Victor. Again I felt the chill this man had brought to my life; I imagined, Branly, a force of infinite distance. The name "Heredia" was the name of a chaotic isolation that merged, and separated, all things. While "Heredia" was talking to me, I saw in my son's eyes the same cruel nonpresence that had frightened me at the cockfight of San Marcos; I was sure Victor was somewhere else, and that my eyes, when "Heredia" was speaking to Victor, condemning me to my own solitude, were not very different. What did Victor and "Victor Heredia" say to one another that I couldn't hear? What pact did they seal, Branly? We will never know with any certainty, because you can never know more than I am telling you. But my intuition tells me that in those moments Victor ceased to be mine; he passed into the hands of "Heredia," and because I loved my poor son, I had to follow him wherever that devil led.

What did "Heredia" say to me? He used fewer words than I will need, Branly, to repeat his terrible offer. We had something in common: the secret desire to resurrect our dead, We cannot forget them. The living must serve the dead;

there are certain things the dead cannot do. But as we serve them, we must be sure that we ourselves will be served at our deaths. You and I spoke of imperfectly restoring a past; those were my words, but "Heredia" spoke them that afternoon as he offered my son a choice of *atoles*, chocolate or strawberry, accompanied by powdered-sugar-sprinkled crullers.

"Don Hugo, may I offer you something a little more substantial?"

There was something gross about his courtesy.

I said no, I didn't want anything. Not even what he had to offer? A drink? Oh, no. He laughed. My wife. My son, Antonio. No, not for nothing. He, "Heredia," needed people in exchange. His problem was considerably more complex, if he might put it that way; while I desired the return of persons who had lived, he required the materialization of someone who had never been. Did I understand what he was saying? I had to say that I did not, and something that had been holding me there—all this happened within a few minutes, not more than five or six, I'm sure—was shattered. I thanked "Heredia" for the tea—which had turned out to be *atole*. I told him we had wanted to satisfy my son's curiosity and that now we must leave.

"Come back any time you like," said "Heredia," patting Victor's head.

"I don't think so. This was merely a whim of my son's. A game."

"Ah, but he won't be coming alone. My dealings are with you, Don Hugo. Think over what I said. I will see you tonight at your hotel."

This time I said nothing. Something prevented me from mocking him in Monterrey, as I had mocked him in Caracas. I nodded, took Victor's hand, and left without further word.

That night, I tucked Victor in and, in spite of myself, went down to the bar. What would you have done, Branly, after such a day, so rich in chaotic impressions? Is there anyone you have forgotten and would like to have back? Then think about the things I pondered during the hours following our meeting with "Heredia": I am forgetting Lucie and Antonio, that is inevitable; soon they will be a vague memory recalled only with effort, the aid of a photograph, the prod of a sudden scent. On the other hand, Victor is here. I don't have to remember him.

Why doesn't Victor help me remember? I have asked him so often. I felt an overwhelming hatred for my living son.

That was the very question "Heredia" asked me that night. He was sitting near the bar at a table beneath the frosted-glass mirrors from the early years of the century, preserved there by an appreciation of the past rare in Monterrey. The large blades of the ceiling fans failed to ruffle the abundant white mane of this man with the fine features and graceless body, tonight wearing a yellow corduroy suit too heavy for the climate of Monterrey and a ridiculous celluloid collar, with not even a tie to cover flagrantly bared bone buttons, Why, he said, why not let Victor help me remember? Victor is capable of remembering everything. He is living; with the proper complement, Don Hugo, you could see all your theses fully realized: a living past, actual, irrevocable. Victor, and someone else; Victor, united with another. To-gether they will have that memory; they will *be* that past. Victor will have more life than his dead brother; he will re-member Antonio, as if he were still alive. But he will also live his dead brother's life; he will remember what Antonio knows because he is dead. What is needed? A perfect space, Don Hugo, an ancient space where my dead and yours can meet through the living young Victor.

"A new brother for Victor," said "Heredia" in the Ancira bar. "That is what I am offering."

He raised his glass, a Veracruz mint julep, in a silent toast. He waited for me to do the same.

"What's on your mind, Don Hugo?" asked "Heredia," his glass still held high.

"A few months ago, in a fit of rage, Victor broke an artifact we found at some ruins," I replied despondently. "I was just thinking that what you are offering is to a degree what I wanted then, though I didn't realize it until this minute. And do you know what that was? I wanted the halves of that object to be rejoined; I wanted their wholeness to become a part of art, of history, of the past, of culture, of anything you can name."

"Does that mean you accept my pact?"

"I mean that, as an act of good faith on your part, I would accept the restoration of the object my son destroyed."

"Would it be enough if you found half?"

I replied that it would. It would offer renewed hope that the object would be whole again. He said that Victor would find the lost half at Xochicalco; that would be the guarantee the other half would be found later, that the object would be restored.

"And what am I to do when my son finds half of what he destroyed?"

"From that moment on, everything will proceed in a manner I would not want to call fatalistic; no one likes to use that word. Let us say, in an orderly sequence of events, eh? One thing will follow another. You, Don Hugo, will understand what is happening; you will always make the correct choice, I am sure of that."

He rambled on, telling me stories about his family, which had lived in different parts of the Antilles. I became increasingly confused, for there were glaring inconsistencies in his stories, none of the dates coincided, and, finally, I wondered if the man with the stubby fingers and pale eyes wasn't simply selecting names and dates at random to fabricate the genealogy that best served his purpose. He mentioned a number of names of his family, and of persons I assumed were family friends. I heard, though I really couldn't follow the thread, stories about a certain Francisco Luis and his two wives, a French merchant named Lange, and a mulatto nurse. I never understood whether this "Heredia" was the son of Francisco Luis's first wife—a physiological impossibility, for that would mean I was talking with a man who was more than a hundred and sixty years old—or the second: even then, he would have been born sometime between 1850 and 1900, when Heredia's second wife died—at what age I don't know. Nevertheless, he insisted on referring to his father's first wife as "Mother."

"Did you know Mademoiselle Lange?" I dared ask.

"I spent nine months in her belly," he smiled disagreeably, "aware of every sip that passed the dear lady's lips."

"Where were you born? Where were you christened?" I asked in a neutral voice.

"That's of no importance," he said defensively.

"But it is," I persisted, in a conversational tone. "How were you christened?"

At that moment, Branly, "Heredia" shed all semblance of fraud or grotesqueness. He stared at me with a terrible expression, which I had the sense to recognize as a strange kind of sorrow, totally alien to me. Why alien? I answered my own question. I have lived life. My only regrets are that at times I made the wrong choices; I celebrate the times I chose well; I lament the things that are lost to me, especially my dead wife and son; I can laugh a little at my setbacks, at the passing years themselves; I lament, celebrate, and laugh at my own death, which I accept because I have always known it could not be avoided, and because I have been convinced that to have lived a little, like Toño, or a lot, as I have—don't you agree, Branly, you who have

[193]

lived so long and so well?—death is a small price to pay. I thought about my dead wife, our nights together, her words of love.

No. "Heredia" had known none of this, and because I knew what my life had been, I knew that the life of my companion that night in the bar of the Hotel Ancira was defined by the absence of these things. That's why I think I understood his next words, spoken with disturbing overtones of self-pity shocking in a man in his position and with his intentions.

"Have I been forgotten? You tell me, Don Hugo. Does anyone remember me?"

I didn't know how to respond to such obvious self-commiseration. "Heredia" himself must have realized he was making a fool of himself, for he added: *"Tant pis, mon ami;* so much the worse for the person who forgets. I will see to it that I'm remembered."

He sucked noisily at the dregs of his rum-and-mint drink, and asked me to lead him to the room where Victor was sleeping. We went up, but as I unlocked the door, this heavily built man pushed past me and slammed the door in my face, and when I began to beat on the door and ring the bell with indignation, I heard "Heredia" 's voice through the chinks of the polished mahogany door.

"Don't interrupt me, Don Hugo. Come back in half an hour. I'll be finished by then. Everything depends on your leaving me alone. Please. Do it for your son. And never tell anyone what happened between us. Do it for your son."

I stopped pounding at the door, and stepped back. But I did not abandon my vigil in the hotel corridor. I counted the minutes on my watch. I waited five minutes past the thirty minutes. Again I knocked at the door, calling to "Heredia" to come out, as he had promised. The door opened at my touch. I went in and found my son asleep. He was alone. I never saw "Heredia" again.

You know the rest of the story, Branly. I told you that in the Ancira bar that night "Heredia" mentioned names of his family and people connected with his family. The names meant nothing to me at the time. But I was startled when Jean introduced you that day in Xochicalco. Your name rang a bell; "Heredia" had spoken of you. I swear I've tried to remember in what context; my impressions are as vague as "Heredia" 's references, Branly: a house of ill repute frequented by the French army in Mexico; a ravine; a woman in a shallow grave; a park in Paris; a window; a boy. Does all this mean anything to you? I haven't been able to make any sense of it.

Besides, I prefer to think of you in terms of the aura of mystery that surrounded you the day you entered my life and precipitated the chain of events. That was the day Victor found half the artifact. I associate you above all with that moment. Something created to last, a piece of art intended for something other than commerce or the bedazzlement of the senses or the celebration of the transient, an object emblematic of that presence of the past that has given meaning to my life, was about to be restored to its pristine beauty and unity. Amends were about to be made—at great cost, but amends, nonetheless—for an angry, stupid, barbaric, capricious act of destruction.

I don't know, Branly, what you may have forgotten about yourself, about your past, your family line—obviously, considerably better documented than our own. With better reason, what have we Heredias forgotten? Now I spend entire nights trying to evoke things I no longer know: a desired violation, all the transgressions of the flesh, the ambition, money, power, and caste that shaped and kneaded the lives of people like the Heredias are forgotten, yes, perhaps because we couldn't live with the constant consciousness of the lives we have sown, the fortunes we have usurped, the misery on which those of us who are anything in the New World have built our being. Lucie will be proved right. A black utopia devoured by a bloody epic; you see what has happened to that dream of a rediscovered Eden, and its noble savage.

In contrast, an object is never cruel, Branly, it has no passions, it harms no one; rather, it gives testimony to permanence, glimmering with the twin lights of a yesterday and a today indistinguishable in art.

"Who was just here, who were you talking to?" I asked, brutally shaking my son awake in our bedroom in the Hotel Ancira.

"André," my son replied. "André . . ."

I don't care about his name. He was a child with us, and will grow old with us. I hope that, thanks to me, my son will enjoy whatever time he has with that boy he so fervently desired to see, or be, or have, I don't know which verb to use, as I, thanks to the boy, will enjoy my time with Lucie and Antonio.

And if I have understood correctly, one day the four of us will be together, because somehow Victor will be with us again. Then we can all be partners in mourning.

But everything depends on your understanding the words. You had a past, but you do not remember it. Try to recapture it in the little time you have left, or you will lose your future.

This is the obligation shared by all of us who were actors in this story. I pass it on to you, Branly, hoping you will accept it as proof of my gratitude. It is because I am grateful that I have told you everything I know—no more, no less. I know I am exposing myself to a terrible fate if you betray me by repeating what I have told you. But, between gentlemen, that question doesn't arise.

You see, Branly, you and I are bound together by a

shared rejection of the death of the past, the present of civilizations. "Heredia" and I were bound by the Pragmatic Sanction, if I may call it that, of the same attitude: our will to serve the dead, so that someday the living will serve us. Through me as intermediary, you and that demon were finally allied in a common goal: the recovery of an angel.

21

When Branly finished his long account of the words of Hugo Heredia in Xochicalco during the vigil of All Saints', its final meaning, like a ball of paper tossed into the sea, was slow to sink to the depths of my consciousness. First, it had to be saturated with water and sun, the vapors of iodine and salt, the agents that allow us to convert what is said into what is known, and what is known into something more: the fate contained in every word, as well as what, prophetically, it announces.

Consequently, the only question that then occurred to me to ask Branly was whether the boy Victor had told his father anything more at their first meeting after being separated by "Heredia" in the Hotel Ancira. But my friend seemed not to hear me; I sensed from his faraway gaze, his murmuring lips, that he had not completely returned from the mournful celebration in Mexico.

I dared not interrupt his strange self-absorption. When he did speak, the words did not sound his own, it was as if Hugo Heredia were still speaking through the voice of my friend.

"Everything depends on your understanding the words. You had a past, but you do not remember it. Try to recapture it in the little time you have left, or you will lose your future."

Again his eyes focused on a point near me.

"Branly." I spoke with a certain anxiety. "Are you all right? Is something the matter?"

"It was the eve of All Souls' Day, the day of the dead," he said, once more in his own voice.

"I know. You told me."

He had told Hugo Heredia that eve of the departed, in Xochicalco, that he had come to hear the truth from his lips because he had greatly admired him when they met, and he could not believe that a man of Heredia's intellectual caliber was a barbarian.

"I had to face him, and force him to face me. I had to know his reasons for acting as he did, for participating in the trickery of that savage "Heredia," for bribing my servants and deceiving the authorities of my country with his report of the drowning of his son on the Normandy coast. He could, my dear friend, tell me nothing I did not already know about the vulgarity of that man you have glimpsed on a carnival night in Caracas, in a tasteless silver-painted apartment, a hotel in Monterrey, and, finally, his own domain, the Clos des Renards."

Branly's eyes clouded at the mention of Enghien-les-Bains. He spoke somewhat incoherently, as if to another person, of the circles, the mute laments, the gray wounds of that tormented city "Heredia" seemed to carry with him, opening the chasms that are the scars of this story, in order to give voice to an intolerable universe of harsh sighs, strange tongues, appalling gibberish, tones of rage, and fields of ashen misery beneath a sky barren of stars.

I knew that my friend was still quoting, reproducing the voices and murmurs associated with the spiritual journey of the night spent amid murmurs and voices on a hill alight with blind lights. What more had Hugo Heredia said, I pressed him. Finish the story, Branly. What did he say?

My friend looked at me as if he scarcely recognized me.

[198]

"Hugo Heredia? Hugo Heredia told me that he was passing on the story to me, asking me to accept it as proof of his gratitude. 'I know I am exposing myself to a terrible fate if you betray me by repeating what I have told you. But, between gentlemen, that question doesn't arise,' he said that night."

At last Branly's words settled into the depths of my consciousness. I did what I had never done before because of my affection, my respect, for this eighty-three-year-old man. I seized him by the shoulders, I shook him violently, I told him to tell me the truth. Were those the words Hugo Heredia spoke to Branly when he told him the story, or were they words Branly meant for me today, here in the solarium of the Automobile Club pool?

My action was motivated by sudden terror. I didn't want to be the one who knew, the last to know, the one who receives the devil's gift and then cannot rid himself of it. I didn't want to be the one who receives and then must spend the rest of his life seeking another victim to whom to give the gift, the knowing. I did not want to be the narrator.

The watery paleness disappeared from Branly's eyes. He hadn't even noticed my violence. I felt ashamed. I removed my hands from his shoulders, but I did not avert my eyes.

"Branly, do you hear me?"

"Perfectly, my friend." And he nodded with absolute composure.

"Then tell me. Tell me the truth. I've listened very carefully. Now I must know what you knew before you talked with Hugo Heredia. I want to know what you knew but haven't told me. I asked whether all the small coincidences, the implicit analogies, had escaped your attention."

My friend started to rise from his chair, then sank back.

"Yes, the portrait of my father beside my bed; the clock made by Antoine-André Ravrio, in whose workshop several men died from contact with the mercury used in gilding; the

Empire-robed woman playing the harpsichord . . . I nearly destroyed both, my friend. I, too, suspected that in some mysterious way the photo and the clock with its gilded bronze figure linked my destiny, much against my will, with the story of the Heredias."

"Why didn't you, Branly?"

Before replying, my friend shrugged. "I did, it is true, finally see the relationships among certain objects. What I still do not know is why those relationships exist. You see, I too, have lost the power of analogy, of seeing that correspondence among all things that for Hugo Heredia was the most meaningful symbol of our early cultures. Perhaps one of my ancestors in the fourteenth century, with no difficulty, understood the homologous relationship among God, a hart with burgeoning antlers, and the hunter's moon. By the sixteenth century, another ancestor would not have known this; he could not see the correspondence among these things. Art, you see, and especially the art of narration, is a desperate attempt to reestablish analogy without sacrificing differentiation. This is what Cervantes, Balzac, Dostoevsky accomplished. Proust was no different. Surely no novel can escape that terrible urgency."

Branly added that the essence of every work of art is that the solution of its enigma creates a new enigma, and he quoted the poet René Char saying that the time is approaching when the only questions left to ask are those that must remain unanswered.

Again I noticed Branly's urge to get up from his chair. But I was not disposed to be silenced by a few literary flourishes from my friend. "Since we're speaking of Cervantes, I should tell you that you have always reminded me of that paradigm of courtesy, the gentleman in green, Don Diego de Miranda, who offered hospitality to Don Quijote when everyone else denied it. But didn't you outdo yourself with the Heredias? Understand, Branly, I am not reproaching you."

"A reproach is the last thing I need." My friend laced his fingers beneath his thin, amicable lips.

"I agree. But you did receive them with more than ordinary hospitality . . ."

"I do not regret that," Branly interrupted, without looking at me.

"Why?" My question was impertinent.

Branly did not shift his position, he merely let his hands fall to his lap. He told me he was indebted to the Heredias for three things. He had dreamed about a woman he had loved in the past, and though he could not identify her, he had experienced emotions from a time when being hopelessly in love was enough to make one happy. And he had recaptured the imperious innocence, the unanswered questions, of his childhood. "Do you remember my fear when I realized how near I had come to refusing young Victor's invitation the time he turned my salon into a sumptuous cavern of blazing candles, silver, and bronze? I swore then I would never refuse any of Victor's requests, for they were the same as those of my own childhood. And, you see, I was right."

"And your third debt?" I asked, hoping to hasten the conclusion of Branly's story.

He looked at me strangely, saying that, after all, it was I who had guessed and expressed that debt with precision. Many years ago, he should have taken that extra step in the Parc Monceau. Seventy years was a long time, but finally he had held out his hand, he had returned the ball to the melancholy child who watched from behind the beveled windows of the house on the Avenue Vélasquez.

"I do not know why I feel that the sins in this story, if sins they are, are those of omission, of absence, more than action and presence. Francisco Luis de Heredia may have been the one person who acted, even though he deceived himself, believing his efforts could wound, humiliate, avenge, decide the course of events. None of the others, no; things happened because *no* actions were taken. I believe, my dear friend, that I have atoned for my childhood sin of omission. If the boy to whom I did not offer my hand in the Parc Monceau was named André, that child now, thanks to me, through my mediation—because I invited the Heredias to my home in Paris, because I played the game of names in the telephone book, because I drove Victor to the Clos des Renards, and because in the final act I did not interrupt the confluence of events—that boy, I say, will never be alone."

I made no comment, but Branly could see my expression. He turned away, his gaze fixed on the distant horizon beyond the glass walls of the solarium, the robed and slippered club members drinking in the bar, attended by young waiters.

"Do not believe that because I am grateful my conscience is entirely clear," he said, avoiding my eyes.

"No," I replied. "Of course not. But I am surprised that though you feel you owe so much to the Heredias you have violated the obligation you accepted so solemnly."

"Obligation?" said Branly, turning to look at me, and laughing dryly. "You jest, my friend."

I did not allow myself to be annoyed by my friend's cool, haughty tone. I held his eyes, in fact offering him my silence if he preferred it, letting him know my curiosity was not as strong as my respect for him and what he considered his secret. But as his eyes met mine, pride blazed even more brightly. I had not expected this.

"After listening to you, I am certain of one thing," I persisted. "This story should never have been known by any except those who lived it. Why have you told me? You promised not to tell it to anyone. You have broken that promise. Why? If seventy years ago you erred in denying friendship to a lonely boy, you have atoned for it today by erring anew. Will you have time to atone for this new sin, Branly?"

With this, Branly sprang to his feet. "What right do you have to speak to me in that tone?" he asked.

"The right that comes from being the guardian of the Heredias' story, and, because of it, committed to the pact of silence you have violated this afternoon."

"Do not delude yourself," he replied with icy pride. "There is something you have not understood, my friend, which is that the real story of the Heredias is not finished."

"Do you mean that what you have told me isn't true?" I asked, my exasperation mounting.

"The events may be true." Branly sighed quietly. "But the essential truth is hidden, the hatred of Hugo Heredia for his son Victor. Victor hoped his father and his brother would die, so he would be left to weep with his mother. And, too, Victor hated the stones; he injured the past Hugo venerated, and, at least according to Hugo, capriciously destroyed the perfect object he found at the ruins of Xochicalco. Hugo Heredia despised his son when he realized that Victor had not learned his lesson. He scorned men, but he did not love the stones. He did not deserve to be the heir of the Heredias."

Branly paused a moment, and looked at me with something akin to compassion.

"Allow me to continue," he said. "I have been disloyal, if that is how you want to define it, to a cruel man motivated by hatred and scorn for mankind, a hatred redeemed in his own mind by his love for the past. On the other hand, I have been faithful to the two boys who were reunited for reasons that escape my logic and his. I offered them my hand. I can know no more. Hugo Heredia wanted to condemn his son to the past. By telling you the story that should have remained untold, I have taken the responsibility for damning Hugo Heredia. He himself said it: his life depended on my silence. You and I do not matter; what is important is to destroy Hugo Heredia and save the boys. I told him that as we said goodbye, before Jean's driver took me from Xochicalco to Cuernavaca. I am at peace. The last time I saw Hugo Heredia, he was barely visible in the dying glow of the candles of that yellow night. You see, my friend, I could not help but notice among the shadows certain faces that brought me nearer to the fulfillment of my desire, the faces of young and old gathered on that candlelit, flower-covered hill, men and women and children gazing at Hugo Heredia with secret, long-buried hatred. Patient crimes, my friend."

"And the other Heredia, the old man?"

"He had no reason to hate me. I recognized him. He got what he wanted."

"Forgive my stupidity; what did he want?"

"The child was born, don't you see?"

He removed his bathrobe and tossed it on the chair. His body was firm, his pale flesh revealed few signs of age except the vivid tracery of blue veins. I watched my friend Branly, clad in blue bathing trunks, walk toward the pool, and something in me argued that I owed him an apology; but the fact that I had learned the story of the Heredias gnawed at me like a strange malady, a tumor in my imagination. I did not want to be the last to know the story, and even though my imagination was racing with fear, I did not know why the knowing burned me like the reunited halves of that object Branly had touched in the Citroën as Victor and André made it whole.

Branly walked toward the pool, and I followed, admiring how completely he had recovered his military bearing. He reached, before me, the fiber matting that rings the enormous, olympic-sized pool notable for a beauty both palatial and bucolic. The pool of the Automobile Club de France should not be reserved for its members—wealthy financiers, government officials, businessmen—but for nymphs and satyrs. Its green mosaic walls suggest a sylvan glen, the golden rim a Roman bath. The cascade of crystalline waters spilling from a seashell-shaped fountain would transport us to ancient times were it not for the strange construction that shatters this heraldic enchantment like the broad stroke of a fountain pen on medieval papyrus: an iron catwalk that spans the pool some nine or ten meters above its surface, near the dome of the skylight that in the daytime illuminates this extraordinary pool sunk in the heart of Paris between the Place de la Concorde and the Rue St.-Honoré, the Hôtel de la Marine and the Hôtel Crillon.

I watched Branly dive into the pool and begin to swim with measured strokes. He was alone in the pool and the water welcomed him with unusual concentration; only he broke its stillness, but, in turn, only he offered himself to the water, delivered himself to its tranquillity. Like the pool and its bridge, water and steel, my friend, I knew by now, was living in a dual state of receptivity and hermeticism that accentuated both his generosity toward others and the exacerbated ritual of his idiosyncrasies.

It was at that precise instant I looked up and saw the waiter walking across the iron catwalk suspended above the pool. I wouldn't have noticed him if he hadn't stopped, his empty tray in his hands, a peculiar expression on his face, instantaneous and indescribable, his eyes narrowed and feline, strangely incongruous with the aureole of curly bronze hair, the similarly golden skin, the smiling moist lips. It was as if parts of his head and body—which, I knew intuitively, was at once tense and relaxed, like the bodies of certain animals whose calm we merely imagine because in the presence of man they adopt a cringing, begging pose— belonged to different creatures.

Suddenly the water in the pool erupted. For an instant I stood paralyzed by the phenomenon; the tranquil lake was transformed into violent waves, and I saw Branly lift one arm, struggle against the roiling, tumultuous water, and then succumb. I dived after him. I cannot swear that my presence calmed the fury of the pool, but I do know that by the time I reached my friend, cupped his chin in my hand, and swam toward the side of the pool, there was no movement in the water except in our wake. I looked up at the catwalk. There was no one there. Attendants came running to help us; club members turned toward us from the bar; some rushed to see what was happening; someone commented that Branly should be more careful, that he had not been himself these last few weeks.

With the attendants' help, I carried my friend to a chaise longue in the dressing room, where he lay back without a word.

Later I drove him to his home. His housekeeper, a beautiful woman of about forty, met us at the door. I hadn't seen her before, as she had been hired to take the place of José and Florencio. As I say, I had never seen her, and I was struck by the fact that, although she was smiling and she seemed perfectly natural, her eyes glistened with tears. I know people like that, especially women, who seem always on the verge of weeping, and in fact they are individuals of unusual kindness, restrained emotions, and extreme shyness. What I had yet to learn was that they are also acutely sensitive to the pain of others.

The photograph of Branly's father was missing from his bedside table. I noticed its absence as we helped him into bed. He apologized for the accident, smiling, saying that perhaps at his age he should forgo sports.

He held out his hand. I took it. I was surprised by its warmth.

I left his room bearing an impression of eyes that were both near and faraway, which is perhaps another way of saying that his eyes saw something I could not see. In any case, I felt vaguely uneasy, as if in leaving I were abandoning my friend in his stubborn, never-ending, and, most of all, unequal, battle with something or someone who had banished from the room the photograph of the young Captain de Branly, born in 1870, and dead in 1900 of a germ that could not have withstood an injection of penicillin.

Later I walked through the salon. Once again I admired the wedding of bronze, marble, plaster, and silver with amboyna, oak, beech, and gilt, and I compared the incredible luxury of the silver candelabra, the malachite vases, the mirrors crowned with winged figures and butterfly medallions, with Branly's description of the interior of the Clos des Renards, its suffocating sensation of flayed skin, its smell of leather, and damp whitewash. The comparison led me, unconsciously, to seek, though in vain, the magnificent clock suspended from an arch of gilded bronze, with a seated woman playing an ornate harpsichord with griffin legs, in a sumptuous mounting of motionless draperies and doors. The absence of the clock caused me to remember something else: the tune the clock played as it struck the hours, a timeless madrigal. How did it go? Where, only recently, had I heard it?

It was perhaps this spirit of inquisitiveness that led me to Branly's library. I had asked the housekeeper to call my friend's physician, and I wanted to wait to assure myself that he was all right. With aimless curiosity I ran my finger along the backs of the volumes on shelf after shelf of that small but splendid library. I paused with bitter pleasure as I recognized the titles of certain books that had appeared in the course of this narration: *La Duchesse de Langeais*, by Honoré de Balzac; the *Méditations poétiques* of Lamartine; *Poésies*, by Jules Supervielle; *Les Chants de Maldoror*, by Isidore Ducasse, known as the Comte de Lautréamont; *Les Trophées*, by José María de Hérédia; *Imitation de Notre-Dame la Lune*, by Jules Laforgue; and the *Mémoires* of Alexandre Dumas.

I was intrigued by the presence among this special group of books of a volume my friend the Comte de Branly hadn't mentioned in the course of his account—but then I remembered that the two boys, Victor and André, had spoken of *The Count of Monte Cristo, The Three Musketeers,* and *The Man in the Iron Mask.* A yellow silk bookmark slit the gold that dusted the page edges. I held the volume in my hand, stroking the creamy leather cover and maroon cornerpieces. The spine cracked as I opened it and scanned a page on which the print stood out as if embossed by reading and by time; the letters in old books seem to want to free themselves from the pages, to take flight like a flock of migrating birds.

What I read was not actually part of the memoirs of that powerful writer, whom fortunately no one—though Flaubert wished it, ironically—had with a wave of a magic wand transported to the cult of Art. I have always believed that Dumas's books are like men themselves—intemperate, merry, lavish, generous, limpid but secretly erotic and insatiable. The page before me records that as he was dying, the elder Dumas gave a louis d'or to his son, author of the *Dame aux Camélias*, saying: You see this coin? Your father may have had the reputation of being a profligate, a spendthrift who threw away a fortune on his castles on the road to Bougival, an unrepentant lover of women who, wiser than he, asked nothing of him but the blossoms of the day; but look at this louis d'or, he'd had it when he arrived in Paris and he'd held on to it until the hour of his death.

Alongside this page there was another, purple ink on

graph paper, carefully glued to the endpaper. "In 1870, shortly before his death, A.D. came in his tilbury to my home in Enghien. In his arms, as promised, he bore a beautiful blond boy child. At my direction, C. went out and handed him the black child. A.D. took the child in his arms, and sent this message by C.: the ancient debts of honor, money, exploitation, and revenge are at long last settled. He added that perhaps this date should be commemorated; each, finally, had his own. I saw no reason to disillusion him. I inscribed his initials and the date over the door. Before he could see them, he died, dreaming, for all we know, of the forests of his childhood in Retz, or, perhaps, of the mountains of his father's childhood in Haiti. I admire this celebrated writer, but I am not obliged to take in the son of a slave woman from the plantations forfeited by my stupid father-in-law. I do not know what became of the black child. Poor L. She had grown fond of him, and she weeps the day long."

Why was it only then that I recalled the last lines of the timeless madrigal: *J'ai trouvé l'eau si belle, que je m'y suis noyé.* "So beautiful were its waters that in them I did drown." I will never be able to forget that I heard those lines for the last time at the club pool, that they were being sung by a waiter with a face like a wildcat, whose features seemed strangely at odds with the configuration of his head, and who was standing, tray in hand, on the iron catwalk above the waters cascading into the swimming pool.

22

Several days later I visited the Clos des Renards. It was a scene of great activity, a tumult of trucks and laborers. Entering through the great gate, I approached the house along the avenue of oaks and chestnuts. The dead leaves had been swept away. The beautiful grove of birches is still standing. But, inside, the house is being completely renovated. Ornamentation, walls, paint, wax, plaster, ebony fall before my astonished eyes: a huge pile of smoldering skins lies at the end of the terrace of the lions, and carpenters are fitting new frames on doors and windows.

I hear a peculiar sound and I peer through one of the newly refurbished windows. A crew of women dressed in full skirts and heavy denim blouses, their heads wrapped in coarse kerchiefs that hide their hair, are scraping down the floors and walls of the house. They don't speak; they don't look at me.

Though the inscription above the door, A.D. 1870, remains untouched, I notice that workmen are attacking the French garden, digging a large pit exactly at its center. Of course. This will be the long-missing pool. Because of the excavation, one can no longer see—if in fact it ever actually existed—the sulphurous, burnt gash Branly said he saw from his bedroom window and, barefoot, walked through that last time the gift of simultaneity was granted him by dream, time, and the physical space of the Clos des Renards.

I ask the workmen the owner's name; no one knows anything. I feel frustrated. We leave behind that house being stripped of its curses as in medieval times dwellings were purified of the plague.

I return to Paris that afternoon, after a leisurely drive through Enghien, Montmorency, Andilly, Margency, and other places where I have friends and memories. Corot's autumn has appeared, crowned with silvery mist. I decide to visit my friend Branly, who is suffering from an acute bronchial infection.

"You must get well quickly," I tell him jokingly. "I don't want to be the only person who knows the story of the Heredias."

He looks at me with doleful eyes, and says I mustn't worry, that memory is a faithless creature and nothing is more easily forgotten than a dead man.

"If you only knew how difficult it is for me to remember the faces of my first wives. Nothing closer in life. Nothing more distant in death."

"Don't you have photographs of them?"

A wave of his hand tells me that anything that cannot be remembered spontaneously deserves to be entombed in oblivion.

"On the other hand, how well I remember Félicité, my nurse when I went to my grandfather's castle for vacations. I remember her. She told me that my grandfather, too, was a military man, first during the July Monarchy, and then during the Second Empire. But he never told me any of this, so I am not sure."

"Perhaps that's what Hugo Heredia feared," I dared suggest.

"What?"

"That he would forget his wife and son in the same way."

Branly turned to look at me with the concentrated but impotent fury of the elderly, more terrible than a young man's rage because the absence of physical menace suggests something much worse.

"Have you had news of him?" he asks, his voice congested.

"No," I reply with surprise. "Should I have?"

"He told me that his life depended on my silence. But I broke that silence; I told you everything. My only hope is that Hugo Heredia is dead."

Branly speaks these words with some passion; he is overcome by a fit of coughing. As he composes himself, I mention the beauty of the November afternoon, a little cool, but radiant, like the afternoons he always loved on the Île de France when as a child he paused on the bridge over the river and experienced that miraculous moment that disperses the phenomena of the day, rain or fog, scorching heat or snow, to reveal the luminous essence of this favored city.

"Don't change the subject," Branly scolds me, his handkerchief in his hand. "The French Heredia told Hugo not to tell anything, because Victor's life depended on it. But he did, Hugo told me the story."

"And you told me, Branly. Actually, I wasn't changing the subject. One morning in this very house, Victor invited you to join him in a game, and you nearly missed the opportunity."

"That is true. Stupidly. Because of my passion for the order and reason that wear the solemn mask of maturity and veil one's fear that one may recover one's lost imagination."

As I open wide the tall beveled windows of Branly's bedchamber overlooking the garden with the solitary sea pine, I tell him that I visited the Clos des Renards that morning.

"I went to your bedroom, my friend. The clothes you were wearing the night of the accident were still there, tossed into a corner. What did Etienne carry away the morning he and your Spanish servants came for you? What did Etienne have in his small black suitcase?"

Branly looked at me with terror. His gaze was lost in the distance, as were his thoughts, floundering in a pool of clear water.

"She asked me to dream of her. She said we would never grow old as long as I remember her and she remembers me."

I feel a sudden sense of remorse. I walk toward the windows to close them, but Branly stops me with a movement of his hand, saying no, I mustn't worry.

His voice is choked, but he manages to say: "You see: I always believed that even when I found her I would continue to look for her, to wait patiently for her to reveal her true face to me. I did it for the boy, I swear it. It was through him that I was able to remember my love. I could have died without remembering her. I am eighty-three years old. Do you realize? I came very close to forgetting her forever. I wanted to repay him. Perhaps he, too, thanks to me, will remember the person he forgot. Perhaps it was not in vain."

"I hope to God you were not mistaken."

"We shall soon know, my friend. What do you think?"

I look at the sadly illuminated figure of Branly sitting listlessly in his threadbare brocade chair, wrapped in an ancient plush bathrobe, a man without descendants. I am seized by compassion, but refuse to be governed by it; I remember what his heritage is: the Heredias, Mexico, Venezuela, the story of which he is gladly divesting himself to give to me— who do not want it.

Even so, a kind of contrary compulsion, irreversible and irresistible, forces me to insist that my old friend tell me everything, as if exhausting all the possibilities of the narrative might mean the end of this story I never wanted to hear, and the resulting release from the responsibility of telling it to someone else. This is the only explanation I can offer for my next incredible questions.

"Isn't there anything more, Branly? Are you sure you aren't forgetting something? I must know everything before . . ."

As my elderly friend hears these words his eyes clear. He looks at me with a profound, almost mordant irony worthy,

I say to myself, of his greatest moments of pleasure, intuition, presence, and power. This is how I imagine him looking that last time at Hugo Heredia, through the dusk of a solitary, sacred barranca where the gods of the New World lie slumbering.

"Before I die? Ah, my friend. Not quite yet. For a number of reasons."

He sighs; he drums his fingers on the shabby brocade chair arm. I realize now that my questions were counter to my best interests: as the gods will one day rise from the rotting mangrove thickets where long ago they were murdered, so my questions sprang from my irrational desire to know. I must know everything before Branly dies and can no longer tell me, cannot bequeath me his story, condemning me to wander like a blind beggar pleading for the few verbal coins I must have to finish the story I inherited. If he died before I knew the conclusion, I would never be free. I had to know everything before I could transmit the story in its totality to another. But Branly was not aware of the chaos of my thoughts; he was enumerating the reasons he would live a while longer.

"No, I shall not die as long as I remember her and she remembers me. That is the first reason. The second, and more important, is that my death will not be borne on tonight's wind; I sense the warmth of a St. Martin's summer. Autumn will be detained a little longer, my friend. You remember that St. Martin was sainted because of his generosity. Did he not share his cloak with a beggar?"

Now he stares at me with disquieting discernment.

"Tomorrow is November 11th, Fuentes. Your birthday. You see, I am not yet senile, I remember the birth dates, the dates of the deaths of my friends. No, you must not worry. You and I are living but one of the infinite possibilities of a life and of a story. You are afraid to be the narrator of this novel about the Heredias because you fear the vile demon who may take revenge against the last man to know the story. But you are forgetting something I have tried to tell you more than once. Every novel is in a way incomplete, but, as well, contiguous with another story. Take your own life. In 1945, Fuentes, you decided to live in Buenos Aires, near Montevideo; you did not return to your native Mexico; you became a citizen of the River Plate region, and then in 1955 you came to live in France. You became less of a River Plate man, and more French than anything else. Isn't that so?"

I said yes, he knew that as well as I, though at times I questioned the degree of my assimilation into the French world. He touched my hand with affection.

"Imagine; what would have happened if you had returned to Mexico after the war and put down roots in the land of your parents? Imagine; you publish your first book of stories when you are twenty-five, your first novel four years later. You write about Mexico, about Mexicans, the wounds of a body, the persistence of a few dreams, the masks of progress. You remain forever identified with that country and its people."

"But it was not like that, Branly." I spoke uncertainly. "I don't know whether for good or ill, but I am not that person."

With a strange smile, he asks me to pour him a drink from the bottle of Château d'Yquem beside his bed. Shouldn't he, I ask, go back to bed? Yes, he will; later, when he decides it is time. Would I like a glass of that late wine, the fruit of the autumn grapes?

I join him in a toast.

"To your other life, Fuentes, to your contiguous life. Think who you might have been, and celebrate with me your birthday and the coming St. Martin's summer days with a wine that postpones death and offers us a second vintage. St. Martin has again divided his cloak to shelter us from the winter. Think how the same thing happens with every novel. There is a second, a contiguous, parallel, invisible narration for every work we think unique. Who has written the novel about the Heredias? Hugo Heredia amid the ruins of Xochicalco, or the boorish owner of the Clos des Renards? I, who have told you the story? You, who someday will tell what I have told you? Or someone else, someone unknown? Here is another possibility: the novel was already written. It is an unpublished ghost story; it lies in a coffer buried under a garden urn, or under loose bricks at the bottom of a dumbwaiter shaft. Its author, need I say it? is Alexandre Dumas. Have no fear, my friend. I know how to survive terror."

I press his hand. As I leave, he asks me to tell the housekeeper that she can go to bed, he will not be needing her. He wants to sleep late. But I really have no desire to speak with the woman whose eyes shine with the glimmer of unshed tears.

Yet, as I walk along the hallway leading from Branly's bedchamber to the salon, I notice an open door that had been closed when I came to visit my friend this St. Martin's eve.

As I left Branly in his bedroom, I had been thinking of the luminous, warm city, the renewed summer he had promised for the following day. As I pass the open door, I feel attracted as if by the light in my imagination, light that disperses the phenomena of the day, rain or fog, scorching heat or snow. I turn, curious about the source of the light, and watch as one tiny flame after another begins to flicker in the candelabra I had earlier, with surprise and dismay, noticed were missing from the salon.

I can dimly discern a pale hand in the shadows, moving from candle to candle. I remember how once young Victor in broad daylight, but behind drawn drapes, had lighted these same candelabra in this same house, but now, to my sudden awe, the room is transformed, transported to a different space, its axis equivocal, its symmetry questionable.

I enter the room. In vain I try to penetrate the ecclesiastic gloom enveloping the figure lighting the candles. Dazed, I retreat to the farthest corner, as far as possible from the candelabra with their bronze ram's-head bases, the garlands of blindfolded girls whose bodies serve as candle holders, the bronze serpents whose fangs fasten on glass shades, the melted wax on the argentine backs of a pack of hunting hounds.

The dolorous hands light the last candle. The room is filled with light; a woman kneels before the table by her leather-canopied bed. On the table is the object I had always before seen in the salon, the clock suspended in an arch of gilded bronze, with the figure of a seated woman playing an ornate piano with griffin legs, in a sumptuous mounting of motionless draperies and doors. On the same bedside table is the sepia photograph of Branly's father.

The woman is weeping, still on her knees, her hands covering her face.

In this instant, all the defenses of humor, innocence, and rationality I have placed between myself and Branly's narrative fall away. It is of little consequence that the woman is dressed in black rather than the high-waisted, décolleté white ball gown with the long stole. Can we call intuition our sudden nakedness beneath the sun of a North African desert or the torrential downpour of an equatorial jungle that, as it strips us of the umbrella of logic we carry through well-lighted streets as we boldly enter shops, routinely step off buses, confidently sign checks, forces us to accept the inevitability of what confronts us? Intuition? Or awareness of something that never happened to us which yet encompasses a truth we did not even want to suspect, much less admit into the orderly compartments of good Socratic reason: someone has lived constantly alongside us, always, not just from the moment of birth, but *always*, a being fused to our life as the waters of the sea are with the sea. And to our death as our breath is with the air we breathe. During our lifetime, this being accompanies us with never a sign of its own life, as if less than the shadow, a tiptoeing murmur, the sudden, almost inaudible whisper of ancient taffeta against the knob of a half-open door, though this something—I know it in my mind as I pry away the strong hands that not only hide but disfigure the woman's face— lives, parallel to our own, a completely normal life, taking meals at regular hours, counting its possessions, casting glances we never see, yet in it jealousy and tenderness battle to exhaustion in a neighboring nonpresence: contiguous, bodies and their phantoms; contiguous, the narration and its specter.

"Lucie," I say. "Lucie, rest now. Leave him in peace. He has helped you. He did the best he could to return your son to you. Be grateful to him for that; he is a good man."

The wife of Hugo Heredia is possessed of an awesome force, a steel mesh woven more of will than of true strength, and I can do nothing but prevent an ever greater calamity. I fear she will claw at her face until it dissolves beneath tears indistinguishable from blood. But I fear even more that the hypotheses born of the intuition that stripped away my defenses as it plunged me suddenly into the horror of an eternal oblivion belonging to another woman like this one, another Lucie, my own, a woman unknown to me who like Branly's phantom was constantly by my side, would obliterate my friend's companion before I could see her face. I knew that the key to her secret was on her face and not in all my hypotheses—which were nothing but unanswered questions. Does everyone have an invisible phantom that accompanies him throughout his lifetime? Must we die before our phantom becomes incarnate? Then who is with us in death, the phantom of life, the only being that truly remembers us? What is that phantom's name? Is this phantom somehow different from what is simultaneously phantom and death during our lifetime: youth?

The moment I realize that these enigmas, if not their solutions, are written on Lucie's hidden face, I know that I have missed my opportunity to know this woman; I can know her only by looking at the face of my friend the Comte de Branly, not at her. If anywhere there was to be found the reality of the eternally tentative woman who floated along the magical paths of the Parc Monceau, it is in the waxen face, the pale hands, the intelligent eyes of the man who will be visited by the woman's spectral presence only if he does not know she is dead. Branly. Is it only through him that all the manifestations of the wife of Hugo Heredia exist? the sweetheart in the park of my friend's childhood, the French Mamasel, the girl who a hundred eighty years ago was seen by Branly's specter in the same park at the same hour in the same light?

As soon as I think I have resolved one enigma, the solution itself creates a new mystery. Any explanation that Lucie could offer me is obstinately withheld by the Heredias. Finally, I understand only one thing, that from behind the beveled windows of a house on the Avenue Vélasquez one presence has watched over everything, known everything, eternal, persevering, cruel in its pathetic will to bring it all back to life.

These thoughts flash through my mind as I struggle to move the hands away from the face of the woman who perhaps at that very instant, spontaneously, freely, with light-hearted yet sinister fatalism, was lowering her hands from her face in the abandoned painting in the attic of the Clos des

Renards. I swear that before I forcibly revealed that face I reproached myself for what I was doing. I told myself that my conclusions were too facile, too capricious, born of my need to tie up loose ends, to conform with the laws of symmetry, but that in truth—*in truth*—I did not have, I would never have, the right or power to interpret or vary the facts, to in any way intrude in the labyrinths of this story so imperiously indifferent to my own.

I tear Lucie's hands from her face. I cannot contain a scream of anguish. As I look upon that gaze of vertiginous infinity, I understand what Branly saw at the bottom of the dumbwaiter shaft at the Clos des Renards in the whirlwind of dead leaves and tiny daggers of ice; I know at last why we sell our souls in the pact we make with the devil not to be alone in death.

It was not in vain that Branly called on certain words to conjure up the true subject of his song: harsh sighs, strange tongues, appalling gibberish, tones of rage, and fields of ashen misery beneath a sky barren of stars.

This is Lucie's face.

The woman, too, screams as I reveal her face. Her first cry is one of fear; the second, of pain.

This is not a hypothesis: Lucie will live the moment my friend Branly dies. The trembling face I see before me is that of a beast crouched in ambush, lupine, rabid to devour the opportunity offered by death. It is not, this trembling face on which I gaze, that of a living woman. It is the mortal remains of a phantom in the unspeakable transit between yesterday's body and tomorrow's specter. I feel I must return to Branly's bedchamber, ask whether he knows that when he dies he will be, as until now she has been, a phantom. But even though she may cease to be a corpse, she will never be more than a specter.

My Lucie says, in a fetid voice as dank as fungus: You are growing old, Carlos. You do not belong here; you will never again belong there. Do you know your phantom? It will take your place at the moment of your death, and you will be the phantom of what in your life was your specter. You must abandon hope. You have not been able to kill it, however much you have tried. You did not leave it behind you in Mexico, or in Buenos Aires, as you thought you had when you were young.

The empty eye sockets, fountains of blood, mesmerize me with a blend of nausea and agonized fascination. "I can see it. It is standing patiently on the threshold of this bedroom. Go with it. Leave us alone. Do not come back."

It is an effort now to free myself from that dankness, from that kneeling woman whose face I could not describe without vertigo. I turn my back to the mother of Victor and Antonio. I could swear that she is clinging to my arm at the same time she is banishing me from her room. But this is merely an illusion, a new illusion, my own. She has no awareness of distance in the way we understand it. Her hand touches my arm, but I know that to her my body is not my body. Her presence does not touch me, it touches my phantom, the one that from this moment, the woman has just told me, waits beside the door of the room illuminated in the flickering of funereal silver.

She remains on her knees, weeping. Again she covers her face with her hands. She is singing quietly, in a quavering voice: "It is long I have loved you, I shall never forget you." *Il y a longtemps que je t'aime, jamais je ne t'oublierai.*

23

I will allow it to guide me through this increasingly warm night. It is as if Paris, heavy with forgotten celebrations and unforgettable stones, were regressing to the eternally warm but equally desolate bosom of its creation.

Sculpted in this struggle between the righteousness of the calendar and the savagery of the physical world, the profile of the city stands out like a bas-relief of time-become-flesh. I do not know the identity of this being, unborn, or returned from the dead, who accompanies me, but, because of it, I know that on this balcony Musset took the sun as a respite from the paleness of the secluded Princess Belgiojoso, and that an anguished, tormented Gérard de Nerval hurried along this wet alleyway, and that from that bridge, at the very moment Nerval was writing *"El desdichado,"* Cesar Vallejo was gazing at his reflection in the rushing waters; on the Boulevard La Tour-Maubourg I will hear the voice of Pablo Neruda; on the Rue de Longchamp, that of Octavio Paz; along with my specter I will walk across the footbridge of the Passerelle Debilly across the Seine; dry leaves will hang suspended above the statues in the Galliéra park; the warm night will reverberate along the Avenue Montaigne; a thwarted autumn will seek refuge in the cellars of the Rue Boissy-d'Anglas; as I feared, we come to the Place de la Concorde, the infinite crossroad, the fatal space where one day, one noon in this month of November, I had approached my friend Branly in the dining room of the Automobile Club and suggested we have lunch together.

Do I have a right to the answers to the enigma that has pursued me during my nocturnal walk from the Avenue de Saxe to the Place de la Concorde? How had Lucie recognized me? Was it because she knew that her husband Hugo

Heredia, a man my own age, had waited for me in vain in front of the baroque façade of the Escuela de Mascarones? waited to walk with me to the French Book Shop on the Paseo de la Reforma, to have a cup of coffee with Huguette Balzola in the manager's office on the mezzanine, to leave with the most recent issue of *France Observateur* or Mauriac's latest novel, to walk toward the French Institute on Nazas Street through the restless dust of a Mexican twilight, to see an old Renoir or Buñuel film, to talk for hours, to compare notes on exile and belonging, on possessions and dispossession, on fatalism and freedom, on beings and nonbeings, on tenderness and cruelty, on accord and discord: on resentment rescued by recognition? Because I chose to live in Argentina, did Hugo Heredia never have the friend he needed? Was he the friend I never knew in the lonely crowds of my youth beside the River Plate?

As I cross the square toward Gabriel's *pavillon*, the night grows measurably warmer. I don't know whether to trust what my eyes tell me. I hurry forward, and a breath of air from the Tuileries gardens carries the scent of magnolias in bloom. I see windows in the Hôtel Crillon being thrown open in the suffocating heat, guests peering with disbelief into the night of this St. Martin's summer.

Normally, the club concierge would not have admitted me at this hour. Tonight, however, I find him in his shirt-sleeves, lounging against the black iron grating of the unlocked vestibule door. He has the look of a prisoner who can't decide whether to escape or choose the security of what he knows.

He recognizes me, and, panting from the heat, allows me to enter. He sniffs something uncommon on the air, and I, at least, am a known factor. He feels he must say the obvious: "What a scorcher! Not your ordinary night, eh?"

I tell him that I had carelessly left some important papers

in the pool dressing room. I can find the way. He had better tend to the door. Indeed, this is not an ordinary night.

I know my destination, know where I am being propelled by my invisible companion. I can smell freshly cut pineapple slices, black-splotched ripe plantains, the buttery red flesh of the mamey. My mouth waters with forgotten, anticipated flavors melting on my burning tongue.

I think I hear the faint sound of singing. I expect to hear the madrigal of the clear fountain, but instead there is only the melancholy Mexican ballad sung to the *llorona*, the weeping woman who wanders the night like a soul in pain, *ay llorona*, how cruel the years have been, *ay de mí, llorona, llorona de ayer y hoy, ayer era maravilla, llorona, y ahora ni sombra soy*, today less than a shadow am I.

I walk through the bar to the swimming pool. The pool itself is obscured in a tangle of lush plants, ivy-covered trees with fragrant bark, climbing vines curling from the green mosaic pillars up to the great dome of iron and glass blinded by matted foliage. There is an overpowering aroma of venomous, ravenous flowers. Gunpowder trees: I had forgotten them, and now the scent reminds me that their bark was used to make the munitions of the Indies.

I make my way down a few steps toward the pool concealed behind the profuse greenery. I seem to be dislodging nests of tiny hummingbirds. I startle parrots into flight, and suddenly find myself face to face with a monkey whose visage is an exact replica of my own. He mirrors my movements, and then scampers off through the branches. I tread on the moulting body of a huge snake swollen with the mass of its own eggs. My feet sink into the moist earth, the yellow mud of the edge of the swimming pool of the Automobile Club de France. Suddenly there is no sound but the chatter of howler monkeys deep in the jungle.

Quickly I climb to the catwalk above the pool, where a

young servant with a feral face had watched a rehearsal of Branly's death.

A hush descends over the deathlike stillness of the water. A film, which could be the fumes of the jungle, covers the verdant pool. In the middle of that sperm-colored scum float two bodies, embraced, two fetuses curled upon themselves like Siamese twins, joined by their umbilicus, floating with a placidity that repudiates all past, all history, all repentance.

The faces are ancient. I stare at them from the iron catwalk. These are preternaturally old fetuses, as if they had swum nine centuries in their mother's womb. I strain to see the wrinkled features, and if in the fleeing simian I had seen my own reflection, I see now, with photographic clarity, the faces of two boys become old men in the floating fetuses.

I had never known them. But the voice beside me whispers into my ear not who they are but who I am.

"Heredia. You are Heredia."

Heavy of heart, I retreat, never turning my back, as if bidding a last farewell to an imprisoned hero, to a god interred in life, to drowned angels. The voice of my phantom pursues me to the iron door of the vestibule and to the square where autumn is beginning to recover its fleetingly usurped rights.

The St. Martin's summer is dying. No one remembers the whole story.